# DAUGHTERS
## *for a* TIME

Published by Amazon Publishing
P.O. Box 400818
Las Vegas, NV 89140

ISBN-13: 9781612182926
ISBN-10: 1612182925

# DAUGHTERS
## *for a* TIME

Jennifer
Handford

**amazon**publishing

# Prologue

With my nose pressed against the glass of motherhood, I was on the outside looking in, consumed with a want so big I would wake in the night, craving the fleshiness of chubby cheeks and equally chubby thighs. I had it all planned out. I *knew* what kind of mom I wanted to be. I'd name her Samantha, but I'd call her Sam, Sammy, Samarooni. I'd give her sloppy, wet, suck-on-her-bottom-lip kisses. I'd blow raspberries on her tummy while she convulsed in giggles. My husband, Tim, and I would laze around with her in bed on Saturday mornings, squishing each other, arms and legs crisscrossed and tangled.

*What a big girl you are!* I would coo, kissing the bottoms of her feet. *What a big girl!*

In the early years of trying, I had become conspicuously present at the house of my older sister, Claire, bouncing her new baby on my knee, logging each moment with my niece as on-the-job training for what lay ahead. I furtively tore recipes from *Family Circle* and *Woman's Day* at doctors' and dentists' offices, stowing away in my bottom desk drawer recipes for jack-o'-lantern-on-a-stick cookies, gummy-worm pudding, and cupcakes baked into ice cream cones.

Plans were made. Claire and I would mother together, a tag team of kisses, juice boxes, and promises. Loving arms circling our daughters with assurances that their childhood wouldn't be cut short, like ours had been.

Years passed, though, and then I became *that* woman, the sad and desperate one. The one who overstepped her boundaries, the one in the checkout line who couldn't help but touch a strange baby's foot dangling from her mother's Baby Bjorn, just to get a quick fix of that new silken skin. An anger and sadness consumed me, but of course, the babies themselves were always exempted from my fury. Them, I still loved. It was their mothers—those women who could do the one thing I couldn't—who I grew to despise.

More years passed, and still nothing. A single pink line, a viscous swirl of blood, an ache in my heart that nearly split me in two. "Not you," my body would cackle. "Anyone but you."

For my three daughters

# PART ONE

PART ONE

# Chapter One

*Get up! Get out of bed!* my mind blared.

*Forget it!* my body countered. I was warm, the down comforter was as soft as a cloud, Tim would be gone soon, and most of all, I had cramps and the pillow jammed under my abdomen felt good.

*Get up,* my mind admonished again, *before your husband loses his patience with you and packs his bags as your father once did.*

*He wouldn't do that,* some other part of my mind reasoned. *He's nothing like my father.* I flipped over, blotted my tears on the pillow, and gave myself five more minutes.

On the toilet, I peered between my thighs, watched blood swirl to the bottom of the bowl, and said good-bye to another month. Statistically speaking, each month was another fifty/fifty try, an even flip of the coin, but I was the idiot who couldn't tear herself away from the roulette table, so certain that there had to be redemption for the loser who kept placing bets. Four years of trying, forty-eight months—now forty-nine—had to build up some sort of probability karma. Surely, next month would land in my favor, wouldn't it?

*Not if you're broken,* my body jeered. *If you're broken, then it'll never be your turn.*

I changed my pad, chose a super-maxi, and waddled out of the bathroom and down the steps to the kitchen.

In the hallway, I caught my reflection in the mirror, saw the sadness that now resided in the purple shadows under my eyes. I reached for my face: Zits *and* wrinkles? There ought to be a law that forbids a thirty-five-year-old from enduring adolescence and aging at the same time. I gave myself a once-over: gray sweatshirt, flannel pajama bottoms, my hair as matted and drab as wet poodle fur. In the kitchen, another mirror, this one hung by the door so that I could check my face before leaving the house. Today I lifted it from the wall hanger and placed it facedown in the junk drawer.

⌒

I walked into our kitchen, slipped into Tim's cooking clogs, and bored my toes into the soft wool. Our kitchen was small, a space about the size of the walk-in refrigerator at Harvest—the restaurant that Tim and I owned. The restaurant that had now made Tim nearly famous, and the place from which I'd recently taken a leave of absence, after the depression brought on by infertility had left me ineffective at work, as impossibly flat as a deflated soufflé.

Tim was pedaling on the stationary bike in the exercise room. I could hear the cranking of the bike through the floorboards, along with Bobby Flay's muffled voice. Tim would click back and forth between the Food Network and CNBC as he put away twenty or so miles. I peered out the window over the sink. Spring was showing off its wares: pink and red tulips, grass greening, shiny leaves cloaking bare limbs. More evidence of the fertile ground all around me. I rinsed and wrung out the sponge to wipe down the countertop. A dusting of flour. Tim must have been baking.

Our house was a cozy and quaint Cape Cod, one of a few small houses nestled among grander ones in our northwest

DC neighborhood, one of the few houses that was actually occupied by a warm body in the middle of the day. Most of our
neighbors were workaholics: lawyers, lobbyists, councilmen,
doctors at the various hospitals, Capitol Hill staffers. Profes-
sionals who left early and returned late to their brick Colonials,
faux chateaus, and Tudors. Breeders who popped out children
like gumballs and then hired a staff of nannies to raise them.

Claire, who was never short on opinions, occasionally commented on how someday Tim and I would "trade up," once the
restaurant became profitable. But I was happy in our fifteen-
hundred-square-foot home, and Tim was too busy to care. The
last thing I needed was more square footage to ramble around
in.

Claire had Maura, my three-year-old niece, an exceedingly
adorable brunette: cuddly, loving, accessible, and warm. Kryptonite for a seemingly barren woman like me. The type of child
who brought me to my knees with her peachy little-girl skin
and watermelon kisses.

Claire was an excellent mother, the type who always had
a clean tissue in her pocket, a Band-Aid in her purse, and a
bag of Goldfish crackers in the glove box. She'd been perfect-
ing her mom skills for over two decades, the result of having
responsibility heaped on her at the early age of twenty, when
our mother died and she became guardian to me, a defiant
fourteen-year-old.

I poured myself a mug of coffee and peeled three Tums
from their foil wrappers. The artificially flavored orange chalk
mixed with the strong French roast actually tasted good, like a
hazelnut-and-Grand Marnier torte that I used to make—and
Tim's current pastry chef, Margot, sometimes still did.

I padded down the hallway to the baby room. The baby
room with no baby. A room painted and wallpapered years
earlier, when my naive optimism fueled the false belief that I

would be pregnant in no time. I sat on the edge of the bed, let gravity pull me down, and lay curled on my side with my knees pulled toward my chest. I hugged a teddy bear and let the tears flow easily. These days I was like a faucet.

Was it so wrong to want a family? To imagine a Norman Rockwell life where the three of us ate dinner around the same table every night, laughing, jockeying for turns to talk, a heated game of Candy Land afterward, a marathon reading session before bedtime. *Just one more!* our child would beg, crawling over Tim's chest, her hands cupped around his face, while I fluffed her pillows and straightened her comforter, ready- ing her cozy nest for a good night's sleep. Later, as Tim and I curled into each other, we'd laugh over a memory from the night. "God, she's so funny," Tim would say. "A little comedian," I'd agree, nudging closer to him.

Three years ago, after a year of trying to get pregnant, I had been diagnosed with endometriosis, which the doctors suspected to be the cause of my infertility and painful periods. Surgery followed, and then two more years of trying, but still no luck. This year's theory was that my egg quality was poor. "The eggs might be there," Dr. Patel, our fertility specialist, had said, "but they don't want to come out."

Lazy, good-for-nothing, squatter eggs.

Dr. Patel prescribed drugs to jump-start the ovulation pro- cess, a shocking dose of hormones to give my eggs a swift kick in the butt. Each month, Tim and I made a trip to the fertility clinic and I endured the humiliating experience of intrauterine insemination, a process whereby Dr. Patel strapped me into stirrups and used a turkey baster to direct my husband's sperm to the right location. There, they rambled around looking for an egg to penetrate. *Hello! Anybody home?* Little did they know that my eggs were freeloaders, sponging off the system without doing an ounce of work.

"I just don't get it!" I cried to Claire one morning after I'd gotten my period. "Why can't I get pregnant?"

"You can! You will," she insisted, though it seemed like she was starting to doubt it.

"I knew this round wouldn't work. Dr. Patel was out of the office on an emergency procedure and a resident had to do the insemination. The idiot couldn't even find my uterus. Ended up injecting the sperm into my cervix! My cervix! *Tim* could basically do that!"

"Everything happens for a reason," my sister said. "Maybe this is God's way of telling you that you're not meant to birth a child."

"Thanks a lot, Claire! So God finds crack whores and single teenagers suitable to birth a child, but not me."

"That's not what I meant. I'm just wondering if you should consider some alternatives."

"Alternatives?"

"Like adoption."

I shook my head decisively. "Adoption is great," I said. "I *love* people who adopt. But I really want to have my own child."

"But if you can't, it's an alternative. A baby's a baby. Love's love."

"It wouldn't be the same," I said defiantly.

"Why are you so determined to perpetuate our gene pool? What's so great about our family's DNA? Poor Mom, dead at the age of forty."

"You *have* a baby, Claire," I said, now angry. "How can you not get that I want to birth a child more than anything in the world?"

"Of course I understand," she said softly, setting a cup of tea on the table next to me. "I just hate seeing you in so much pain. How far are you willing to go?"

"To the end of the earth."

I plopped into the corner of the sofa, sliding my body down the length of it. I placed my hands on my sternum where the gnawing pain was usually located, a nagging ache that had plagued me since Mom died. Acid churned in my stomach, the pressure lodged under my rib cage. Tums, Tagamet, Axid, Pepcid...Nothing worked. I needed something much stronger to extinguish the self-doubt that I was feeling. Today I needed an entire medicine chest: something for the cramps, something for the acid, something to dull the pain altogether.

If my mother were here, she'd smooth back my hair, make me a cup of cocoa with a heaping spoonful of fluffernutter, and assure me, "It's okay; your time will come." But Mom wasn't here and that left Claire, and Claire would never say that. Claire was a problem solver. She'd give advice, recommend reading, tell me to buck up and think of a new plan. "Did you get the article I sent on the couple who adopted twins?" Claire would want to know.

The basement door squeaked when Tim came up from exercising. I wiped my eyes, slid off the sofa, and tried to lift my mouth out of its frown. Tim's shirt was soaked with sweat and his disheveled sandy hair stuck up in every direction. His cheeks shone red. *Vibrant* was how he looked. The opposite of me. Every time I caught my reflection in the mirror, I couldn't help thinking how much I resembled my father, Larry. *Defeated* was how I remembered him looking.

"How are you?" Tim asked in a careful voice. Dealing with me these days was like walking on eggshells.

"I'm fine," I said, retrieving a Gatorade for him from the refrigerator.

"Thanks." Tim had the boyish looks of a model in a Polo advertisement, like a prep school lacrosse player fresh off the field. He wiped the sweat from his face with a wet paper towel and then looked at me. "How are you, really?"

"Just the usual. Got my period in middle of the night."

"Of course you got your period." As if there wasn't a chance in hell that I would turn up pregnant. "We need to start the process. There's a daughter waiting for us. Focus on that."

Tim had a childhood friend who adopted from China last year and their daughter was doing beautifully. Tim had already done some research, contacted the same agency that his friend had used, and requested the paperwork. It sat untouched on my dresser.

*This is my daughter from China*, I had tried saying once, but the words got caught in my throat, like eating too much corn bread with nothing to drink. The *daughter* that melted in my mouth like a chocolate truffle was the one that I was unable to conceive.

"Helen, come on," Tim said. "Anyone can have a baby, but it takes a special woman to adopt."

The burning behind my breastbone flared. It was never Tim's intention to hurt my feelings; he was just able to do it so well. As if these four years we'd spent trying to conceive had been just a silly exercise in biology and chemistry that didn't really matter in the long run.

"Not anyone can have a baby," I reminded him.

"You know that's not what I meant."

"Sorry," I said, wishing I didn't take everything Tim said so personally.

He exhaled and offered a smile. "Let's start over. What are your plans for today?"

I bit into a cranberry scone he'd whipped up earlier. My recipe. Though back when I was the pastry chef in our house,

I'd used currants. It was buttery and light and the cranberries were tangy and chewy. Baking was my personal alchemy. I loved how the science of yeast, flour, and liquid could produce such delicious results. I liked, too, the reminder that there was a fine line that separated miracles from disasters. How all the skill in the world still required a dash of luck.

"Let's see, I'm going to do some laundry, pay some bills, go grocery shopping," I said, trying to sound efficient, like Tim. But what I really wanted was my flannel pajamas, my down comforter, a couple of these scones, and a pot of coffee. I had a week's worth of soap operas recorded upstairs. I wanted to hear the opening music for *Guiding Light* because it reminded me so much of Mom that I could almost feel her.

"Do you think you'd have any time to come into the restaurant?" Tim asked. "You know you're always welcome to come in and work, whip up something for the night's tasting menu."

"I know. I'll think about it."

"It'd be good for you to get back to work a little, you know?"

"Meaning?"

"Just that it would be good for you to get out of the house for a while. For you to remember how much you used to love baking."

"True," I said, wistfully remembering what it was like to spend a morning at my stainless steel workstation, my mixers, pans, and tins organized neatly in front of me, a giant marble slab covering a refrigerated space below. But true, too, was the memory of my last day at work when the devastation of starting my period flung me into a rampage, setting into flames with my blowtorch an entire rack of chocolate-hazelnut tortes.

"We have rehearsal today at eleven o'clock, for tomorrow's show," Tim said. "I could always use your help with that."

For the last year, following a glowing article on Tim and Harvest in *The Washington Beat* magazine, my husband had enjoyed the status of a celebrity chef. Now, once a week, he prepared a gourmet meal in a five-minute bit on *Good Morning Washington*. Last week he seared foie gras, slid it onto pointed toast, and topped it with caviar. The bleached-blonde, C-cupped newsperson, Melanie Mikonos, was nearly orgasmic as she savored Tim's creation, leaning into his arm. Unassuming Tim—a guy who was a thousand times cuter than he realized—just shrugged his shoulders like it was no big deal.

"It still cracks me up that you have to 'rehearse' cooking," I said, instantly regretting my snotty tone.

Tim raised his eyebrows, probably wondering where the woman he married had gone. I used to be funny, but now I was just sarcastic, as if I'd forgotten the mechanics of a good joke.

"Sorry." I walked toward Tim and took his hand. The clot in my throat left me unable to say more.

Tim kissed my forehead, and for a second, I wished that I could burrow into his chest and go to sleep. I wished that things were as they were when we'd first met. The two of us, broke and in love, traveling through Europe following our graduation from cooking school, lying side by side in our sleeper cabin as the train thundered through the night. Back when having children was just a fantasy. We'd split our time between DC and Paris. Our children would be so *international* they'd speak three different languages. It would be no big deal to pull them out of school for a holiday in Naples.

We'd exhale, lying back with our arms crossed over our chests, dreamily resolved in our plans. Back then, anything and everything seemed possible. Our love and curiosity and iron-clad loyalty to each other insulated us from any wrong turn.

Those were happy days for me, two special years spent overseas with Tim, traveling with no itinerary, an unfolded map spread out before us. Those were the years when I actually found some peace following Mom's death. Something about feeling so small in comparison to a gigantic world gave me a perspective I hadn't had before. After years of blaming Mom for leaving me too early, I was finally able to mourn *her* loss, finally able to see that she was a woman who had been robbed of her future, too, and forced to leave her girls to fend for themselves.

"Sorry I'm such a crab," I said. I wrapped my arms around Tim and let my head rest on his chest. Closed my eyes. Breathed. More tears ran down my cheeks.

Tim hugged me back, unwrapped my arms, and went to the cupboard for a coffee cup. "If I don't see you sometime today, then I won't see you until late tonight." He feigned sadness, turning his bottom lip over.

"On a Wednesday? Why can't Philippe close the kitchen?"

"We have a special group coming in. I want to be there 'til the end, just in case."

"I'm sure Philippe could handle it."

"I'm sure he could, but I'd rather stay. If you need me, just call. Or even better, come in and work."

"I don't think so."

These days, feeling sorry for myself reigned supreme. Somewhere below the self-pity was a nagging guilt I felt for shirking my responsibilities at the restaurant, welshing on our "co-owner" arrangement.

"I'm sorry I'm not more helpful," I added.

"It's fine," Tim said. "By the way, I looked at the draft of the new menu format you designed. I think it looks great."

"Thanks." I had spent hours on the Internet, pulling up actual menus from restaurants in France and Italy, getting ideas.

"And when you come back to work, you'll be even more help," he said.

"Yeah. Sure."

*When you come back to work.* The words splashed a wave of acid in the bowl of my stomach. More evidence that there would be no baby in my future. Tim was never one to initiate a fight, but he was a champ when it came to putting his foot in his mouth, always pushing the buttons that hurt me most.

"What are Claire and Maura up to?" Tim asked. "Maybe you could get together with them."

Four years ago, my sister and I started trying to get pregnant at nearly the same time, only Claire succeeded and I failed. Claire got the starring role and I was cast as the understudy, the one who only got to play mom while babysitting my young niece.

"I'll be fine," I said to Tim. "Maybe I'll get outside, do some gardening."

Tim smiled, more smirked. Not even he bought that load of crap.

"Is there anything I can do?" he asked, shrugging, palms up.

"No, of course not," I said, forcing my face into a smile. "I'm good." I rose from the table, kissed Tim on the cheek, and then submerged my hands into the warm, sudsy water. Tim walked up behind me and wrapped his arms around my waist and kissed my neck. I closed my eyes and waited for him to say, "Don't worry, maybe next month will be ours," but instead he said, "Take a look at the adoption packet, okay?"

Once Tim left for the restaurant, I walked through the three-bedroom, two-bathroom house we'd lived in for the last six years, opening all of the blinds and a few windows, letting the breeze hit my face, smelling the wet grass from last night's rain. Feeling something.

I went upstairs and sat at my vanity, a walnut Queen Anne antique we'd purchased in Hong Kong. I rummaged through the top drawer. Brand-new lipsticks, pencils, blushes, all designer names: MAC, Estée, Bobby Brown. Claire showered makeup on me regularly, singing, "It's gift time at Lancôme." The one-ounce containers of makeup were invariably accompanied by at least two ounces of uninvited commentary: "Helen, if you line your lips in a lighter shade than your lipstick, you'll have a much fuller, natural look."

I stared in the oval mirror and took inventory of my face. Where had my color gone? I looked gray, the skin under my eyes translucent and bruised. My naturally curly hair was dry and frizzy, in desperate need of a cut and moisturizing treatment. Claire had a natural, girl-next-door beauty: perky cheekbones, rosebud of a mouth, shiny thick hair. My looks verged more on the exotic: darker skin, almond-shaped brown eyes, unruly hair.

I opened a tube of lipstick, dabbed the rose color onto my lips, and then tossed it back in the drawer. "I always find that when I'm down in the dumps, a fresh face of makeup and a nice outfit perks me right up!" Classic Claire. I squeezed a dot of a beige concealer called Disaster Cream onto the tip of my finger and dabbed it under my eyes. Now my bags looked like bruised fruit covered in a layer of primer.

I picked up a silver frame with a photo of Tim and me in St. Tropez, arm in arm, beaming. I was wearing a turquoise batik halter and a wrap skirt. My body looked good: tight, tanned, and healthy. My curls were piled atop my head, with loose tendrils falling around my face. Tim was in a salmon-colored Tommy Bahama shirt. We were glowing, we were having fun, we were happy. I looked to the ceiling, recalling the date—2008. Only four years ago. Things were so different.

We had just begun our efforts at getting pregnant—month four, and already I was growing anxious. On a whim, Tim cashed in some airline miles and whisked me away for a long weekend in the South of France. "We'll get pregnant here," he had said. Looking out at the tangerine sunset, I had nodded, certain he was right. Though a pinch of worry had already dug in her first claw, I was still optimistic. Never could I have imagined that four years later I'd still be empty-handed.

Tim and I had met in Lyon, France, where we both were enrolled in culinary school. It was a two-year program designed to impart a classical education in French culinary skills, cuisine, and pastry. On our first day of class, when it was my turn to introduce myself, I said that I was from Arlington, Virginia, that this was my first time abroad, and that I had a weakness for good bread: I was liable to eat an entire loaf in one sitting. I saw Tim look up and smile. A few students later, it was his turn. He looked right at me when he said he was from Fairfax, Virginia, that he was a smothered only child to well-meaning parents who flew him around the globe, and that his weakness was red meat and red wine. I smiled, looked down, blushed. There we were, halfway around the globe, two kindred spirits from Virginia.

By the time summer rolled around, Tim and I were nearly inseparable. We'd spend our weekends exploring the city, navigating our way through the cobblestoned old town, accosting one pastry shop after another, devouring brioche and lemon tarts. We'd visit wineries, olive groves, outdoor markets; stroll into galleries, churches, antique shops. Summer came and we ventured farther, boarding trains and buses for the adventure of experiencing each other, trying the unknown, eating interesting food, and mingling with the local culture.

Our first week was spent in Paris. We did what all young tourists do. We toured the Louvre, lit prayer candles at Notre Dame, walked hand in hand along the Seine. We smoked French cigarettes; we gorged ourselves on crusty loaves, creamy Camembert, and fruity Beaujolais. We ditched our originally booked hotel in lieu of a quaint little inn with second-story, wrought iron balconies in the red-light Pigalle District. Prostitutes solicited on the corner, and sex shops and shows lined the streets. We felt naughty and exhilarated, embarrassed and invigorated, all at once.

On our last night in Paris, Tim and I lay on our backs on the cool grass surrounding the Eiffel Tower, dozing on and off, kissing and cuddling each other. As day turned to night, fireworks were ignited against the backdrop of the great Tower as the city celebrated Bastille Day.

"I think I love you," Tim said tentatively.

"Oh, thank God," I exclaimed. "Because I am madly in love with you."

# Chapter Two

Lately I had been driving by my father's house—my father whom I hadn't seen in seven years. He lives in Arlington, mere blocks and a thousand memories away from where I grew up. Only blocks from where, once upon a time, I had a mother and a father. Now Larry lives in a bungalow on a tree-lined street that circles a park. The park isn't big, but enough for a playground and a walking trail and a few scattered benches. A perfect park for grandchildren, if only my mother were still alive or my father were someone else.

Today I parked across the street, the closest I'd allowed myself to get. His house has a substantial porch with a set of Adirondack chairs and a hanging swing. The landscape is well done, shrubs and grasses and colorful annuals; it seemed like a lot of work for a guy who had a history of walking away from living things. His carport was empty this time. Last time it was occupied by his Buick LeSabre, the very same car he'd had when Mom was still alive. The very same car that we had used for family trips, Claire and me hunkered down in the back-seat, slapping down our cards in heated games of War. The very same car in which he drove away from his family.

After Mom died, Claire had decided that we would stay where we were, in the house in which we'd grown up. She fig-ured that it was best—at least until I finished high school. At fourteen, I was just a freshman; Claire had graduated a few years earlier and was taking her core courses at the community college.

Larry would come around every now and then. Claire kept him at an icy distance, always getting right to business. She'd give him a list of expenses that needed to be covered. "I paid to have the loose brick on the walkway fixed. I wasn't sure if you'd think that was important or not. But *I* didn't want anyone to trip over it." Larry nodded, assured her that of course he'd reimburse her, that it was smart of her to get it fixed. At the time, I didn't fully get why she was so curt with him, but later it was easy to see that she was hurt and angry, and martyrdom fit her better than grief.

Back then, I always wanted to get between Claire and Larry and say to my sister, "At least he's trying now!" All I knew was that I was sad, I missed my mother, and I wanted someone else to be sad with me. And Claire had no interest in being that person. Each of us had been broken by Mom's death, but we mourned differently. Claire shifted into overdrive, pushed herself forward with the steam of efficiency, productivity, and accomplishment. I remember so well how *rushed* I felt by Claire's antiseptic process of boxing up, giving away, and saying good-bye to Mom. That was her way.

My way was to wallow. I found comfort in walking through the dark house, opening and closing cupboards, staring at odd items like Mom's favorite coffee mug. I'd sit on the rug in Mom's closet, brushing my hand through the drape of her clothes. I'd slip on her shoes. I'd go through the pockets of her purses. The smells would bring her right back: an old piece of bubblemint gum, a tiny bottle of Tresor, a Lancôme lipstick.

I was sad, and I thought I'd recognized the same sadness in Larry. Part of me felt like he and I could have done some good for each other—fellow wallowers. But the three of us were each coping in our own way, and the path of least resistance was to drift apart.

One day he stopped by to give Claire the monthly child-support check. Claire was on her way out. "You can't stay," she told him. "I've got to get to class, and Helen has the day off from school."

He agreed, and I didn't argue. I knew that Claire would never let Larry visit with me alone, without her watchful eyes serving as chaperone. He waved to me as he walked back to his car. Ten minutes later, after Claire had left for school, Larry knocked again on the door. "Do you want to talk?" he asked.

I let him in and for the next two hours we sat at the kitchen table with Dr. Peppers, poring over a tattered pink photo album: Claire's kindergarten school picture, in which she wore a plaid dress with a wide white collar and her hair in pigtails; me as a baby, finger-painting with orange squash baby food; Mom displaying a chocolate cake with sprinkles. We turned the page: Claire riding her Barbie bike; me playing dress-up in Mom's heels and clip-on earrings. Now older: Claire in her soccer uniform; me cooking with Mom, smocked in a too-big apron and floppy chef's hat. The next page: Larry with Claire, sitting at a table. He was still in his suit and tie from work. An insurance salesman, he always dressed sharply in starched shirts with French cuffs and shined wingtips. Claire was wearing blue leggings and a turquoise tunic. He was quizzing her on multiplication tables with index cards. Her mouth was pursed and serious, showing her concentration, but her eyes were bright. I peeled back the sticky, clear cover and gently pried the photo from its spot, leaving a visible square in its place. *Claire—nine years old* was written on the back. A happy girl, basking in the glow of her father's attention.

*He's not so bad*, I remember thinking at that table with him. *Why does Claire have to be so hard on him?*

Now, I looked again in the direction of my father's house, wondered if he ever thought about me as I thought about him. All these years later, and I still felt so alone. Even with Tim and his loving family, and Claire and her family, in the same town. It *should* be enough. But it wasn't. I missed the family I had had as a kid. I wanted to remember. And while Claire had filled nearly every void in me over the years, the one thing she was unable to do was to talk about Mom and Dad. It was her way; I got that. She wasn't a talker. She didn't wear her heart on her sleeve. She had no intention of letting her guard down. That left Larry, the one person who might want to remember with me. But Claire and I remembered our father differently. I remembered more good times than she did. If I attempted to reconnect with him, Claire might not forgive me.

I took one last look, wondered if my father had any dad-telepathy that made him feel my pain, wondered if he ever thought about Mom, wondered if he missed her even a fraction as much as I did, wondered if he had a hole in his heart that matched mine.

I looked at the clock and then drove in the direction of the Target shopping center. Nestled in the corner was Gymboree, a tumbling haven for little tots. My niece Maura's class was just starting. I ducked into Starbucks for a latte and then slipped into Gymboree, pulling up a chair next to Claire.

Claire looked at me, then at the handful of little girls tumbling in front of my eyes, and pulled her mouth tight, like she wondered whether it was a good idea for me to be there—an addict so close to the open drug cabinet.

"What have you been up to today?" she asked.

"Nothing much," I said, my voice sounding odd. Certainly not driving by our father's house.

All of the waiting moms bustled about. Former lawyers, CEOs, and lobbyists who had chosen to be full-time moms now crowded the lobbies of gymnastics and dance classes, selling candy bars and wrapping paper. One of them was passing out catalogs. "It's for the school," she said primly. "We could really use your support."

I took her catalog, but after she'd gone, I whispered to Claire, "These women make me want to vomit. The way they all flaunt their mommy-hood like a badge. Look at me! Devoted Mommy. Gave up my career *and* I'm raising money for the PTA!"

"I know," Claire said. "They're a little overboard."

Claire was different. She'd smoothly transitioned from being a top investment advisor to a mom, and had never looked back. But that was Claire. Claire slipped into motherhood like she slipped into everything else—with perfect ease. She wore her roles as comfortably as her size-four jeans. I was anything but smooth. Everything I did required a certain amount of tailoring to fit me just right. And even then, the trained eye could see how many times I'd been taken apart and put back together.

Claire was six years my elder and, at five foot four, a good four inches shorter than me. At Goldman Sachs, her boss had nicknamed her "Dynamo" for the indomitable energy with which she'd worked fourteen-hour days, brought in big clients, and held her own with the big boys. With a bouncy brown bob and giant chocolate eyes, she'd be mistaken for sweet and pliable. But Claire was the toughest person I knew, the type of mom who would find the adrenaline to lift an SUV single-handedly to free a pinned child.

I had spent most of my high school and college years trying to be different from Claire. Claire was conservative, wore Ann Taylor, and carried a day planner; I wore vintage clothing, shopping at the Army surplus store or the Salvation Army, balked at convention, and showed up late. Claire would bristle, offended by my behavior—just the response I was looking for.

The weird thing was, I never disliked Claire, nor did I *not* want to be like her. I just knew I wouldn't be able to "do Claire" as well as Claire did Claire.

In class, the kids practiced somersaults, looking more like overturned turtles than gymnasts. Maura had the typical body of a three-year-old: arched back, distended belly, and bowed legs. Her underwear crept from the legs of her shimmery blue leotard. She was adorable, with pigtail knots on top of her head and eyes as bright as diamonds.

"There are my genes at work," Claire said, pointing to Maura, who was on her side, hugging her knees and yelling in her mother's direction, "I'm an armadillo! I'm in a ball!"

"I love how she checks in with you every three seconds. Makes sure that you're watching."

"Maura's a little lovebug," Claire said. "But I worry about her. She could use a little toughness, a little fortitude." Claire made a fist and hammered it through the air.

"She's only three years old, Claire," I said. "She's supposed to be cuddly and vulnerable. You're not raising a Navy SEAL."

Claire smiled, offered me a bite of her peanut butter cookie. It tasted good, slightly burnt, crumbly on the outside, chewy in the middle.

"Not as good as yours," Claire said. "I love when you make the peanut butter–chocolate chip cookies."

"Mom's recipe."

"Really?"

"Actually," I said, remembering, "it was in a recipe book that Mom's mother had made for her before she got married. So technically, I guess it was Grandma's recipe."

"Grandma died when I was pretty young," Claire said. "I don't think you were even born."

"All of the women in our family die young," I said, trying to make a joke, but it was true. Our loving and affectionate mother had been taken from us way too early, after a yearlong battle with ovarian cancer.

"The family curse," Claire agreed.

"If Mom had known she was going to die at forty, do you think she still would have wanted to have kids?"

"I don't think anything would have stopped her from having kids," Claire said. "But if she *had* known her fate and been able to make an adjustment, I'm sure she would have liked for you to be a little older by the time she died. Leaving you just as you were starting high school had to have been the hardest part for her."

"I didn't make it any easier on her," I admitted, remembering how I used to sulk around the house, feeling sorry for myself, cloaked in my usual armor: earphones blaring The Cure's maudlin music, barricaded behind my sketchbook and bad attitude.

"That's because you were only thirteen when she was sick," Claire said. "That's my point."

Mom had been a natural when it came to mothering. We couldn't leave a room without her saying, "I love you," or leave the house without a hug and a kiss from her. She was still tucking me in at night when I was in junior high school, brushing the hair out of my face and whispering the same prayer she'd said since I was a toddler: "May the Lord bless you and give you peace..."

Claire and I stared into the gym, watching Maura tumble.

"Sometimes I look at her and I feel like I'm looking at Mom," I said.

It was true. Maura is a clone of our mother, all eyebrows and a thick mop of wavy, brown hair.

"Looks like her. Acts like her," Claire said, pulling out her cell phone and checking her e-mail.

"How does she act like her?" I pressed.

Claire sighed, tossed her phone back into her designer bag. "Maura's sweet and trusting and naive." Claire listed those qualities as if they could someday get her daughter into trouble.

"Mom was a good egg," I said, and my heart gave a familiar lurch at the thought of her.

"No doubt. But she was a doormat for people like *Larry*. She could have used a little more backbone to walk out on him after his affair."

"Maybe it took more backbone for her to stay."

Claire gave that a dismissive shrug. "I just don't want Maura's good nature, her trust in everyone, to get her into trouble."

"It won't last long. You'll scare the trust right out of her." I smiled smugly at my sister.

With all her self-assurance, Claire was a helpless worrier, probably thanks to me having been dumped in her lap. By the time Mom died, the paperwork that appointed Claire as my guardian was already growing dust in some lawyer's file cabinet. She and Mom had taken care of that early on, leaving no chance that I would end up anywhere other than in Claire's care.

Now Claire was the mom who did weekly Internet searches for sexual predators in her neighborhood and around Maura's preschool. Claire was the mom who walked her daughter into class each morning, while all the other moms handed off their kids at the curb to the teachers' assistants. If it were socially acceptable, Claire would have a GPS chip implanted under Maura's skin.

"I don't want to scare her," Claire said, picking off a piece of cookie. "I just don't want her taking any unnecessary risks. I want her to learn to play it safe. God knows that life can clobber you, even if you're doing everything right. Look at poor Mom."

"Yeah, I know."

Claire turned, looked me square in the eyes. "How are you doing? Anything new on the adoption front?"

"I think we'll give it a few more months. The doctor increased the dose of meds I'm on, so maybe this'll be our month."

"It's fine to keep trying," Claire said. "But you need to get in the right frame of mind. Rambling around in your house all morning and hoping for a miracle is not the best plan."

"Do I look like I'm rambling around the house?"

Claire raised her eyebrows, inspected my makeupless face, my blondish ponytail with too-dark roots, jeans, and sweatshirt. "This is what you need to do," she said, waving her hand before me as if I were an exhibit. "Catch a yoga class, get your hair done, and start filling out the adoption paperwork." Claire put her hand out like a stop sign. "Just as backup. Seriously, Helen, you'll feel completely better."

And just like that, Claire was bossing me around like we were kids again. A lifetime of Claire played through my memories: "Helen, I'm not saying they're *ugly*, but you may want to rethink those pants." Or, "Helen, algebra really isn't hard. Let me think of a way to explain it so that *you* might understand."

Claire dug through her Fendi bag. "I almost forgot. I brought you some new eye cream. Retinol. It'll plump your skin right up."

"Subtle," I said, taking the cream.

"Trust me, you'll feel better if you clean up a bit. If you want to come over this week, I can do your roots. And pluck your eyebrows, and wax your legs, and exfoliate that layer of dead skin off your face."

"I'll check my schedule, Elizabeth Arden, and let you know," I said, reaching for my face, thinking that Claire's assessment of my skin wasn't exactly fair. Just the other day when I was in the shower, I'd scrubbed my face with Tim's Clinique shaving gel with exfoliating beads.

"And come with me to the gym. I've been spinning and kickboxing, and Enrique's got me on a new strength regimen." Claire was a fitness freak who worked out with her personal trainer four times a week, keeping her hundred-pound body in Madonna shape. Even when Claire was pregnant with Maura, there wasn't an inch to pinch.

"Sounds horrible."

"And I went on the adoption agency website and looked at the packet of information," Claire went on. "You'll need letters of recommendation, so I went ahead and drafted one for when you're ready."

"Fine, Claire."

"And read those books I got for you!"

I thought of the stack of books on adoption, none of which I had cracked open, sitting on my side table next to the bed. "Okay, Claire," I said. "I've got it."

Just then, Maura bounded out of the classroom and onto my lap. "Aunt Helen," she said, hooking her fingers around my neck, her face only a centimeter from mine. "Guess what?"

"What?" I asked, inhaling her sweet breath, something like animal crackers and jelly beans.

"Did you know that Michael is allergic to peanuts, and if he eats them, his throat will close?" She clutched at her neck to illustrate.

"No way!" I said. "What else?" We jokingly called Maura "Running Commentary" because she couldn't help but give everyone a blow-by-blow of the goings-on in her day.

"Peanuts aren't really nuts, and daddy long legs aren't really spiders—six legs!" Maura said, her eyes open so wide that her eyebrows almost disappeared under her hair.

"That's fascinating, munchkin."

"Aunt Helen, guess what?"

"What?" I said, leaning into her, resting my mouth on the soft velvet of her forehead.

"I love you."

"I love you, too," I said. I closed my eyes, inhaled my wish, and exhaled a prayer: *Please.*

"I'll see you Sunday," Claire said, standing up and stretching side to side. "I'm sore."

"Tell Eduardo to lay off."

"Enrique."

"Whatever," I said, hugging Maura against my chest. "Mommy's in no position to take care of you," I babbled in a cartoon voice. "So that means that you're mine, all mine." I nuzzled my nose against Maura's until she squealed.

# Chapter Three

Cilantro. Strong coffee. Bacon. I flipped over onto my side, grabbing a handful of down comforter and burrowing deeper into my pillow. I was on a boat, a canoe in the middle of a lazy river. Who was cooking bacon? Where was the coffee? I looked around for an oddly placed herb garden, for a campfire with a tin coffee pot over it like the one Huck Finn used as he rafted down the Mississippi.

The current picked up and the canoe bumped toward a fork in the river. I scrambled for the oars, desperate to make the right decision. *Which way?* I pleaded. *Which way?*

*Helen*, I heard Tim saying. I pried my eyes open and found him standing before me holding a tray.

"Good morning," Tim said.

I took a breath, tried to let my heart rate settle. "What time is it?"

"Eight o'clock."

"Oh! Really?" I yawned, stretching my arms over my head, trying to shake off the sleepy fog. "I didn't even hear you get up." I scooted myself up against the pillows and headboard and looked at Tim. "What's all this?"

"Happy 'Almost' Mother's Day!" Tim sang, placing a tray of huevos rancheros in front me. My all-time favorite breakfast: a fried tortilla topped with fluffy, cheesy eggs, black beans, fresh salsa, and thick slices of creamy avocado.

"Wow!" I said. "Look at this."

"Just think, if we work quickly, this time next year we might be celebrating your first real Mother's Day. Wouldn't that be great?"

I glanced over at the adoption paperwork, stacked neatly on my dresser, untouched. I had planned to open it, but this last cycle seemed especially encouraging. Tim and I had had sex a number of times, and with the new medication I was on, I should have been a target-rich environment for his eager sperm. And this morning I was feeling decidedly pregnant: the tender breasts, the urgency to pee. There was a chance that I was pregnant right now, placing my due date in a solid nine months. By next year at this time, I'd have a sweet three-month-old.

Tim settled onto his side of the bed with the Sunday paper. I reached over and rubbed his shoulder. "I love you," I said.

"I love you, too. I hope you have a great Un-Mother's Day."

"I think I'm going to have a great day," I admitted, pocketing my plan of doing a pregnancy test later tonight.

It was past noon when I pulled up to Claire's Great Falls mini-mansion. She was sitting on the front steps, her face tilted toward the sun, the "G" on her Gucci sunglasses shimmering like diamonds.

"Not a bad day, huh?" I hollered to her as I walked up the path.

"It's gorgeous!" Claire exclaimed. "Why can't we have weather like this all the time?"

"Because we live in DC, where it's either swamp-ass hot or freezing cold."

"Nice language."

"Ready to go?"

"You bet!" Claire stood up, perfectly pulled together: indigo-colored skinny jeans, ballet slip-ons, and DKNY T-shirt.

"You have the stuff?" I asked.

"In the trunk of my car. I can drive. It might be easier."

"Sounds good."

I slid into Claire's Mercedes. The earthy smell of leather and the warm sun baking the seats made for a luxurious cocoon. I considered the possibility of a three-hour nap.

On a beautiful day like today, our sisterhood seemed so natural. When I was in high school, the age difference had been too big. There was no way for me to consider Claire other than a mother figure, a guardian. After graduation, I begged Claire to let me get my own apartment. I needed to get out of the house where it all had happened—where Mom died, where Dad left. But I needed her help, so I had to go along with what she wanted. Waging an argument against college would have left me out of luck. So when she insisted that I enroll at George Mason, I agreed, even though studying Greek philosophers and German psychologists held little interest for me. The payoff of having my own apartment was worth it—my own space where I didn't need to censor my feelings, two hundred square feet where my grief could emerge as often as it liked, rearing its ugly, familiar head like a hungry monster. I needed my privacy, where I could cry just because it felt good, even though it had now been five years since Mom had left us.

Claire was like the Gestapo, checking in on me daily, so I was forced to shed my flannel shell each morning to attend my classes and do my homework. I didn't really mind, though. I actually enjoyed some of my classes, including some I'd been certain I'd hate, like accounting. There was a deep satisfaction in balancing columns, some cosmic or karmic assurance that what went in would equal what came out. A hopeful thought that my pain would someday be reconciled with happiness.

I studied most of the time at the corner coffee shop and that was where I met a group of alternative students who seemed to have the world figured out. They smelled of clove cigarettes and patchouli oil. They spouted their philosophies. *Buddhism is so enlightening,* I remember them saying. *No dogma.* At the time, I felt that their free-living lifestyle was the antidote to too much Claire and to missing my mother. When I was with them, I didn't think about Mom when she was sick and Claire pounding down on me the importance of going to college. They were recovering Catholics. Some of them fancied themselves anarchists (though I never knew them to do anything but talk). Everything about them showed disdain for social convention, and Claire was the poster child for social convention. Meanwhile, my sister continued to check in on me, and I continued to tell her what she wanted to hear—that everything was fine, that *I* was fine—and not one word about my new group of friends. The last thing I wanted was my conservative, goal-driven sister telling me that my current lifestyle was unacceptable.

One night, four of the guys in the group were arrested for possession of cocaine. The group cried foul, saying that the arrest was bogus, that drugs should be legal anyway. We should be able to do what we want with our bodies, they argued. I might have lacked direction, but I'd never done drugs and was put off by their defense of these guys. Where I once saw them as evolved, progressive, and revolutionary in their opinions, I now saw them as aging dropouts with few prospects. All of a sudden, Claire and her day planner, her tax-deductible IRA, and her five-year goal chart didn't seem so stupid.

The next year, I convinced Claire that I could handle a job. I scoured the want ads, though I wasn't qualified to do more than bus tables or answer phones. Then I came across an ad for a prep cook at the Arlington Country Club. I'd always liked cooking next to Mom. In fact, standing next to her at the counter was one of my fondest memories. *First soak your bread in buttermilk*, I could still hear my mother say as we made meatballs. I loved the way she always hummed as she worked, the way our conversations flowed easily while our hands were busy chopping or mixing, the times when she revealed something new about herself that I'd never known, like the miscarriage she had had between Claire and me, how she still sometimes woke in the night wondering about her lost child.

I was hired, and for the next six months, I did every bit of grunt work that was asked of me. Early one Sunday morning, Chef asked me if I wanted to learn how to make hollandaise for brunch. I whisked while he gently spooned in clarified butter, explaining the risk of the sauce "breaking." Then I watched as he poached the eggs in water and vinegar, cradling each one as gently as a baby bird. I shadowed Chef for two weeks, at which time he promoted me to the resident eggs Benedict maker. A perfect hollandaise was now my responsibility.

After five years of going to school and working part-time, I was finally ready to graduate with a degree in accounting. When Claire and I met for lunch one Saturday, I told her what I'd been thinking about.

"You're going to think it's stupid," I said, feeling my heart thump. "I know you are."

"Try me," Claire said, as calm as a career counselor.

"I don't want to be an accountant," I said. "I can't sit in an office all day."

"What do you want to be?"

"I want to be a chef," I said, and then turned away, waiting for Claire's barrage as to why that was the stupidest career choice in history. How, with my luck, I'd end up stocking the salad bar at Olive Garden or flipping pancakes at IHOP. How I'd never have health insurance, paid vacation, or a 401(k) this way.

"At the country club?" she asked.

"No," I said. "Well, maybe. But I want to be a *real* chef, not an assistant."

"Okay," she said slowly. "I don't think that's stupid at all. I know you hate to sit still. I actually think that's a pretty good choice."

"Really?"

"Yeah, really."

"They offer cooking classes right here at George Mason," I said, growing more excited by the minute.

"How about we dream bigger?" Claire said. "Maybe France? Or Italy?"

"Are you *kidding*, Claire?" I gasped. "How on earth would we pay for that?"

"I have some money set aside for your education, from Mom's life insurance. Plus, Larry's on the hook to cover some of it, too. I think you'd do really well to get out of Virginia for a while."

"Thank you, Claire!" I said, flying into her arms. "Thank you so much."

―⌒―

Claire started down the winding streets that led out of the neighborhood, and pulled onto a road that ran parallel to the Potomac River. "I ordered a bouquet from Flowers Galore," she said. "It's right down the road. There's a coffee shop next door. We can grab the flowers, get a coffee, and then be on our way."

We got the flowers and coffee and then headed back to the car. I rested my coffee on the roof while I wrestled the gigantic bouquet of flowers into the backseat. Claire was prone to over-kill. The odiferous bunch stood taller than Maura's booster seat. If it were up to me, I would have opted for a subtle bunch of wildflowers.

The overly sweet scent of lilacs perfumed the air.

"What are Ross and Maura up to?" I asked.

"Ross took her to see the new Chipmunks movie. Promised she could have her own bucket of popcorn, plus gummy worms." She smiled.

"Tim fixed me breakfast this morning," I said. "For Un-Mother's Day."

"Any headway on the adoption?"

"Since the last time you asked, two days ago?"

Claire shot me one of her raised-eyebrow glares. "No need for sarcasm."

A half an hour later, Claire slowed nearly to a stop as we eased our way through the wrought iron gate that was the entrance to Oak Creek cemetery. Mother's Day was a busy day for visitors. My sister and I shared a sigh before we looked at each other, said, "Ready," and opened our doors. Claire carried the bouquet, and I carried the potted daffodils from her trunk, along with a hand shovel, gardening gloves, and a bottle of water.

We climbed the hill that led to Mom's gravesite. It was a good site, on the crest of a perfectly manicured hill that offered sweeping views—if such things mattered once you were dead and buried. Claire stood with her hands on her hips, taking in the view, and then bent down to pick a few weeds.

"How do you want these?" I held up the tray of daffodils.

"I'd say split them equally on either side of the headstone, don't you think?"

Claire was fond of ending sentences with "don't you think?" even though it was clear that she had already made up her mind.

I plopped down on my knees. Claire pulled a dishrag from her purse, poured some water on it, and rubbed at the top of Mom's headstone, pulling away cobwebs, dirt, and grime that had accumulated since the last time we'd visited. *When was that?* I wondered. *Did we really not come at Christmas?*

"When were we here last?" I asked.

Claire looked up from the headstone, made a visor with her hand, and said, "I came at Christmas, but I don't think you did."

"You don't think?" I said.

"Okay, I *know* you didn't."

"Why didn't you tell me that you were coming?"

"I did tell you," Claire said. At once, I remembered when Claire had called and how I'd been huddled in bed following another disappointing month.

"So I just came alone." Claire went back to rubbing the headstone, scraping at a patch of moss.

"Real nice, Claire." I threw the words like daggers, but they might as well have been made of rubber the way they bounced right off of her.

"Whatever," Claire said. "We're here together now. So start digging."

"Remember how Mom was at Christmas?" I asked, a warm memory sliding through me like a sip of hot cocoa.

"You mean all of the presents?" Claire smiled, her face opening, bringing to mind Maura's innocence—allowing me for a split second to see my sister as a child, before the stress of adulthood claimed her much too soon.

"She went nuts," I said.

"You couldn't get anywhere near the tree. And she was just as excited as we were. She'd swear that we'd have to wait until Christmas, then as it got closer, she'd start with, 'Okay, just one!'

By Christmas Eve, we'd have at least a dozen presents already opened."

"Do you remember Christmas Eve dinner?"

"Yeah, of course. We'd always go to that little French bistro."

"That was after Mom died," I corrected. "That's where you and I went. I'm talking about when we were younger, still a family. It was Chinese food every year! I hated it, remember?"

"Oh, yeah." Claire nodded, remembering. "So Dad would run into McDonald's and get you a cheeseburger beforehand."

"And a box of cookies that Mom let me eat during midnight Mass, remember?"

"She would have never let you eat cookies in Mass," Claire said. "You must have put them in your pocket like a little sneak."

I stared out over the treetops, dug my hands deep in my sweater pockets, and felt Mom's hand wrapped around mine. "We were a pretty normal family back then, huh?"

"It was a good childhood," Claire said, willing to concede only so much. "But we don't know what Mom was going through that whole time. She put on a happy face for us, but she couldn't have been too happy inside."

I dug into the dirt. It was soft and crumbly, like a cupcake falling apart, completely unlike the red clay that I had to deal with in my yard. Did the cemetery put a soft layer of soil around the gravesites to make it easy for weary family members? I wondered whether that was mentioned in the brochures: *Soft Soil! Easy to Plant!*

When we were finished, there were two neat clusters of daffodils on either side of the stone tablet, and the gigantic bouquet propped against Mom's now clean headstone. Claire and I stood back and took stock.

"We love you," I said for the two of us.

"Happy Mother's Day," Claire added.

"And Happy Mother's Day to you, Claire," I said, giving her a hug.

"And Happy Un-Mother's Day to you, too, little sister," Claire said. "I've got something for you." Out of her purse, she pulled a neatly stacked bundle of letters, tied with a ribbon.

"What are those?" I asked, even though I kind of knew already.

"These were the letters you wrote to me while you were at school and traveling afterward."

"You saved them." A chill ran down my arms.

"They're beautiful, Helen. They meant the world to me. Every day I would check the mail to see if another had come. I lived your adventure alongside of you. Your happiness and zest for life popped off the pages."

"Geez, Claire," I said, almost embarrassed by her sentimentality.

"I thought maybe you'd like to read them. To reconnect with that part of yourself. Or just for the heck of it!" she said, lightening her tone.

"Thanks, Claire. Thanks a lot." I hugged her tightly, breathing in her expensive rosemary shampoo.

A few minutes later, we turned and began walking down the hill. I glanced back once, only to see that the impressive bouquet had already slid onto its side. I slung my arm around Claire and pointed to the car, hoping that she wouldn't look back to see that even the sturdiest bunch of flowers could be overcome by its own weight.

Inside the warmth of the car, I pulled out the stack of letters. The first one was written inside a card I bought from a peddler on the street. It was a typically Parisian scene: couples strolling along the tree-lined bank of the Seine, Notre Dame in the background, one of the impressive bridges straddling the river. I started to read it to myself.

"Read it out loud," Claire said.

Dear Claire,

I'm now settled in at the culinary school's chateau—
you've never seen a "dorm" quite like this! I cook all
day, and at night, a small group of us students who
have become friends sit around on the patio of the
manor house, looking out over the hillside covered in
lavender, sipping the most delicious Beaujolais. You
wouldn't believe this group—everyone is from somewhere different. The accents, the translations, the hand
gestures we all use to communicate what we're saying. It's so much fun! We're tentatively planning a trip
through Greece and Turkey after graduation.

Believe it or not, there's this one guy—who is SO good
looking, so totally not my usual type (dark, brooding,
dangerous). This guy has sandy blond hair and a square
jaw and the greenest eyes—very "boy next door." Guess
where he's from, Claire? Fairfax! I traveled all the way
to France to meet a guy from Fairfax, probably ten
miles from where we grew up.

Anyway, we'll see what happens. He laughs a lot. I like
that best. I mean, I laugh a lot when I'm with him. It's
like we're two kids, the way we think everything is SO
funny. You'd roll your eyes at us, guaranteed, telling us
to "grow up."

So, Claire. Here's the thing: I sit with this group of great
friends, and I laugh all night with this new guy, Tim,
and I love what I'm learning all day long, and while
I'm as happy as can be, I can't help feeling sad for you.

I can hear you already, reading this, saying in your most indignant voice, "Don't feel sad for me!" But I do because I just wonder: When was your time for fun? Mom died and you stepped right into her shoes caring for me in so many ways I never deserved. I know that I wasn't good to you and I also know that you never gave up on me. I owe you my life, Claire. You're the best sister/surrogate mom in the world and I truly hope that now that I'm older and not such a wretched brat all of the time, we can finally be more friends than anything.

I love you, Helen.

I refolded the letter and wiped the tears from my face. Looked at Claire to see how she was doing. Saw a single tear easing down her cheek. I exhaled noisily, blew my nose, and packed away the letters.

⌒

That night, while Tim was in the exercise room, I slipped into the bathroom with two pregnancy tests. I read the directions carefully, though by now I was a pro. I locked the door, spread out the contents, and peed into a cup. I dropped the urine into the test area and then waited. A few minutes later, I had the results. One lonely pink line. One very definite negative sign. I held up the tests at different angles, looked at them in different lights, squinted. Maybe it was too early to tell. I waited another five minutes but nothing changed. The negative sign hadn't miraculously turned positive; one line hadn't turned to two. I threw the tests away, buried them in the garbage. Five minutes later, I dug them out, just in case the results had changed. They hadn't. This time I wrapped the remnants in a brown paper bag, crumpled it, and shoved it to the bottom of the garbage under tissues and dental floss so I wouldn't be tempted to look again.

I waited for the tears to come, but interestingly, they didn't. An eerie stoicism had taken their place. Could it be that I was all cried out, that my water supply had dried up? Or maybe, could it be that the adoption idea was starting to settle in me? Was it finally sinking in that my infertility might be related to whatever had eventually led to Mom's ovarian cancer, that my body just wasn't capable of doing what I wanted it to do? Was it time to admit that I was the end of my line, the last bead to drop from a withered strand of DNA?

In the bedroom, I walked to the dresser, put my hand on the stack of adoption papers, and took a deep breath.

# Chapter Four

June rolled in, then July. My period continued to earn perfect attendance, showing up every twenty-eight days. *We may not do much,* my slacker eggs seemed to be saying, *but we're still here.*

In a quiet moment, I finally acquiesced and opened the adoption packet, read it through. Then I went onto the adoption agency website, read, and scrolled through the photos. The site described the children: orphaned, abandoned, vulnerable, waiting for a home. There was one photo in particular—a string of glossy-haired toddlers lined up against a cinderblock wall, holding hands and offering pick-me grins. They were so adorable and perfect. I just stared into their eyes, thinking neither she nor she nor she had ever felt the safety of a mother's arms, had ever nuzzled into a father's neck, had ever fallen asleep bookended by two people who would move heaven and earth for her.

It hit me hard. At once, I wanted to be someone to one of these girls.

The tears came, tears made of the same sadness that I had cried for the baby I couldn't have. I cried—no, I blubbered—freely, as one does in the company of only herself. I read, scrolled, and traced the cursor over the photos. I cried, blew my nose, scrolled some more. Before I knew it, an hour had passed. During that span of time, my pile of Kleenex had grown into a mountain, and the strangest thing had happened. My heart was pounding and my hands were shaking and I had cried a year's worth of tears. It was undeniable: I had been touched, my heart warmed by an entire society of abandoned baby girls from China. *I could do this*, I thought. *Maybe I could do this.* Before Tim got home from the restaurant, I had already drafted our essay for the application.

But my openness to adoption was tempered only a week later, when I felt a twinge in my ovary that suggested that my disappointing eggs were trying to twist and claw their way back into my good graces. *Don't forget about us*, they seemed to be calling. *We've let you down before…but give us another chance. Maybe we'll make something of ourselves this time.* And since a mother never loses faith in her children, I once again allowed my burning desire to have a baby kindle hopes in my heart and mind. I called the doctor, asked him about a new medication I had read about that seemed highly effective at stimulating ovulation.

"Helen," he said, his weariness with me audible over the phone. "I'll prescribe it to you, but don't get your hopes up."

"My hopes are not up," I said. "In fact, we're looking into adoption. But there's no harm in trying a few more times."

As I hung up, I placed my hand over my left ovary, gave it a pat, and told it that this was its last chance. Hail Mary time.

A few weeks later, my cell phone rang and it was Tim, saying that he'd be home early for once—by seven o'clock. Tim was never home that early, so I took it as a sign. Today happened to be Day Sixteen of my cycle, and according to my temperature rise and ovulation kit, tonight would be a good night to try. With Tim coming home early, we could put some real effort into it, rather than the usual routine of Tim getting home at midnight, me waking up from a deep sleep, and trying to get things going. This would be our last try, I negotiated with myself. If it didn't work this month, I'd give in to the adoption.

I decided to reward Tim for coming home early—and butter him up for a good effort tonight with a batch of cream puffs, his favorite. I went into the kitchen and began pulling out ingredients. Once the pastry batter was out of the saucepan and cooling in a bowl, I preheated the oven and baking sheet. Then I prepared the custard and set it aside. Next, I piped onto the baking sheet twenty-four circular mounds. Once they were in the oven, I melted chocolate in a double boiler.

While the puffs were baking, I ran upstairs to freshen up. I washed my face and brushed my teeth, dabbed some foundation under my eyes and around my mouth, swiped some mascara over my lashes, and smeared a layer of pink gloss onto my lips. I pulled on some clean yoga pants and a tank top, throwing my oversized T-shirt and jeans into the laundry basket.

Back in the kitchen, I removed the puffs from the oven, and while they cooled, I opened a bottle of Cabernet Franc, Tim's favorite, and let it breathe. Then I piped the custard filling into the center of the cream puffs, closed them up, and dipped the tops in chocolate. I popped one into my mouth and smiled, thinking about how excited Tim would be when he saw a plate of these. I poured a glass of wine, took a long sip, and closed my eyes as the notes of cherry warmed their way down my throat. My last glass, I reasoned. Just in case.

At six thirty, I went into the family room, fluffed the pillows, folded the afghan, and started a Coltrane CD that Tim liked. At seven o'clock, I heard Tim pull up. I went to the window and saw that Tim's car was there, but so was another car behind him—a minivan. I watched as Tim waited while a man, woman, and baby got out of their car. Tim offered to carry a bag. As they got closer, I saw that it was Danny Meyer,

Tim's friend from school, and his wife, Ellen. And, of course, their gurgling adopted baby from China.

I squeezed my eyes tightly and gritted my teeth until my face shook. Damn you, Tim! Bringing home the faithful to proselytize.

I plastered on a fake smile, met them at the door. "Hello," I said. "This is a surprise! Good to see you guys." I had met Danny and Ellen a couple of times years ago.

"I happened to be talking to Danny today," Tim said. "And we thought that it would be a good idea for you to talk to them about Sasha, their new daughter."

"Great," I said, fuming inside, thinking that if I had Tim alone right now, I'd throttle him and then make him watch me flush his cream puffs down the toilet.

Ellen looked at me with a nervous face. "Sorry for just popping in like this."

"Oh, please," I said, waving away her concern. "Come on in. I just opened a bottle of wine and made a batch of cream puffs. Please, help yourself."

"Another benefit to adoption," Ellen said. "You can drink through the entire process."

Adoption buffs were always saying stuff like that: You can drink the whole time! No morning sickness! No need for those awful maternity clothes! Never mind that I fantasized about paneled denim, imagining my protruding belly, my supportive hand on my hip as I backed my way onto the sofa.

I laughed, smiled, and when Danny and Ellen hovered over Sasha, I sent Tim a look that told him that he was in serious trouble. He shrugged at me like I wasn't too scary.

We settled in the family room and spread out a blanket for Sasha. I stared at her while Ellen rambled on about the logistics, the paperwork, and the travel. How waiting for the INS approval was the hardest part. How Danny's fingerprints got confused with a petty thief's doing time in Georgia. How once there was an error in the file, it was like moving mountains to fix it.

At some point, I stopped listening and began to wonder, tried to conjure up an image of a little Chinese baby, rattling around in a crib with others just like her. What would it be like to hold a baby who had never been held by a mother or father who adored her? I thought of Maura, how she had been welcomed into this world in a warm hospital, nestled at her mother's breast, swaddled tightly in soft blankets. How wildly her start differed from the scenario that Tim was proposing: adopting a baby born...where? On the dirt floor of a hut in rural China, her parents disgusted when they saw that she was a girl? An old saying described Chinese females as "grass born to be stepped on." It wasn't as if I hadn't read *The Good Earth*, and the entire collection of Amy Tan books. I knew how girls were treated there. I knew that it was only the lucky ones who were abandoned in open marketplaces or on the road leading up to the orphanage.

"With children, you write on a blank slate," Claire always said. But if I acquiesced, if I gave into an adoption, we'd be getting a baby whose slate was anything but blank. A year in an orphanage could certainly mar one's slate, if not warp, crack, or break it altogether. Not to mention the shoddy, possibly nonexistent, prenatal care that the birth mother had likely received. Smoking, drinking, drugs, poor nutrition, disease—who knew what a baby's nine months in the womb were like, without even considering what the following months brought.

While a baby like Maura was having love lavished upon her by two parents who wanted a child more than anything in the world, I was being asked to consider loving an orphan who might not love me back. And while I was fully cognizant that being a parent meant being selfless, meant giving of myself in exchange for nothing in return, I wasn't ready to strike that deal in such bleak terms. I needed what Maura gave to Claire: bright smiles, uninhibited displays of devotion, velvety cuddles. I needed the pure adoration, little possum hands hooked onto my shirt, endless strings of kisses. I wasn't strong like families I'd seen on the news, adopting ten special-needs kids, shaking off praise as if it were nothing. I stood in awe of those parents, but it wasn't me. I needed to acknowledge my limitations.

I needed my daughter to love me back.

*Here's the thing, peanut,* I'd say to my prospective daughter. *I'll love you until you cry uncle. You won't know what to do with the amount of love that I'll have for you. But it's vital, it's essential, that you love me back. Because you see, we're the same. I have a hole in my heart, too. I'll fill yours. But I'm counting on you to fill mine. Do we have a deal? Pinky swear?*

But what if the answer was no? What if the answer was maybe? Not now? Perhaps in a few years? What if it was never? What if all the nurturing in the world could not restore what was robbed from the baby I got? What if the separation from her birth mother caused irreparable damage to her ability to trust? Who was I to think that I had the ability, talent, patience, capacity to care for a child like that? What evidence did I have that I was strong enough? I hadn't exactly healed well after Mom died. I hadn't exactly fared well during my failures with infertility. I wasn't Claire.

Having a biological child seemed easier. I would know where she was coming from. There would be no mysteries about scarred hearts or pain or longing. Having a biological child seemed doable, like making pancakes or biscuits. But adopting a child seemed much more difficult, excessively difficult, like layering paper-thin pastry dough in order to make a perfectly flaky phyllo.

I sat down on the floor next to Sasha, held out my finger for her to grab, and made silly, googly faces at her. She smiled and clapped and squeaked the cutest sound. When she looked at me, my heart issued a percussive beat, and I felt compelled to look away, as if I knew that looking at her for too long was as dangerous as staring directly into the sun. She was beautiful, and if her start had been a rocky one, I certainly couldn't tell. Was it possible that she had made it through her beginnings unscathed? Was being adopted a magical tonic that granted these girls a do-over, erasing any trace of hurt?

Sasha looked at me as if to say, *I'm loveable, don't you think? You can find a space in your heart for a baby like me, couldn't you?*

*Maybe*, I thought.

___

That night, after the Meyers had left, Tim lay against his pillow with his clipboard on his lap, working on the week's menu. Though I was still furious at him for bombing the Meyers on me unexpectedly, meeting Sasha *had* been eye-opening, and plus, I needed him tonight. I rolled over toward him, began rubbing his chest, working my way downward.

"Helen," he said, putting his hand over mine. "I thought we were done trying."

"Almost," I said, freeing my hand from his, tracing a figure eight over his stomach. "I think we might have a good chance this month. I'm really doped up on drugs."

"You say that every month. You're setting yourself up for pain."

"Please, *please*," I begged. "Have sex with me."

"Didn't you think little Sasha was adorable? Didn't that spark any interest in you?"

"It did," I said. "Really, she was a doll and I could totally go in that direction. But we might as well give it one more try, right?"

That night, my exasperated husband made love to me and, afterward, stuffed pillows under my bottom. Meanwhile, I closed my eyes and did what I always did: visualized Tim's sperm meeting up with one of my juicy, viable eggs, a Botticelli beauty that had been trapped in a war zone. Now she slid easily from my ovary and down my fallopian tube, ripe for a union with a handsome sperm.

Then I said a decade of Hail Marys, just for good measure.

Afterward, Tim got up, went to the bathroom, and brushed his teeth. He slipped into bed, smelling of Irish Spring and Crest, crisp scents that made me think of our first summer together. Only hours after we'd reached Athens, we caught the first ferry out, destined for the white beaches of Paros. Once there, we checked into a quaint beachside villa.

We swam in the turquoise water and stuffed ourselves with local delicacies. We explored the white stucco Orthodox churches and shopped for sea sponges and souvenirs as we ambled along the cobblestone paths through the marketplace.

On the eve of our departure, we sat on the patio outside of our villa, staring out at the azure Aegean and sipping chilled white wine. Tim reached into his pocket and pulled out a tiny silk pouch. He knelt before me as I pulled open the little strings.

"Oh my God," I gasped, staring at the glistening silver ring.

"I love you," Tim said, his green eyes watery.

"I love you, too."

"So will you marry me?"

"I would die if I didn't."

*Oh, the romance*, I now thought. "I would die if I didn't." That's how our life was then, one romantic adventure after the next, one exotic trip after another, not a worry in the world.

___

Sixteen days later, for the first time in my life, I stared down at two pink lines on a pregnancy test. For good measure, I repeated the test—twice. Ten minutes later, I had three tests beaming positively at me: two pink lines, a plus sign, and one that spelled out "pregnant."

I was speechless, as though if I spoke a word or moved a muscle, everything would change. Even though I was a fair-weather Catholic—only a fraction as faithful as my sister was and my mother once was—I fell to my knees and thanked God. At once, it seemed that true divinity was at work. I sobbed and sobbed, grateful giant tears of joy. "Thank you, thank you," I cried, "I promise to be the best mother in the entire world."

When I gathered and then slid the stack of adoption paperwork into my bottom desk drawer, a shudder of shame snaked down my back. I flipped the agency brochure over so that I couldn't see the photo of the little girls. *I'm sorry*, I whispered, and then shook off the uneasy feeling and went to the kitchen for a prenatal vitamin, a tall glass of milk, and some slices of cheese.

___

Two months later, just as the zipper on my jeans was starting to pull tight, I sat down on the toilet seat and watched a clump of blood sink to the bottom. An ultrasound confirmed that the baby had been lost. A D&C followed the next day.

I stayed cloistered in my bedroom for nearly a week. The sonogram photo of my little bean lay on the pillow next to me. *What to Expect When You're Expecting* sat on my end table, Post-it notes fanning from the pages.

Tim was helpless to ease my pain. In my grief and selfishness, I never once thought that he might be hurting, too. Claire visited every day and tried to help, but in her usual way, which, in my frayed state, seemed too intrusive. She'd dump my tea before I was finished, fluff my pillows when I liked them flat, and change my sheets while I was still in the bed. She meant well; of course she meant well.

But she was pushing me through the steps quicker than I could handle. It was her way, and I recognized her method of dealing with grief. I'd seen it before, as she dealt—or didn't deal—with Mom's death. Claire's eerie calm, steely resolve, and uber-efficiency was too much for me, and everything she said hit me wrong.

"Miscarriages are blessings in disguise," Claire said. "It's nature's way of weeding out unviable pregnancies."

I wanted to smack her across the face for using the words "weeding out" and "unviable" when describing my baby. I didn't want to hear her dissertation on baby Darwinism, how my baby had to endure the dog-eat-dog world of survival of the fittest before she was even born. *She.* Of course, it was too soon to know. But somehow I just did.

I wanted my mother. My mother, who would let me cry until the well ran dry; my mother, who wouldn't try to rationalize the biology of a miscarriage; my mother, whose faith was so potent that only a drop would leave you convinced. I could just hear her telling me that my baby was in the arms of angels, that there she would grow big and strong, that someday I would see her again.

Two weeks later, I announced to Tim, "I'm done. No kids. I'll be back at the restaurant in a few weeks. And let's plan a trip. And let's get drunk. And eat oysters."

Tim looked at me with his pity face, the one that said he didn't buy a word that I was saying.

"Helen," he said. "You were this close to jumping on board with the adoption. You saw Sasha, you read the literature. You said yourself that you could see it working for us."

"And what if we go through the process, and in the end, we don't get a baby?" I asked, my voice shaking. "How would that be any better than the hell we just went through?"

I stayed in bed for another week. Waited for the open wound on my heart to dry out and scab over. Waited for the truth to sink in: Being a mother wasn't in the cards for me. It was time that I accepted that fact.

*Back to work*, I thought. Something that I could do successfully.

On the morning of my return, Tim had left the house before I did. I told him that I'd meet him at the restaurant a little later. When I went downstairs for coffee, I found a note from Tim: *Love you. See you at the restaurant. Let's get going on this paperwork. The sooner we get it going, the sooner we'll get a baby.*

The stack of adoption forms sat on the counter.

I poured my coffee, stared out the window, and then systematically crumpled every single paper. Then, just for good measure, over the stainless steel sink, I burned them.

Each day, I went to work. Clouded by a certain numbness, I went through the motions of my day without a clear consciousness of each step. I'd get to Harvest, but not remember driving there. I'd eat, but not taste. I'd carry on conversations with Sondra, our hostess, and the other workers without having a clue what was being said.

Behind my workstation, I felt safe and warm. Cloaked in my apron, I felt disguised. With my hands pushing through dough, I felt comforted. Each morning, I would take inventory of my supplies, plan my recipes, calculate the needs for each night's dinner sitting. Then I would start. In my own little world, in a frenzied cloud of grief, I baked. I did the work that couldn't be seen: the prep, the proofing, the careful kneading of the dough. I made biscuits and loaves and cookies and pies until the racks were filled. I needed to witness the conversion of flour, yeast, salt, and water. I needed to see how the mingling of these ingredients, when exposed to heat, produced something nourishing, something that filled holes in stomachs and hearts.

Most days I drove home alone because Tim came later to the restaurant and stayed later. But this night, we drove home together. Tim had decided to call it an early night. I peered out the window at Embassy Row: Peru, Trinidad, Chile. Tim and I used to take late-night walks all the way down to Dupont Circle to have a drink on an outdoor patio. It had been years since we'd done that. Now that we weren't going to be parents, there would be plenty of time.

"I called the adoption agency today," Tim said.

I whipped my head in his direction, sent him a treasonous glare. "Why'd you do that?" I asked through clenched teeth.

"Because you won't do it," he said. "And I know that it's the right thing to do. I'm intervening, Helen. I'm intervening on your behalf."

"We're *childless*, Tim. That's all there is to it. I'm accepting it, why don't you?"

"We don't need to be childless. There are thousands of babies out there."

"What makes you so sure that an adoption will go through?" My voice cracking, tears filling my eyes. "How do you know that I'd pass the tests? I mean, hell, Tim. Look at my history—a mother who died, a father who left, and me—not particularly stable during a crisis. What makes you think that some social worker is going to say, 'Yeah, sure, let's give that nut a baby.'"

"Helen," Tim said through his own clenched teeth. "What about the good stuff? We're a happily married couple, business owners, homeowners. We're good candidates."

"These children," I said. "They're orphans. They've been left. We might get a baby who isn't capable of loving us."

"Why would you think that?"

"You're not the only one who has been on the Internet, Tim. I read an article by a psychologist who believes that adoption is like a trauma that produces a wound that never heals. *Ever.* She said that the separation between birth mother and child essentially leaves a hole in the baby's heart. What if that's true, Tim? What if we get a baby who has a wound that can't be healed by us?"

"With two parents who love her, how could she have a hole in her heart? This baby is going to have so much love she'll be waving a white flag."

"But what if two parents who love her isn't enough?"

"It's two more than you had for much of your childhood," Tim said, looking at me. "And you still turned out pretty good."

"That's debatable," I said, thinking that I was far from whole. "Even if she's happy with us, who's to say she won't leave us someday? Someday she might want to return to China."

"She's not going to be an exchange student, Helen. She's going to be our daughter."

"She might leave us, though. We're not her blood. She might go looking for her real parents someday."

"Is that what you've been worrying about all of this time?" Tim asked. "Her leaving?"

"People leave," I said flatly. "Statistically speaking, one way or another, everyone leaves."

"You're wrong, Helen. Not everyone leaves. Just because your father left and your mother died, doesn't mean that's all there is to your track record. I'm not leaving. Our new baby isn't leaving, either." Tim shrugged, palms up. "Do you even believe that someone can actually stay? *I'm* staying, Helen. I'm not going anywhere. And our daughter will stay, too." He shook his head. "Do you need to know more than that?"

"No."

"No one's leaving," he repeated.

"No matter what?"

"No matter what."

# Chapter Five

The next night I found myself behind the wheel, heading in the direction of Arlington. Tim wouldn't be home for hours, and other than diving into the packet of adoption materials, I didn't have anything to do. I zipped through the drive-through at Starbucks for a caramel latte and a piece of coffee cake and turned onto the road that led to my father's house. I slowed to a stop in front of the park and squinted to see through his front window. There was light inside. He was in there, moving around, but I couldn't make out much. Next time I would remember to bring binoculars. I squinted again at the window. What was he doing? Putting away his dinner dishes? What did a guy living alone even *eat* for dinner? A frozen pizza? A steak fried in a pan? Maybe he had more skills than I was giving him credit for. Maybe someday I'd cook him a big pot of chili with a batch of corn bread muffins. That would last him all week. He'd like that, wouldn't he? A home-cooked meal?

I stared at my father's house as if it held the answers to all of my questions. Why did my mother die when she would have done anything to live to see us grow up? Why did my father live but leave when we needed him so badly to stay? Where was my family when I needed them to fill the hole in my heart?

*If you want a family so badly*, some pesky intruder in my head chimed, *then make it happen.*

⌒

The next day, I pulled the adoption packet out of my bottom desk drawer, flipped over the brochure, and stared into the eyes of the girls who needed mothers. *I get it*, I wanted to tell them. *I've been left, too. I have a hole in my heart, too.*

With the completion of each form, a new eagerness rose in me, a resounding assuredness that this might work. But as quickly as the hope would rise, I'd push it back down. *Not yet*, my heart seemed to be saying, as if it knew that it was safer to keep some distance. The file of paperwork grew. Soon it was so thick that I transferred it to a box, a tangible pile of evidence pointing in the direction of a baby. But still, there were no guarantees, my skeptical mind would remind me. I was afraid of opening my heart completely until she was in my arms. Just in case she never was.

Nonetheless, with each completed form, I felt my body calm, my shoulders drop, my heart heal. Some nights, when I closed my eyes, an image of a precious porcelain-faced baby with lacquer-black hair popped into my mind. I could almost imagine her rosebud lips and almond-shaped eyes. I'd see her a few years down the road when she was Maura's age, regaling me with her stories from the day. *We got to paint, Mom! With our fingers!*

The adoption paperwork was voluminous. We produced tax returns, pay stubs, investment summaries, medical exams, police screenings, fingerprints. We collected letters of recommendation, wrote essays, swore that we would feed, clothe, educate, and never hurt this child. Each form required our signatures, a notary public witnessing them, a certification stating that the notary public was indeed a notary public, and authentication. While unfit parents everywhere were popping out babies, we were being scrutinized in order to adopt a baby nobody wanted. The irony was rich.

One day, I was outside collecting our mail. My neighbor, Kathy, was at her mailbox, too. We chatted and she stepped easily into my personal life, asking how the "fertility problems" were going. Before I thought it through, I told her that we were putting in to adopt.

"Mark my words!" she said in her know-it-all voice, wagging her finger at me. "You'll adopt and no sooner get pregnant. You watch! It happens all of the time."

I nodded, refraining from arguing that thousands of adoptive parents out there would beg to differ with her theory. Infertile was infertile, as it were.

Back in the house, I sat down with a cup of tea and considered Kathy's point. Maybe, I thought, Kathy and her cohort of intrusive, busybody women who spouted their philosophies whether you asked them or not were correct. "Just watch!" I'd heard them cluck a thousand times. "Your body will relax and you'll get pregnant!" they'd said, laughing with their mouths open, as if it were the most delightfully ironic thing in the world. How I could have punched them in the mouth, those women who sprouted babies from their hips and arms like eyes on a potato.

And while there was no science to back up Kathy's claim, it was true that it happened all of the time.

Tim was elated that I had finally come around and that we had submitted the last of the paperwork to the agency. And truly, I *had* come around. My continuing efforts to procreate now sent an uneasy shiver down my spine, as if I were betraying the Chinese orphan whom I had never met but was somehow already growing to love. But still, I was split. I was courting two lovers and was flanked with the attendant guilt. I desperately wanted the baby in China, but I also couldn't help reserving a glimmer of hope for a last-ditch effort, a secret plan to tempt fate, confuse karma, and trick my body. I pocketed my plan as my own little treasure, something I clung to in private, something I would take out if I ever achieved pregnancy again. *See!* I'd say. *I told you not to count me out.*

In September, we met with our social worker, Dr. Eleanor Reese.

"Call me, Elle," she said, standing at our front door, fluffing her nest of wild auburn hair.

We asked her into the family room, offered her coffee. She sat in the upholstered chair in front of the fireplace. Her eyes were greenish, feline, and her body was voluptuous, with a pendulous bosom and curvy hips. She was dressed in flowing fabrics of bright hues, three-inch heels, and a pound of jewelry. She looked like an advertisement for Chicos. She was so vibrant and I was so *anything-but* in my khaki pants and blue sweater from the Old Navy Boring Department. The juxtaposition was glaring.

I was already squirming. Her eye contact was *too* good. What if she could detect that I wanted to adopt, but that I wasn't quite finished trying to get pregnant?

"It's so nice meeting you both," Elle said, waving her arm in the air, her bangles falling like dominoes down her wrist. "I enjoyed talking to you the other day on the phone."

During that phone conversation, I had told her a bit about Tim and me, our desire to adopt.

"Tell me more about yourselves," she said now. "How long have you been married?"

"Seven years."

"And how did you meet?"

I told her about meeting at cooking school in France—two kids from Virginia falling in love halfway around the globe.

"A real love affair," Elle said, shimmying in her chair, bracelets chiming.

I looked at Elle, wondered what it would be like to be so *jolly*, to wear such bright clothing, to laugh so loudly, to feel so much joy.

"Once you were married, did you have conversations about having children?"

"All the time," I said. "We both have always wanted a family."

"And seeing that you both went to cooking school, are either of you chefs?" Elle asked.

"Tim and I own a restaurant—Harvest, on Seventeenth Street?"

"Harvest!" Elle roared. "I have dreams about the braised pheasant and parmesan polenta." She opened her mouth and let out a gravelly laugh that caused tremors throughout her body.

"Yeah, that is pretty good," I admitted, imagining the slow, thick bubble of the deepening sauce sliding into the earthy polenta.

Tim and I looked at each other, smiled through our eyes.

"Why don't you tell me what brought you to the decision to adopt."

We told her about the years of trying, the infertility, the miscarriage, the baby room that was dulling with age.

"I just want to be a mother," I said in a pitiful voice. Elle Reese's killer eye contact operated like truth serum on me. With her, I wanted to bare my soul.

"Have you had a hard time accepting your infertility?"

I looked at her, paused before I answered. What did she see in me? "I admit, I wanted to have a baby badly. And I haven't yet completely mourned that loss. But I'm ready to adopt," I said. "My heart is in it."

"Tell me about your family."

"My family spans the spectrum," I said. "I have a father who left us early on—so, not a good thing. But I have an older sister who carried her responsibility to me like a torch, so she's definitely a 'positive' in my family column. And Tim has two parents who are just lovely, incredible people."

"Where does your mother fall?" Elle asked.

"My mother just fell, period. She died of cancer when I was fourteen."

"I'm so sorry to hear that," Elle said, and pulled a thin box of Kleenex from her bag. "For you, raising a child as a 'motherless mother'—a mother who lost her own mother at an early age—will have its challenges. I recently read a study that showed that these mothers worried more about 'getting it right' than mothers who still had their own mothers around."

"I want to be a good mother," I said. "I know that."

"When you lose your mother early on, as you did, having your own child is remarkably healing, in that it can restore what was taken from you. But it also forces you to face your demons. There's no running away."

We worked with Elle for a few months. She told us that the wait to get a baby would be about twelve to fourteen months from the time that our paperwork was approved. A pregnancy, plus some. When all was said and done, on the first day of November, the adoption agency sent our dossier of paperwork to China, requesting on our behalf that we be matched with a baby. If all went well, in about a year's time, Tim and I would fly to China and return with a baby girl.

Months passed, Thanksgiving and then Christmas. Before we knew it, the New Year was upon us. With each passing day, the adoption grew closer. *My daughter*, the words that used to get caught in my throat as I thought about adoption were now smooth and welcoming, like a caramel melting in my mouth. Each month brought us closer to getting our referral, the document with information about the baby with whom we had been matched. Each day, my fixation with having a biological baby eased. What was once an obsession was now like a part-time hobby.

My efforts to get pregnant became halfhearted, at best. Some months I would be aware of my cycle and would make an effort to seduce Tim on prime nights. But most months, I wasn't paying attention. The desperation was gone. A new calm had infiltrated my being. One morning, when I was feeling particularly strong and well adjusted, I cleaned out the cabinet below my sink, tossing the ovulation and pregnancy tests in the garbage. I tossed, too, the dog-eared books on the mechanics of getting pregnant and understanding fertility that had filled a bookshelf. Finally, I threw away the ovulation-inducing medication.

Claire urged me to get the baby's room ready. "I'll take you shopping," she said. She knew everything that we would need, every piece of gear that could possibly be required. Finally, I acquiesced and we went shopping for the big items: stroller, crib, dresser, car seat—impersonal items that could be returned if we ended up empty-handed. Still in their boxes, I lined them against the wall in the baby's pale-yellow room.

"We need to get some clothes, too," Claire said.

"Not yet." Still superstitious, I needed to stay away from the onesies and the OshKosh overalls and the rubber-footed sleeper suits. Falling in love with a piece of clothing with duck feet seemed like a bad idea. My heart was only so strong.

⌒

When Tim got home from work, he found me on the floor of the baby room, lying on my back, taking in the scent of lavender sachets and the crisp air from the open windows.

"For her room," Tim said, holding something behind his back.

"What is it?" I asked, seeing the corners of a frame.

"I found this saying on the Internet," Tim said. "And I had a guy in Chinatown write it in calligraphy on one side and English on the other." It read:

> *Not flesh of my flesh*
> *Nor bone of my bone*
> *But miraculously, still my own;*
> *You didn't grow under my heart,*
> *But in it.*

"Oh my God, Tim," I said, fighting back the rush of emotion. "I love it. I love it so much." That was the end of me holding myself at a distance. I was all in. If the adoption fell through and I ended up empty-handed, I would just need to die from a broken heart. Another broken heart.

"You're going to be a great mom, Helen," Tim said. "I know you will be."

# Chapter Six

Spring came and the weather was schizophrenic. A sunny blanket of sun in the seventies one day, cold and windy in the fifties the next, tumultuous downpours the following week. Today was one of the gorgeous days, the kind that made you forgive the long, humid summers and endlessly frigid winters. I had spent the day baking: a rack full of mini caramelized-onion quiches and prosciutto tortes, trays of focaccia, and three cakes. I had also helped Tim cook for the lunch crowd and prepare for dinner. Once my station was cleaned, I slipped out the restaurant's back door, sat on a crate in the alleyway with a tumbler of iced tea, and watched the sun set. I was exhausted but satisfied, excited but calm. When a cool breeze snaked through my shirt and behind my neck, the feeling was so gentle it almost made me cry.

After saying good-bye to Tim, I left Harvest and headed to Target to get some of the items we would need for the trip to China as well as a birthday present for Maura, who would turn four in a few days. But my car turned left instead of right and I ended up in the direction of Arlington, parked on the opposite side of the loop across from my father's house. His LeSabre was under the carport. I grabbed the bag of peanut M&Ms from the glove box, locked the car, and went into the park across the street, finding a seat on a swing.

My pocket vibrated and I checked my phone. It was Tim.

"Hi," I said.

"I just wanted to tell you that a couple just came in for dinner and they have two little girls from China and they're really cute. I wish you were here to see them."

"That's awesome," I said. "I love you."

"I love you, too."

I once read that girls from broken homes were statistically more likely to choose unsuitable mates than girls from stable homes. The logic was simple: she who knows what a healthy relationship looks like will model that relationship and vice versa. If I had fallen into that statistic, I would have ended up with a cheating husband who walked out on me when times got tough. Instead, I hit the jackpot with Tim and his loving family.

My boyfriend before Tim, a guy named Charlie, strung me along like an overused fishing lure. Even after the Draconian breakup, during which he had looked me straight in the eyes and said with a shrug, "I just don't care about you the way you care about me," he'd still drop by occasionally, clinking two bottles of hefeweizen and a white pizza from Fratelli's. And although I'd practiced a harsh "What do *you* want?" having imagined the moment a hundred times in the weeks since the last visit, I always let him in with an affable hello, hoping that this time would be different. By the end of the night, Charlie would have my buttons undone and he'd whisper into my ear, "I don't want to mislead you." *Then what are you doing here?* I always wanted to say but never did as Charlie shucked off my shirt. Each time, I was left feeling smaller and less worthy than the time before.

When I met Tim, I almost faulted him for wanting me. After a father who had left and a boyfriend who valued me so little, I couldn't figure out what Tim saw in me. There had to be something that he was missing that would soon rear its ugly head, sending him packing.

One night, when Tim and I were on a ferry from Venice to Corfu, we were lying on our backs on the deck of the bow. The sky was blacker than I'd ever seen and the stars were almost blue they shimmered so brightly. It reminded me of the Lite-Brite I had played with as a kid, plugging each little bulb into the board.

"Are you sure you love me?" I asked Tim. "Are you sure you're not going to hurt me?"

"Not all men are evil," Tim said. "You'll see. You'll see how good I can be to you."

In the little park outside of Arlington, I popped a handful of peanut M&Ms into my mouth and chewed, staring at Larry's house. I took a long breath, inhaling and exhaling with force, feeling the tensile edges of my ribs. I imagined walking up to his door and knocking loudly, with purpose. No hesitation. *There are things that I need to know!* I'd demand. I could do that. What could be the worst thing to happen? Instead, I got up and walked the loop around the park. I watched as a teenager took my seat on the swing, his friend handed him a beer, and together, they laughed loudly.

The houses surrounding the park were cute, eclectic. The golden glow of table lamps and porch lights made for a quaint, gingerbread-house effect. As I rounded the last corner, my gaze fixed again on Larry's house. A sense of daring crawled up my back. As if being coaxed, I took a deep breath and crossed the road. I was now standing at the end of his driveway. My heart hammered. I looked back at my car. When I was a teenager, I, along with a group of somewhat derelict kids, had toilet-papered our math teacher's house. I remembered the exhilarating feeling that accompanied that trespassing. This felt the same.

I willed myself to take more steps. Now I was standing at the base of his carport. I reached out and touched the back bumper of his LeSabre. *I rode in that car*, I thought. As a little girl, I sat in that backseat and believed that everything in the world was good and right.

Every October, our family would drive out to the Shenandoah Valley of Virginia to take in the sweeping views of the brilliant fall foliage. Claire and I would hunker down in the backseat, my nose buried in a Nancy Drew, Claire's buried in one of her summer reading selections. *The Catcher in the Rye*, I remember well, as my sister gasped and giggled her way through it and I begged to know what was so funny. Meanwhile, Mom and Dad were in the front seat listening to the soft croon of George Jones on the cassette player. Every now and then Dad would swing his arm back to tap our knees. "Look out your windows," he'd say. "You're missing the beautiful scenery." Claire and I would look up for a minute and then burrow back into our books, more interested in our sleuthy and scandalous stories than the changing leaves.

We were happy then, it seemed. I was, anyway. But I was only nine, maybe ten years old. Claire seemed happy, too. But what do kids know about grown-up things like braving a marriage riddled with sickness and betrayal? At what age does a child learn that her parents might be pillars, but that, easily, they can crumble?

A few more steps. Now I was standing on the concrete entryway. The front door was staring right at me. My heart buckled in a way that made me wonder if it was strong enough to endure such a stress test. I felt nauseated. This wasn't a good idea. I wasn't ready for confrontation tonight. I wasn't ready to hear what he might have to say. I turned and felt the safety of seeing my car. *The shortest distance between two points is a straight line.*

Just then, the front door opened. Larry stepped out, a Hefty garbage bag suspended in the air, his mouth falling open like a ventriloquist's dummy's, his eyes as wide as buttons.

"Helen?" he said, staring at me as if I were a hologram.

"In the flesh," I said, in a stupidly casual voice.

"God, you're looking more and more like your mother."

"That must be weird," I said, for lack of anything better to say.

"Spitting image."

"Everyone always said that I looked like you." When I was a little kid, I used to think that meant I looked like a man with a mustache. Claire got to be the one who looked just like Mom.

"Is everything all right?" His hair was more white than gray; his face was corded with lines, worn and leathery. His voice was more gravelly than I remembered. He wore jeans and a Green Bay sweatshirt.

"Yeah," I said lightly. "Sorry to drop in like this. I was in the neighborhood…"

"Are you hurt? In trouble?" he asked, setting down the Hefty bag.

"No, I'm fine."

"Do you want to come in?"

"I can't stay."

Larry looked hard at me as he raked his fingers through his hair. The side of his mouth pulled sharply to the side. Oh yeah, the twitching.

"So you still like Green Bay, huh?" I said, pointing to his sweatshirt.

"It's too hard to be a Redskins fan," he said, offering a small smile. "How's Claire?"

"Good. Married with a daughter."

"I saw her once at Home Depot. She didn't see me and I didn't say anything."

"Yeah, that wouldn't have ended well."

"What about you? Are you a mom?" He leaned against the doorframe, popped his knuckles.

"No," I said, and then added, "Not yet."

"Do you want to come in?"

"I've got to go."

"Helen," he said. "Why'd you come?"

"I don't know," I said.

"Are you sure you don't know?"

I turned my head, looked across the road to the park. I thought about the reasons why I was there, whether I understood for sure myself.

"Helen," he said again. "It's been a long time. Tell me why you're here."

"I miss Mom," I said plainly. "I was just wondering, don't you miss her, too?"

"I do," he said.

"Claire never wants to talk about her."

"Come in, Helen," he said. "Just for a minute."

I stepped over the threshold and into the front room: blue tweed recliner, leather sofa, television on a stand, a childhood photo of Claire and me at Christmas in red flannel nightgowns. Larry walked to the easy chair in the corner of the room and signaled in the direction of the couch for me to sit. I did.

"I miss her, too," Larry said softly.

"I can't believe that she's been gone for so long," I said. "I can barely remember being fourteen, but I remember every detail about Mom like it was yesterday."

Larry nodded, sitting back and crossing his legs. "Did your mother ever tell you how we met?"

"No," I said.

"Let me get us something to drink," he said, going to the refrigerator and cracking open two bottles of Sam Adams. "It was our first semester of college," Larry said, handing me a cold beer. "I don't know how we found each other in that sea of students, but somehow she and I sat down next to each other in history class. She grew up in Baltimore, right in the city. And of course, I was in West Virginia, out in the country. We were an odd match, but we hit it off right away and started dating."

I imagined Mom and Larry when they were young: a city girl and a country boy. The two of them *wanting* to be with each other; the two of them considering each other like a found treasure.

"Your mother and I had three things in common. One, I was the first in my family to go to college and she was the first in hers. Two, we both had rocky upbringings, both with our fathers. Maybe you never knew that." Larry clenched his fist, spread his fingers, clenched his fist again. "And three, we both wanted a family of our own so that we could do things right."

I thought about that, how they wanted to raise their children differently than how they themselves had been raised.

Larry went on. "We dated, got married during Christmas break. Your mother was pregnant with Claire soon after that. She decided to drop out of school. I always felt bad about that. But she wanted to. Nobody was going to take care of her baby but her. When I graduated, I went to work for MetLife. A year or so later, we tried to have another baby, but we had a hard time."

"She once told me about a miscarriage she had after Claire."

Larry nodded. "Five years later, you came along. Your mother was so happy to have another baby. She really wanted a sibling for Claire. We lived in a small apartment and money was tight, but during those early years, I can say that we were truly happy. For a number of years, I worked in the afternoon and evening, sitting down with folks around their kitchen tables, showing them how much insurance they needed. It wasn't so bad and I got to be home in the mornings with you girls. Your mother had gone back to work part-time. Those mornings with you kids were some of the happiest times in my life." His mouth twitched, and then he looked away.

"We were happy for a lot of years," he said. "Then I went and screwed it all up. I had an affair."

"Why'd you have the affair?" I asked. I took a swig of beer, savored the bitter malt and sweet caramel, felt it travel down my chest and into my stomach.

"There's no reason. None that makes sense. I was just a fool. The woman made me feel like I was young and wanted."

"And Mom?"

"She was devastated, but didn't want a divorce."

"Always a good Catholic," I said.

"That's about the size of it," Larry said. "She said that she wouldn't disgrace her children by getting a divorce. So we stayed married, but she also stayed mad. I was at a loss to make things better. Then, Met was looking for a group of guys to go open an office in Philadelphia. I'd be gone for a couple of months. I took it, thinking that I was doing something good for your mother—giving her some space. What I should have done was stay home and work harder at our marriage. At the time, I thought I was making the right decision."

"Then what?" I asked.

"By the time I got home, your mother had lost faith in me—on many levels. Looked at me like I was less than the man she had married. I guess, after that, I met her halfway by becoming less and less, until she no longer remembered that I was ever anything more."

Larry's face twisted. His hands formed into fists, the white of his knuckles popping like X-ray images.

"Then she got sick," he said. "And that was that."

I watched Larry's eyes well up, and then he shook his head.

I nodded. The emotion was rising in me like milk warming on the stove. I figured I had about five seconds to get the hell out of there before I bubbled over, making a mess that would be hard to clean up.

"I've got to go," I said, putting down the beer bottle on the coaster. "Thanks."

"Helen," he said, following me to the door. "I'm glad you came."

I nodded, looked at him for a split second, wondered whether it was my wet eyes that made his look wet, too, and then ran to my car.

Once upon a time, I thought as I drove away, we were just an average family—a mom and dad, two daughters. Then my father left and my mother died and my sister and I were heavy with grief. Maybe those things were average, too. Maybe heartache was more normal than the absence of it.

# Chapter Seven

The phone was ringing when I walked through the door. It was Davis and Delia, Tim's parents, who were always both on the line when they called. And who were both always in the most cheerful moods.

"How are you, darling?" Delia asked.

"Good. I just walked through the door. I've been at Harvest for most of the day."

"And Tim?" she asked.

"Busy! As usual. He's still at the restaurant. I won't see him for a few more hours."

"We just wanted to check in on you, dear."

"We're good," I said. "Really good."

"And the adoption? Is everything going okay?"

"Yeah, as far as I know, it looks good."

"When you and Tim get back from China, we'll come up and help you out."

"That would be great," I said, thinking that all this talk of China meant that it was getting closer by the day.

"Let us know when you have a date," she said. "We'll book a room."

"No you will not. You'll stay with us. No arguing!" This was our obligatory back-and-forth every time they visited.

"We don't want to burden you, dear," Delia said. "We want to help."

"Burden us? We love it when you're here. End of discussion."

Many people loathed their in-laws. I adored mine. Davis Francis was the retired CEO of a string of manufacturing companies. With broad shoulders and a thick wave of black hair, à la Michael Douglas as Gordon Gecko in *Wall Street*, Davis was a towering man with an equally towering presence.

Tim's mother, Delia, was as petite as Davis was tall, and her presence as mild as Davis's was imposing. A size four with tight brown curls, Delia had a way of looking at me that made my throat tighten and tears pool in my eyes. "You are so special," Delia had said to me at the end of our first dinner together. She placed her petite hand on my cheek and added, "Cancer took my mother, too." I fought for the breath that was stuck in my throat, but it was a lost cause; Delia's words undid me. I cried that night—hysterically, cathartically, painfully—on the quilted down of Delia's four-poster bed. She held me and I remembered thinking how long it had been since I'd found comfort in a mother's arms, how uniquely curative they were, like a warm spoonful of chicken noodle soup on a rainy day.

Davis and Delia regarded each other like fine wine—with reverence and adoration. I watched them in wonder as if I were observing exotic animals at the zoo. What is this creature called "loving husband and father," I'd think. How did Davis grow into this caring human being who valued family more than anything, when my father had been overcome by husband-hood and fatherhood?

Of course, there were no answers, and I didn't really care; I was just so thrilled to be part of a family who loved so deeply and with such loyalty. "God's smiling on us today," Davis said to Tim and me on our wedding day. Davis then walked me down the aisle, and at the altar, he lifted my veil and kissed me on the cheek, his eyes filled with tears. He squeezed my hands and whispered the word *daughter* sweetly in my ear just as I looked up to the back of the church to see Larry, standing in the corner, decked out in a three-piece suit. Against Claire's advice, I had sent him an invitation to our wedding. At the reception, Larry sat awkwardly at a table with some of Tim's relatives. At one point, I saw Claire talking to him in a corner, though when I asked her about it later, she waved it away as nothing. As the night went on, Larry stayed inconspicuously out of sight, blending into the background during the toasts, cake cutting, and first dances. When he said good-bye, he took an awkward step forward as if he wanted to hug me but stopped short and settled for a quick hand on my shoulder. He shook Tim's hand, gave us a wedding card along with his congratulations, and left. That was seven years ago, the last time I had seen my father before this evening.

Davis and Delia's generous manner and easy lifestyle had yielded a wonderful son, albeit one who was a tad naive. Tim believed that there was goodness in every person. I wasn't convinced—a belief bred not of pessimism or cynicism, but pragmatism. Most people had been hurt at some point. Most people had had their faith—in humankind as well as anything divine—tested. But Tim's private-school, loving-and-doting-parents, always-in-a-safe-environment upbringing had left his belief intact.

I recalled one evening in late August when Tim and I were dating, having recently returned from our travels abroad. We sat poolside at Tim's parents' estate, our feet dangling in the cool water, a bottle of Riesling sitting empty between us.

"What's the worst thing that's ever happened to you?" I asked. Though Tim and I had been together for four years, there was a feeling of newness to our relationship now that we were stateside.

Tim thought, looking up at the marbled sky, as though he wanted to come up with something good. "I once invested in this IPO that went sour the next day..."

"No!" I protested, punching him in the arm. "I'm not talking about business. What's the worst thing that's ever happened to *you*?" I considered helping him out, filling in the blanks, offering suggestions. Hurt by someone you loved? Father left? Death in the family? Heart broken? Hadn't he ever been devastated by something, someone? Hadn't he ever felt the earth shift beneath him? Hadn't he ever felt utterly alone?

"I've had a nice life," Tim said with a shrug, rubbing my thigh in a way that told me that he knew I hadn't navigated my first twenty-seven years with a similar ease.

I was dumfounded and yet pleased by my new boyfriend's purity. Yes, next to pristine Tim, I felt so marred, so *seasoned*, yet I was right where I wanted to be—planted firmly in the middle of a family devoid of chaos, absent of hurt. I only hoped that by association I, too, would be purified.

Tim slipped through the front door at midnight. Tonight I was wide awake and eager to see him. He kissed me, said hello, and then headed to the bathroom to take his shower.

I stood on my vanity chair and peered over the top of the shower. The damp steam billowed onto my face. "How was the dinner crowd?"

"Busy—we served two hundred," Tim said, scrubbing his body with a loofah.

Tim's back was lobster red from the heat. He rubbed the bar of soap under his arms, down his back. I used to do this all the time—talk to Tim as he took his after-work shower. I smiled at the familiarity of it.

"But we ran out of the veal," Tim said. "I underestimated how many would want it."

"Did you substitute pork or take it from the menu?"

"I subbed pork," he said. "It worked okay."

"What else went on? Any juicy gossip from Sondra or Philippe?"

Sondra was our knockout hostess, a stunning twenty-five-year-old brunette with high, sculpted cheekbones and pillowy, ruby lips. We'd hired her when we were getting ready to open the doors to Harvest and she was newly graduated with a degree in hotel management. In the space of a few short years, she had grown into a beautiful woman who radiated confidence like she held a thunderbolt.

"You tell me," Tim said. "You talk to Sondra more than I do."

"She told me that she broke up with another boyfriend. I told her that she needs to date a guy her age."

"She likes the guys with thick wallets."

"What about Philippe?"

"Nothing much," Tim said. "He's really learning a lot, though. In a few years I can definitely see letting him run the show."

"You said that a couple of years ago," I reminded him.

"What about you? What's new?"

"Well," I said, a smile stretching across my face, "I went shopping tonight. Got all sorts of stuff for our trip. Whether we, or the baby, happen to have constipation, diarrhea, bug bites, rashes, a cold, or a fever, I've got us covered."

"Great."

"And I got us money belts, and passport holders, and airplane pillows."

"Somehow you and I made it all around the world without all that stuff," Tim said, smiling.

"Yeah, but we were just twentysomethings. Now we're going to be parents. We need to be prepared. No 'winging it' allowed."

"Listen to you."

"I'm getting really excited about this," I said. "And I talked to your parents tonight, too. They're going to come up to help us out when we get back from China."

It was always easier talking to Tim when he was in the shower. The glass wall of the stall cut the tension between us, as if it were a confessional. I hadn't knelt in a real confessional since the month before Mom died, hoping that offering up my sins would somehow open me up to some good fortune. But Mom died, anyway—her faith intact, mine spent.

"That's great, Helen," Tim said.

"There's more!" I said, an uneasy chuckle tumbling from my mouth. I peered at Tim through the steam. "I saw my father tonight. Larry. I walked up to his door and actually talked to him."

Tim was silent for a moment, wiped the water from his eyes. "Why'd you do that?"

"Because he's my father" was the only answer that came to mind.

"And..."

"And when we were applying for the adoption, the social worker—Elle Reese—asked all about him and I didn't have a clue what to tell her. Did you see what she ultimately wrote in the home study? She wrote, 'Father estranged.'"

Tim turned off the shower, reached for his towel, and nodded his head in consideration.

"I don't want him to be estranged anymore," I said. "Especially if we're getting a baby."

"Especially *since* we're getting a baby," Tim corrected.

"I just feel that he deserves another chance. Doesn't every-one deserve a second chance?"

"Helen, I think it's great. I'm all for you reconciling with your father. What will Claire say?"

"She'll say that I'm nuts. Our memories of Larry are very different. I was so much younger. I didn't see the half of it. She dealt with all the grown-up stuff. Mom confided in her, so I'm sure that tainted Claire's feelings, knowing what Mom was going through. So whatever she says, I won't be able to blame her. I just remember good times. Right or wrong, I always liked being around Dad."

Claire and I are separated by six years and our mother treated us very differently because of it. Claire was her confidant, and Mom leaned on her as she would a best friend. Claire once told me that Mom—only days before she died—had apologized to her, saying that she knew all along that it wasn't right to ask her daughter to shoulder her worries, but that Claire was just so capable.

For as much as Mom relied on Claire to act older than her age, she relied on me to act younger than mine. I was her baby, the daughter she could cuddle, a talisman of the early years before her husband and body had betrayed her. Except that, when Mom got sick, I got mad, and because there was no one else to blame, I blamed her. So instead of being pliable and cuddly and childlike, as she needed me to be, I became snotty and hurtful and blasphemous, sprinkling my thirteen-year-old language with Goddamn this and Jesus Christ that, those deities who seemed solidly in cahoots with cancer to take my mom away from me, those deities to whom Mom seemed to be giving a pass.

After Tim got out of the shower, we locked up the house and then crawled into bed together. I pulled out the stack of letters that Claire had given me, and snuggled up against Tim.

"Do you remember where this was?" I asked Tim, showing him the front of a card, a simple sketch of cobblestoned streets, a town square, and mighty church in the middle.

"That could basically be any city in Europe," he said.

"But it was Lyon, remember?"

"Oh, yeah," he said dreamily, and opened the card.

Dear Claire,

I'm writing you from Lyon, the gastronomical capital of the world! I'm sitting in a *bouchon* (a small restaurant), eating an amazing dish called *poularde demi-deuil* (pullet hen with black truffles), along with soft cheese with herbs piled on the most amazing baguette, and washing it down with the most amazing Cotes du Rhone wine. Hilarious! I see that I just wrote "amazing" three times. But truly, this food is AMAZING!

So wish you were here. Do you believe that I miss you? I really do, but I know you're taking the world by storm. I tell everyone about you: MBA, youngest senior investment manager at Goldman Sachs. Someone asked me if you did "arbitrage." I told them I wasn't sure. What the heck is arbitrage? Sounds kind of scary. Don't do it if it's dangerous.

Anyway, I can just see you all put together in your banker-gray, pin-striped, double-breasted suit, pointy heels, and smart chignon, strolling into the office, snapping your fingers for one of your minions to bring you a latte and the *Wall Street Journal*. Just kidding, I know you wouldn't be bossy. Ha, ha. Seriously, I'm sure you're the best to work for and with.

Love ya, Helen

# Chapter Eight

The next afternoon, after I had left Harvest following a morning of baking, I drove straight to Larry's house. There was one more thing that I needed to know. I strode up to his door and knocked, this time with the certainty I had been hoping for the night before. He answered, dressed again in jeans and the same Green Bay sweatshirt.

"Two visits in twenty-four hours," he noted.

"May I come in?"

"Of course," he said, taking a step back, waving me in. "You look like you have something to say."

"A question," I said. "I want to know *why*, of course. Not why you left Mom. I could find reasons for that. I know adults drift apart. But why'd you leave us?"

Larry shifted uncomfortably, walked to the easy chair in the corner of the room. I sat on the edge of the couch.

He kept his eyes in his lap and swallowed once. Twice. "When you kids were little, you thought I was funny." He cupped his chin with his hand and then shuddered, as if the memory were alive in him. "We played hide-and-go-seek. I'd give you ice cream for lunch. I'd crawl on the floor with you and make tents and forts. Then, one day, you girls no longer found me amusing."

"I was fourteen years old," I said. "I didn't think anything was amusing then."

Larry grinned, cocking his chin up.

"We were growing up," I said.

"You grew up, that's for sure. You were always locked in your room, and Claire was already at college and working. Neither of you ever had a word to say to your old dad. I'd ask you something and you two would just look at me like I had two heads. What *use* does a teenage girl have for her dad, anyway?" He laughed, as though the question tickled him.

*A lot of use*, I wanted to say. Having a father around could have done wonders for the choices I made in the years following Mom's death. I gravitated toward boys, then men, who were certain to hurt me because I already knew what that felt like and the devil I knew was comforting in its own way. They were predictable, easy. Real love, I had convinced myself, meant opening up and trusting that my heart would be safe in the hands of someone new. That seemed excessively risky, and failure seemed as certain as the fact that Mom was gone. Love hurt; that was what a girl learned when her father left. And the pain wasn't a quick one-two blow; it was *chronic*, like the flu in your bones, an ache that persisted, a constant reminder of what you used to have. The fact that I found and married Tim, a guy who could look me in the eyes and swear that he would never leave, should go down in history as a true miracle.

"By then I was a lost cause," he said. "I didn't know how to deal with your mom's sickness, especially on the heels of our separation the year before. I didn't feel I had anything to give you girls. All I know is that there were years when I'd drive home, sit in the driveway, and think, 'Who the hell even gives a damn if I walk through the door?' I was in a pretty low spot in my life, thinking that I'd really messed things up."

"Hindsight's twenty-twenty," I said. "But it would have been nice if you'd have stayed."

Larry's jaw shifted back and forth, and he rubbed at the corners of his eyes.

I saw him cry once and it was awful. After Mom had died, Claire and I had met him for lunch. He'd sat slumped in a booth as tears poured down his face, his body jolting as he emitted gulping, wailing groans. "I wish I could take it all back," he had sobbed. He'd sounded like an animal dying.

"I wish that I stayed, too," he said now in a gruff bark. His mouth twitched, and he turned away, facing the fireplace mantel.

"We survived," I said, hoping to navigate the conversation to a lighter place.

"That's right," he said, turning in my direction, straightening himself, his chest puffing back to normal. "By the time your mother was sick, I wasn't clear on whether she wanted me around or not. I had hurt her and I figured I was only making matters worse by staying. I think now that that was just a cop-out on my part. If I had it to do over again, I would have stayed, no matter what."

"The past is the past," I said.

"Nothing I can do about it now," he agreed. "Any other questions?"

"Yeah," I said. "Do you think that I'm more like you or more like Mom?"

"I'm sure you're more like your mother," he said. "When it comes to things that matter, anyway. Taking care of your family, that sort of thing. But I think that you and I are alike, too. Neither one of us is good at accepting the cards that we've been dealt. I think people like us get stuck in the past and have a hard time moving forward. Do you agree with that?"

"Yeah," I said. "I always sensed that you and I might have been able to help each other after Mom died. Well, maybe not *help* each other, but at least we could have kept each other company in our misery. But circumstances...It didn't work out that way."

I thought of something I had just read in my guidebook, about Buddhism, how one could never find happiness while dwelling in the past. I thought of how much I clung to the past, how I loved it in such a personal way, how giving it up for the sake of a future might be too daunting a proposition.

"It was hard to see the forest for the trees."

"I *am* moving forward, though. We're adopting a baby," I said. "From China." Saying the words aloud still sounded funny in my ears, as if I were unsure of the pronunciation.

"That's great, Helen," he said, and then looked away. "Maybe you'll bring her over one day. I'd get a real kick out of seeing my granddaughter."

"Maybe," I said. I had to give him credit for putting himself out on a limb. "See you." I left the house and slid into the car. I turned the key and saw that it was almost three o'clock. If I hurried, I could catch Claire and Maura at Gymboree class.

# Chapter Nine

June's oppressive heat covered us like a wet wool blanket. The kitchen at Harvest was nearly too hot to bear by noon, so I did most of my work in the early morning, adjusting my recipes to accommodate the humidity and heat. Every bread's crust and crumb was affected by these elemental changes.

In the afternoon, I would meet Claire at the swimming pool and keep her company as Maura took swim lessons, splashed in the water, and played with friends.

Today, Claire and I relaxed on the chaise lounges while Maura swam in front of us, her arms buoying her with swim wings, her mouth blowing bubbles, her legs circling like a frog's.

We watched two teenage girls walk by, sipping milk shakes with whipped cream on top.

"Reminds me of when we were kids," I said.

"What do you mean?"

"We used to play restaurant. You were the chef and I was the waitress. Chocolate milk with whipped cream on top was what we always served as the drink."

"I don't remember that." Claire furrowed her brow. "Did we serve real food?"

"Tuna casserole, mainly."

"With potato chips crumbled on top," Claire said, her face opening in remembrance.

"That's right."

"I remember making it, but to whom did we serve it?"

"We served it to Dad."

"When would we have done that? Larry wasn't around that often."

"When we were little, he was. Sometimes he worked nights, so he was home in the daytime. We'd eat an early dinner before he left."

"That is so bizarre," said Claire. "I haven't thought about that in over twenty years."

"It's your selective memory. Larry was a bundle of laughs back then."

"How can you be so charitable? This is Larry we're speaking of."

"He wasn't so bad."

"Mom certainly didn't mention any good times."

"Mom was hurt. What would you expect?" I said. "Don't you ever think about him?"

"Not really. Last time I talked to him was maybe five years ago. He was moving to Chicago for work."

*He's back!* I wanted to yell. *He lives in Arlington. He still drives the same Buick. I sat in his family room.*

"Do you ever think that maybe he could stand another chance?"

"It's too much to forgive."

"He tried, didn't he? After Mom died, didn't he try to keep in touch with us? I remember him coming back."

"That was *after* Mom died. You're right," Claire said. "Before Mom died? He was pure useless. You didn't know the half of it. There was no need for you to get sucked in."

"How bad could he have been? I mean, other than the obvious—leaving while Mom was sick."

"Right before she died, Mom was in so much pain she was begging me to give her too much morphine. She was as frail as a bird, but I can still feel the grasp of her hand around my wrist. 'Please, Claire, please.' It nearly killed me seeing her in that pain, but I couldn't help end her life. I gave her the correct dosage of morphine and waited until she fell asleep. Then I came out of her room and plastered on a smile for you. 'She's asleep!' I cheered, like nothing was wrong. Then I went into the kitchen and called Larry. 'I need help,' I told him. 'I can't handle all of this on my own.'"

"What did he do?" I asked.

"He came over and the two of us stood over Mom and he just cried and shook his head and kept saying, 'What am I supposed to do? What am I supposed to do now?'"

"But how could you fault him for not knowing what to do?"

"Because, Helen, I was twenty! I needed him to know what to do. It wasn't right that he didn't know. It wasn't right that all the decisions were left to me."

"But you took such great care of Mom."

"There was no way I could've known that, though, Helen. I was scared every step of the way that I was making the wrong decisions. I needed him to tell me I was doing the right thing."

"I never thought about that. I'm so sorry, Claire. I knew you made all of the decisions, but it never once occurred to me that you second-guessed any of them. I didn't know you ever second-guessed yourself at all."

"It was a long time ago," Claire said.

"Still. I feel bad. That you dealt with everything." I reached over and squeezed my sister's arm. "I know that we have different memories of Mom and Dad."

"I do remember the tuna casserole, though," Claire said, a softness flushing over her face in memory of a nicer time. "Potato chips on top—that's hilarious."

"Aunt Helen!" Maura hollered. "Come in, come in!"

I looked at Claire, wished that I wasn't such a chicken, and decided to put myself on the hook. "When I get out, I need to talk to you about something," I said, standing and pulling off my swim cover-up.

I bobbed in the pool with Maura wrapped around my waist, zoomed her through the glassy, cool water like a motorboat, tossed her gently in the air, and caught her before her toes dipped. "More, more!" she cried. We went through the routine again, and then I coaxed her out of the pool with the promise of a treat at the snack shack. Once Maura was sitting on her beach blanket with a chocolate sundae ice cream cone, Claire looked at me pointedly.

I smiled, took a deep breath. "Listen, Claire. About Dad. For a while now, I've been driving past his house."

Claire wrinkled her nose like something smelled. "He's back from Chicago, then."

"He was listed in the phone book," I said. "I just searched his name on the computer. He lives only a few blocks from our old house."

"And *why* have you been driving past his house?"

"I don't know."

"You must *know*," she said, "or you wouldn't be doing it."

"I was curious."

"Was?"

"I saw him, okay? I was in his house. I talked to him. We had a drink. He told me stuff I never knew about Mom."

Claire shook her head. "You're crazy."

"He looked good," I said.

Claire stood, pulled off her cover-up. "I can't be part of your little reunion." She reached for Maura, who was still eating her ice cream, and led her to the steps. I followed them into the shallow end.

"He told me stuff," I pressed.

Claire ignored me, held Maura high on her hip, licked the drops of ice cream inching their way down the cone.

"Nice stuff," I continued. "About how he and Mom met. How they had so much in common—at least in the beginning."

"He walked out on us while our mother was dying of cancer."

"I don't think he did that because he was evil. I think he couldn't cope with the situation—dying wife, two daughters. Claire, I really think that he was damaged from it."

"We were all damaged from it," Claire said, her voice cracking. She looked away, cleared her throat, and took a deep breath. "When you're a parent, you don't have a choice. You'll see." Claire raised an eyebrow at me. "You cope, period. It's your job to step up to the plate and deal with whatever is thrown your way. No ifs, ands, or buts."

"That's you, Claire," I said. "You're strong, and you see everything in black and white. But most people struggle with making the right decisions and with having the staying power to stick through the tough times. Larry's not the first parent to leave. Parents leave all the time."

"They do, but it's not right. They shouldn't," Claire said, her cheeks flushing red. "Larry should have stuck around. It was his responsibility. What kind of father leaves his daughters at a time like that? What kind of father lets his daughter carry such a burden?" Now that Maura was finished with her cone, Claire slid her daughter onto her back, held onto her little hands, and swam to the opposite side of the pool.

⌒

The night our father left for good was the same day our mother underwent surgery to see if the cancer had spread beyond her ovaries.

The day had started like any other. Mom sat at our avocado-green Formica kitchen table, sipping Sanka, thumbing through the newspaper, and nibbling on an English muffin. "They're checking the *thing* this afternoon," Mom said to Claire, who was dressed in a pressed Polo shirt, pleated khakis, and loafers, her hair pulled neatly in a low ponytail.

I remember recoiling at the word "thing." At the time, it made me angry that Mom couldn't just say "cancer." It made me angry that Mom spoke only to Claire, as if, at age thirteen, I was too young to comprehend what was going on.

"I know," said Claire. "I have a copy of your admittance paperwork in my purse."

"Can't we go with you?" I whined, setting my cereal bowl down next to Mom. She pulled me toward her and wrapped her arms around me, my scrawny body swimming in a too-big black T-shirt, kissing the nape of my neck. "There's no need, pumpkin. I'll be home after supper. Dad will be with me the whole time."

"You'll be fine," Claire said in her adult way, reassuring everyone involved. "We'll be fine. Come on, Helen. Finish your breakfast and I'll drive you to school so you don't have to take the bus."

I remember being so angry at Claire's bossy, know-it-all tone that I had wanted to scream at her, but I also wanted a ride to school, so I kept my mouth shut.

That evening, Claire warmed up a chicken casserole from the night before, and we sat in front of the television with trays, watching a rerun of *Cheers*. I hated casserole is what I remember, the chicken and cashews and pineapple all tasting exactly the same. Dad pulled in around seven o'clock and Claire and I ran to the door. He carried Mom into bed. She was groggy and tired and far from lucid.

"They let her *leave* the hospital like that?" Claire asked.

"No, she was awake when we left, but she started to have some pain on the ride home, so she took a pill. It knocked her out pretty fast."

I kneeled by her bedside, put my face in front of hers. "Mom, Mom?"

Her eyelids shifted and twitched, but she didn't open them.

We followed Larry into the kitchen, where he poured himself a tumbler of Scotch.

"So?" Claire asked impatiently.

"The surgery went well," he said, trudging through his words as if he were stuck in mud. "She should sleep through the night. If she wakes up and needs pills, she has morphine in her bag." He looked to the window as he spoke, specks of dust dancing in the thin slant of light.

"What did they find out?" Claire asked. "Did the cancer spread?"

"No. It's contained for now. But your mother will have to talk to her doctor tomorrow."

Claire and I followed him into the hall. Without turning on the light, he opened a closet and pulled out a duffel bag.

"Where are you going?" Claire asked.

"Listen, girls, you'll be fine. Your mother will be fine."

"You're leaving? Tonight?" Claire spat the words. It was unfathomable.

"Your mother and I talked about it in the car on the way home. This is too hard, me being here."

"Who is it too hard on?" Claire asked curtly.

"On all of us," he blurted, pulling at his hair. "It's hard for me to see her this way, and I'm sure as hell it's hard on her having me around after all we've been through."

"Where are you going?" I asked.

"I'm staying with a friend for a while," he said, only looking up at me briefly. "Everything will be fine. Your mother will be fine, and she'll talk to the doctor tomorrow."

We followed him into the bedroom. We all looked at Mom, who had turned onto her side, her hands gathered at her chin. Larry placed the duffel on the bed, unzipped it. He opened his dresser drawers and tossed in a few essentials: socks, shirts, underwear. Then he went to the closet to get a suit for work, one still covered in plastic from the dry cleaner.

This would mark the second and final time our father had left. The first time followed his affair a few years back. Then he'd come back home. It was then that Mom discovered she was sick.

"Dad," I pleaded, my voice coming out in a whisper. "Why do you have to go?"

He looked at me, then at the duffel, then at Mom. His face fell. He pressed the heels of his palms into his eyes, shaking his head. "I just need to get away for a while. I'll call you girls tomorrow, okay? I'll call Mom tomorrow."

Lifting the duffel bag, he crossed to the dresser and picked up a framed photo of Mom, another of Claire and me, his silver chain with the charm of St. Christopher, and tucked them into the side of the bag.

Dad walked past us, suitcase in hand, his shoulders slumped. He placed his hand on my shoulder and gave it a quick squeeze.

"Can't you stay?" I said feebly, too softly for anyone to hear.

"This is just top-notch," Claire said, standing firmly with her hands on her hips.

"I'm sorry, Claire," he said. "What do you want from me?"

*I want you to stay, I want Mom to wake up and be healthy, I want us to be a family*, I remember thinking.

But Claire had her own answer. "It should have been you."

He nodded as if he agreed and walked out the door.

# Chapter Ten

The stifling, stagnant heat ended on the last day of August when a slight breeze pierced the oppressive wall of humidity. Soon we were pulling light sweaters from the closet, opening our windows at night. October dropped the first crimson leaves. At the end of the month, we traipsed Maura around the neighborhood, dressed as a jaguar, collecting candy for Halloween. The adoption was drawing near and I tried to temper my wanting and impatience by keeping busy at work. Tim and I worked on a new menu, considered bringing in more organic ingredients. Together, we met with meat, fish, cheese, and mushroom purveyors, sampled their items, and made choices. If my mind was occupied, the days were tolerable, but if there was a moment of pause, a panic would stir, and I'd think, *What is she doing now? Is somebody loving her? Why does it take so long to get the babies into the arms of their parents?*

On the first Friday of November, I drove to Claire's house. We were headed to Harvest to celebrate her and Ross's anniversary. I opened the double doors to the grand foyer. Gigantic stalks of gladiolus adorned the circular table in the entryway. Maura ambushed me at the door, leaping into my arms.

"Aunt Helen," Maura huffed. She was naked except for her underwear, and had pigtail knots on top of her head. "Guess what? I'm a puma!"

"Where are your clothes?"

"I have fur."

"Soft," I said, rubbing her back. "What else is going on?"

"I found a ladybug on my window and I put it outside to fly away, and Aunt Helen, guess what? It flew back to my window. The same one!" Maura's eyes grew huge.

"Awesome, munchkin," I said, kissing her cheek and setting her down.

I found Claire in the gourmet kitchen she'd designed straight out of *Home & Design*: a Viking six-burner range and double oven, a separate brick wood-fired oven in the corner, a Sub-Zero refrigerator, an island covered in butcher's block, and Italian terra-cotta floor tiles. Her gorgeous kitchen was a thousand times nicer than mine, and I was the one with the diploma from culinary school. Claire was bent over the counter, working on her "things to watch out for" list for her mother-in-law, who would be watching Maura.

Ross and Claire had done well for themselves. Claire made a bundle when she sold her investment practice to her partner. And she still received some sort of compensation for "assets under management," which I didn't quite understand. Ross worked in the investment business, too. Municipal bonds, mostly.

Tim and I were different from my sister and brother-in-law in that we never thought about money as a goal. "As long as we're living our passion," we used to say, as we traveled from country to country. "As long as we're doing what we truly love..." Back then, we thought that that was enough: loving each other, traveling with a few bucks stuffed in our backpacks. Now Tim and I carried a double mortgage on our house and a business loan to keep Harvest afloat. So long as the restaurant continued on as it was, booked seven nights a week, we should turn a profit in about three years.

I left Claire to her disaster list and went out onto the veranda, where Martha, Ross's mother, was watching Maura swing on the playset.

"Ever babysat before?" I asked wryly, giving her shoulders a squeeze. Martha was a good sport who had raised three sons. Not much ruffled her feathers. She tolerated Claire's "instructions" better than most.

"Here and there," Martha joked back.

"You might not know this, but you shouldn't let Maura play in the road or juggle fire."

"I'll make a note of that," Martha laughed, glancing around to make sure Claire wasn't listening.

"She's used to me," I said.

Martha smiled and said, "She can't help it. She's a worrier. Fear is a debilitating thing. You can't rationalize it."

"She could probably thank me for all that fear," I said, thinking about the time Claire had to fetch me from a 7-Eleven in a rough part of northeast DC after the guy I was with ditched me, leaving me with no way of getting home.

As we entered Harvest, the warm orange glow of the lighting, the tantalizing fragrance of wood smoke from the kitchen, and the low chatter of the bar crowd enveloped me with a wave of pride, a sense that I had had my hand in something successful. I looked around at the golden frescoed walls, the flicker of candlelight behind the ornate plaster sconces, the Italian tapestries hanging high on the walls. Years ago, I had spent months with an interior designer, discussing and debating paint chips, fabric swatches, lighting options. Rustic, yet elegant was the feel we were going for. Tonight, it seemed spot-on. Our time spent in the South of France, in Northern Italy, had influenced every decision. We needed to be authentic.

Claire was radiant in her strapless ruby dress, and Ross looked so handsome in his teal merino wool sweater. I was wearing a long, flowing skirt with a peasant blouse and boots, an ensemble that, in my mirror at home, had looked stylish. But compared to this chic crowd, I felt more like an actual gypsy than the unconventional Bohemian I was going after.

The lobby was packed and the bar was overflowing with happy hour patrons.

"Helen! How nice to see you," Sondra said, kissing the air next to my cheeks, leaving a wake of exotic and spicy perfume. Her eyelids were lined expertly, covered in smoky gray shadow, and her eyebrows were plucked into exaggerated arches. Sondra looped her arm through mine as she walked us through the restaurant to the kitchen. Her masses of chestnut hair cascaded loosely down her back, soft and silky. I reached self-consciously at my hair, which tonight seemed thick and dense, like cauliflower florets.

"The restaurant looks beautiful," I said, smoothing my blouse.

Nestled in the corner of the kitchen—across from the workstations and next to the fireplace—was an alcove with a corner booth. We called it the chef's table and built it with the thought that some patrons would relish the idea of watching a kitchen in motion while dining. While it was used occasionally for that purpose, the cozy table was used mostly for private luncheons and dinners for DC high rollers. Before we had opened Harvest's doors and custom-built this corner banquette, Tim and I had sat in this exact spot, with folding chairs, a card table, and a bottle of pinot. The kitchen was under construction. Blueprints lay strewn about on the countertops.

As we were scooting into the corner booth, Tim exited the walk-in refrigerator with an armful of what looked like lamb chops and rosemary. His face filled with joy at seeing me, which made my heart warm, to think that he still loved me, after everything I had put him through. He kissed me on the mouth and Claire on the cheek, and then poured four glasses of Dom Perignon.

"I propose a toast!" Tim said, holding up his glass. "To my favorite sister-in-law and brother-in-law. My *only* ones, but my favorite, nonetheless. Here, here."

"Ten years," said Ross, holding up his champagne flute. The crystal flutes joined for a satisfying clink.

"Ten years," Claire repeated, with what sounded like false enthusiasm.

"Go call," Ross told her, swigging at his glass. He looked exasperated. "You'll feel better."

"Just let me check in," Claire said sheepishly. She already had her phone on her lap dialing Martha. "So many things could go wrong."

"Like what?" Ross said. "She's with *my* mother in *our* house. In actuality, very little could go wrong."

Claire opened her mouth to respond but must have decided against arguing. We'd all heard Claire's litany of what could go wrong before: Maura could fall off the back of the sofa, she could slip off the barstool, she could choke on a pretzel, she could drown, she could feel insecure, left, vulnerable, scared. She could feel like Claire and I had felt so many times after our mother had died.

"I'm going to get some air," Ross said, and walked toward the back of the kitchen, where a door led to the alley.

I looked at Tim and he gave me a sympathetic smile. I bit into a piece of crusty focaccia, letting the coarse salt and rosemary melt on my tongue.

Claire clicked her cell phone closed, took a long sip of champagne, and finally relaxed.

"She's fine," she announced. "Fast asleep."

I could imagine Maura sucking on the pacifier that she was still allowed to use at night, pausing occasionally to pull it out and examine it, as an old man would do with a pipe.

"You think you worry now..." Tim said to Claire, with his lighthearted chuckle. "Just wait 'til she's a teenager." He smiled. Poor Tim. Just trying to make conversation, just trying to sympathize.

"Don't even mention it," Claire said, tensing her shoulders. "Besides, I know all about raising teenagers." Claire looked at me with raised eyebrows.

"Here it comes," I said, laughing. "Let's hear how incorrigible I was, how, if not for you, I would have ended up in the gutter."

"Well," Claire said.

"We all did crazy things when we were teenagers," Tim began. "My buddies and I used to swipe the dustiest bottle from my dad's liquor cabinet—usually Schnapps, if I recall—put it in a Coke bottle, and drive around cruising for chicks."

"How'd that work for you, honey?" I asked, leaning into Tim and kissing his cheek.

"They were lined up," he joked. "They knew I was super cool with my dad's Oldsmobile and my bottle of Schnapps."

"We all did reckless things," Claire agreed.

"I doubt *you* ever did," I joked. "If you did, it would have been during the three-minute bell between honors math and honors science."

"You're right." Claire smiled. "I was kind of busy keeping you out of trouble, going to school, and taking care of the house."

"I know, I know," I said. "I owe you my life, Claire. Anything you ever want, you've got it. My kidneys? Liver?"

"You never know," she said. "You might need to save my life someday."

"I'm all yours."

Claire had finished high school before I had even started. Even so, her reputation was still there, like the perky spirit banners that lined the hallways. *Go Team!* Claire was in Advanced Placement *everything*, the president of the student council, a peppy cheerleader. And while I did pretty well in the grades department, I couldn't touch Claire in the attitude department. The teachers, en masse, were effusive about Claire: Future leader! Strong prospects! The sky's the limit! Rather than compete, it was easier to be the sister in the black Van Halen concert shirt who stood across the street from the high school smoking cigarettes before the morning bell, the kid who forged her sister's signature to get out of class, the freshman who hitched rides from seniors. On a number of occasions, Claire was called into the principal's office to discuss my behavior. I'd sit in the hallway, outside of the office, in a hard plastic chair, and listen to Claire lobby on my behalf. "She can do the work," Claire argued. "We just need to get her to focus. She'll do better. I promise this won't happen again. She needs to stay in school. Detention or expulsion will only make her spiral further downward. Our mother died, you remember that, right? Give her a break. She's still grieving. This is just her way."

Ross came back inside. Tim poured more wine, which we all happily accepted.

Claire smiled and then ate a piece of Tim's bruschetta. "Oh God," she gushed. "This is to die for. I am going to *dream* about this taste."

"Not much to it," Tim said. "Just grilled shrimp, avocado, garlic, chili flakes."

"Just sautéed in the skillet?"

"I'd be happy to show you."

"What I dream about," Ross said, "are those potato things that Helen used to make."

"Blini," I said. Blini were one of my specialties back when I worked the dinner shift: potatoes, flour, crème fraiche, eggs. Pure, silky warm, melt-in-your-mouth comfort food.

"I'll make them for you next time you're at our house," I said.

"Why not make them now?" Tim asked.

"Are you serious?" I asked, looking at the kitchen like I was looking into the mouth of a monster. It had been so long since I'd been behind the line during the dinner shift, elbowing my way among the sous chefs, different entirely from my baking station across the way or helping out at lunch. My palms grew sweaty just at the thought.

"Go ahead, Helen. Make your brother-in-law a blini."

"Okay," I said, standing up and smoothing my billowy blouse again. It would be nice to pull an apron tightly around this puffy shirt. As soon as I got home, I planned to toss it into the give-away box.

After I scrubbed my hands and fastened my apron, I slipped behind the stainless steel, thankful that it was a Monday night and only Philippe was on the line. First, I prepared the eggplant and set it to roast. Then I peeled and boiled a couple of Yukon Gold potatoes, the perfect potato for absorbing cream, and pressed them through a sieve. I whisked in the flour and crème fraiche, added an egg, and whisked again until the batter was smooth. Seasoned with salt and pepper, spooned onto the griddle. Once the pancakes were slightly golden, I removed them from the griddle and topped each one with roasted sweet peppers and eggplant caviar.

For the next half an hour, we drank a bottle of wine, ate blini, and reminisced. It was the happiest I had felt in so long. It was definitely the most connected I had felt in a long time, chatting easily with my sister and brother-in-law, leaning in to Tim naturally, knowing that soon enough we'd be on our way to China.

Later, Philippe brought our second course, an heirloom tomato tart with *nicoise* olive tapenade, mixed field greens, and basil vinaigrette. And then sweet potato *agnolotti* with sage cream, brown butter, and prosciutto. Followed by our main course, butter-poached Maine lobster with leeks, pommes, and red beet essence. We ate until we were slouched back in our seats with bulging bellies.

While we rested and let our food settle, Tim slipped out of the booth and into his office. A few minutes later, he returned, holding a stack of papers. His eyes were aglow; a smile had invaded his face, his mouth pulling toward his ears. In all of the years I had known him, I had never seen *this* look on his face, something akin to jubilation and joy and wonder.

"What's with you?" I asked.

"It's here," he said.

"What?"

"The referral from the adoption agency," he said. "It was just e-mailed a few minutes ago."

My heart went into a free fall, ending somewhere in the bottom of my stomach. In Tim's hand was a photo of my daughter.

"Xu, Long Ling, female, was born on the fourth of December, two thousand and eleven," Tim read, "and was sent to our institute by Xuan Cheng Police Station on the sixth of December, two thousand and eleven."

"She was only two days old when they got her," Claire said.

"And how old is she now?" I asked, trying to do the math.

"About eleven months," Claire said. "She'll be just about a year when you get her." Claire covered her mouth; she was crying.

"We named her Xu, Long Ling," Tim read. "*Xu* represented her birthplace. *Long* meant that she was born in the year of the dragon. *Ling* meant clever and spiritual. We gave her the name with many of our good wishes for her."

"What else?" I asked.

"She eats steamed egg or congee with pork and biscuits and fruit. She sleeps fairly deeply and does not cry often."

"Oh, good. No crying," I said.

Claire looked at me skeptically. "Yeah right."

"Xu, Long Ling is fairly outgoing and active. She is a very lovely little girl."

"Pictures, pictures," I said, rubbing my hands together in anticipation.

Tim sat down, slid a piece of paper with three photos in front of me. My hands shook as I reached for the printout. In the first photo, she was sitting in a basket, propped up with blankets, looking upward as if the photographer were shaking a rattle overhead. Her grin revealed two front teeth and a dimple in her left cheek. The next photo was of her in the crib, nestled against another baby who looked much bigger than she did. The third photo was taken in front of an artificial backdrop of cherry trees, as if our new daughter wasn't really in China but instead with us, enjoying the spring blossoms on the National Mall.

I blinked back the stinging tears, swallowed the guilt and shame I felt for all of those months when I doubted that I could love an adopted child. My daughter was gorgeous, and without ever meeting her, I already knew her and could feel what she was feeling and knew that she'd never leave, and if she did, she would have company because I'd follow her to the ends of the earth.

I placed my hand on my heart because it was warm and tingling and I knew exactly what was happening. It was healing.

"Oh God," I said solemnly. "I love her so much." I put my hand over my heart because, truly, it was swelling and the stretch of it almost left me breathless.

Tim, Claire, and Ross looked at me with their own watery eyes and quivering chins.

"Excuse me for a second," I said, and slipped out of the booth, down the hall, and into the ladies' lounge, sinking deeply into the upholstered chair. Through blurry eyes, I smoothed the arm of the chair, remembering how I'd deliberated over the choice of fabric—this one (Tuscan Morning) or another (Florentine Flowers). I slid onto my knees and thanked God. I now knew that love showed no bias where children were involved, that love transcended international waters. That loving a child had nothing to do with pregnancy, labor, and delivery.

After I dabbed my eyes with a wet cloth, I went back to our booth.

"Now, Helen," Tim said. "If you love her so much, give the child a name."

"Sam," I said. "Samantha Ann, named after our mother, if that's okay with you."

Claire hugged me and I felt her chest heave. "That's really nice, Helen," she said.

"I had been saving it—the name—all these years, thinking that someday we would name our daughter Sam. But tonight I realize that the little baby in this photo *is* our daughter."

Philippe brought champagne and we toasted and cheered and smiled until our cheeks ached.

After saying good-bye to Claire and Ross, Tim and I drove home in a giddy silence with only the hum of the car and the occasional clunk when we hit a pothole. There was a quiet and an awkwardness and an electricity to the moment that reminded me of a first date. Finding words beyond "Oh my God," and "I can't believe it," and "This is really going to happen," left us speechless. All these months I had tried to keep some distance, just in case the adoption didn't go through. Now it was here. It was upon us. And I was bobbling my emotions, as though they were slick and impossible to grasp.

Tim pulled into our neighborhood and then into our driveway, pushing the button to open the garage, which was so narrow that it was almost comical. We joked all of the time. "Suck it in," we'd say as we each squeezed through the ten inches our car doors were allowed to open. We entered our house and stood in the darkness. Tim reached his arms around me and I leaned into him, letting the weight of my head bear into his chest, feeling the steady thump of my heart, hearing the drum of his in my ear.

"This is really happening, huh?" I asked.

"This is really happening," Tim said. "I'll be right back."

I went into the family room and sat on the edge of the sofa. Tim returned a minute later with a bottle of wine and two glasses. He poured, lit a few candles around the room, and flipped on the stereo. A Cranberries CD we both liked.

Tim handed me my glass of wine. I took a long sip, letting the earthy notes of leather and dried cherries and licorice slide down my throat. I laid my head back against the pillow, staring up at the ceiling.

"What are you thinking about?" Tim asked.

"Sam," I said, exhaling. "Her first year. How she's been without us for an entire year." I considered the parallels: how she was growing in her mother's womb as our social worker, Elle Reese, walked through our home, inspecting it to see if it was suitable for a child; how she was born and abandoned right around the time our dossier of paperwork was sent to China;

how she lay in her crib, staring at the ceiling day after day, and night after night, while Tim and I, too, stared at our ceiling, imagining what it would be like to be parents to our baby girl.

Tim took a sip of wine, looked at me. "I hope she likes football. I need someone to watch the Redskins with me."

"I hope she's *fat*," I said, thinking of Maura when she was born, her doughy legs and ripples of elbow fat. "As fat as a Butterball turkey, with lots of rolls and dimples."

"I'm going to teach her to cook," Tim said. "I'm going to get her a little apron and chef hat."

"I'm going to teach her to bake," I said, wondering if raising a daughter shared any similarities to baking. I imagined a two-by-four recipe card. First mix your dry ingredients: an abundance of love, understanding, and compassion. Separately mix your wet ingredients: patience, tolerance, and forgiveness. Mix until your batter is as comforting as a set of mother's arms. Pour into your pan. Bake. May take a lifetime.

"I just hope she's healthy," Tim said, striking a more somber tone. "That's all that matters."

"I just hope she likes us."

Tim kissed me and my body went slack. He undressed me, and we made love. For the first time in years, I made love to my husband without the thought of getting pregnant, without visualizing super-swimming sperm penetrating plump eggs, without sending a begging batch of prayers up to God.

It was only our third date when Tim and I first made love. He'd cooked me an incredible dinner of filet mignon and lobster tails; we drank an endless supply of Chianti. I could still recall the buttery taste of his mouth, the roughness of the stubble on his cheek, the salt of his skin. It was at that moment that I realized how lonely I'd been my whole life: a father who left, a mother who died. I knew that, one day, I would tell Tim how I felt so alone. And while sleeping with him so early in our relationship was a patently risky move, I never once felt nervous that he wouldn't still be around the next day. I curled into Tim and tried to hush a lifetime of Claire blaring in my head, "One or two drinks, maximum! Make him ask you for another date! Don't give it away for free!"

With the referral photos in hand, I slipped out of bed next to fast-asleep Tim, went downstairs, and logged onto my computer. Now that I had the name of Sam's town and orphanage, I typed them into a search box. First, I clicked on a website for the town—a small rural village three hours from an industrial hub in southern China. It boasted of the region's temperate climate, the rich landscape, the picturesque mountain range with unrivaled views. It told how numerous wars had been fought over this strategic location, the contemplative pull of the many Buddhist temples where one could witness the monastic life, the festivals that set the streets ablaze with activity for the New Year. *What a lovely place to visit*, one would think.

Then I clicked on the website for the Children's Welfare Institute, just a homemade site: an address, a few photos of the outside of the white cinder block building. There was a picture of the road that led to the orphanage. If we hadn't been told, we never would have known that that was the road along which so many of the newborns were abandoned in their first days of life. Clearly, Sam and the others like her deserved some publicity. Shouldn't the PR guys spin their story, too? *Must see! Beautiful baby girls! Take one home today. Guaranteed to fill your home with happiness, good luck, and many blessings!*

That's okay, I thought. The country of China might have forsaken these girls, but parents like Tim and I weren't. All I needed now was for the adoption agency to call with our travel arrangements. I needed to get there, urgently. I needed to get my daughter in my arms.

*Hang on, baby*, I prayed. *Mommy's coming.*

# PART TWO

# Chapter Eleven

Tim's parents, Davis and Delia, arrived at four o'clock on the Wednesday before we were scheduled to leave for China. They lived five hours away in a gated golf course community on the North Carolina coast, only a mile from the beach. When Delia hugged me, she broke into tears and then pulled back to reveal her happy face. "Oh, Helen, this is the most wonderful day in the world."

My chest hiccupped and my eyes welled with tears because she was right. In just a few days, I would have Sam in my arms. We were scheduled to leave for Beijing on Friday, landing us there sometime on Saturday. We would travel together with a group of other adoptive couples. The babies would be delivered a few days later, bundled and transported by bus to our hotel.

While Tim and his father drank a beer out on the deck, I showed Delia all of the items I had collected to take with us to China. Inside the baby room, we gazed at what looked like a pharmacy: Tylenol, Mylanta, Gas-X, ipecac, Dramamine, Alka-Seltzer; a smattering of diapers, wipes, tissues, Band-Aids, gauze, hand cleaner, surface cleaner; cans of formula, boxes of Cheerios, teething cookies, bottles, liners, sippy cups; a thermos, camera, video recorder, gifts for the orphanage director and her staff; pacifiers, lots of pacifiers.

"This is a lot of stuff," Delia said. "And now I feel badly that I have something else for you to bring." Delia pulled from her pocket a little rubber photo album. The edge of it was hard and ribbed, like a teething toy. Inside of it were pictures of all of us: Tim and me, Davis and Delia, and Claire, Ross, and Maura. "I read online that adoptive babies like to look at pictures of their new family members."

I choked back my tears as I hugged Delia. "Thank you," I whispered.

Delia and I went into the kitchen. She chopped vegetables while I gathered the ingredients to make cornmeal biscuits to serve with ripe peaches, candied walnuts, and fresh whipped cream. The smell of barbecued pork chops with an apricot glaze filled the air.

When dinner was ready, we carried the food to the deck. Davis, who was leaning against the railing with a bottle of Sam Adams, looked at his wife of forty years as if he were seeing her for the first time. "Darling, can you believe this meal? Can you believe this beautiful weather?" he exclaimed. I smiled. Davis and Delia were excessively kind to each other, respectful, as if each knew the dangers of taking the other for granted. I wondered whether my parents ever had moments like that, when they looked at each other in wonder. Treasured. I remembered a happy childhood, but then the fighting started, and then Dad left. Mom getting sick overwhelmed every memory at that point. I now wondered which memories were reliable and which were false, a blur of reality coated in want, rolled in despair.

That night, I hardly slept. Every hour I would wake, roll over toward my side table, and reach for the photo of Sam. *Just a few more days, baby.* When I was still awake at two o'clock, I went down to the kitchen and quietly made brioche bread dough. The butter-rich bread was always best to start the night before, to give it time to rest in the refrigerator.

The next morning, I showered and dressed and, once in the kitchen, turned out the dough onto the floured counter, luxuriating in its coolness, and spread evenly onto it the pecan paste. In the greased loaf pan, I baked the bread for forty minutes.

By the time Tim and my in-laws descended on the kitchen, the bread was ready and the coffee was brewed. Now I chopped chervil, whisked eggs, and cut smoked salmon into small pieces, cooking them lightly with a spoonful of Dijon mustard.

"A fabulous dinner followed by a fabulous breakfast!" Davis proclaimed as he dug his thick pieces of bread into the rich eggs.

"Wow, Helen," Tim said.

"I couldn't sleep," I admitted.

"Too excited," Delia said.

I smiled and nodded because I couldn't explain that "too excited" didn't do justice to the feelings that had my heart racing, my hands shaking, and eyes tearing. The reality that I was actually close to getting what I wanted was almost too much for my little heart to bear. Too much liquid for the dry ingredients to absorb. Keeping my emotions at bay was like holding up a dam when I knew that there were cracks on the inside, hairline fissures that would soon make their way to the outer layer, an imminent burst.

An hour later, Claire arrived to pick me up. She was treating me to a day at the spa, a milestone moment of pampering before I shipped off and then returned a mother.

At the spa, Claire registered for us and poured us each a cup of green tea. Our first treatment was a mani-pedi. I nestled into a black leather massage chair that kneaded my back and neck. My feet soaked in a blue bath of water. A young Vietnamese girl scraped at my heels, sending pieces of skin sailing through the air like shavings of parmesan. Next, she cupped my toes in her hand and shook her head, as if untended cuticles reflected badly on me as a woman.

Claire reached into her purse and popped open the bottle of Advil, poured three into her palm.

"Headache?" I asked.

"No, just *pain*," Claire said, twisting in her seat. "Enrique has really been working my core."

"You're a masochist."

"The hot stone massage will feel really good," Claire said. "A few days from now when you have a baby in your arms and you're begging for sleep, you'll remember the massage and think, really, was that me? Was that really my life?"

*A baby in my arms.* Five words threaded together and tied with faith. They still hit me as false.

"I cannot believe that you're leaving tomorrow!" Claire said, squeezing my forearm. "Can you believe it, Helen? You're getting a baby!"

"I'll believe it when she's in my arms." It was difficult to explain that, yes, I understood that I would be getting a baby—Sam, specifically—but the notion still seemed just that, a notion. My mind was doing its part, conjuring images for me of Sam. And my heart was all in, too, squeezing and tightening and issuing heat at the thought of holding her. But my other senses were on standby, waiting to be invoked. I wanted to smell her babyness, taste her sweetness, touch her softness. Until my mouth was on her tender skin, none of this would be real.

"In a mere few days, you'll believe it when you're doing everything in your power to get your baby to sleep."

"I won't care," I said. "She can cry, scream, and yell. As long as she's mine."

Claire smiled. "It's going to be great, Helen. *She's* going to be great. *You're* going to be a great mother."

"Hopefully you and Mom have rubbed off a bit."

"So, Helen," she said, giving me a sidelong glance. "I've thought about your shenanigans with Larry, your little stalking escapades."

"Yeah?"

"Why are you doing it? What's your objective?"

Claire always had an objective.

"Curiosity," I said.

"Just curiosity?"

"No," I admitted. "I kind of want him back in my life. Preferably, I want him back in *our* life."

Claire reached for her cup of tea and took a careful sip. "So what's he look like?" Claire asked, her eyes closed. "*Our* father."

"He looks exactly like I remember him," I said.

"What else?"

"He looks sad. Like he knows he missed out. There's regret in his eyes like you wouldn't believe."

"Well…" Claire started and then stopped. "Well."

A massage, facial, haircut, and color later, the woman I saw in the mirror hardly resembled the fractured person I had become. I looked pretty. My hair was a shiny chocolate brown with lighter brown highlights falling in soft waves around my face. My skin looked glowing and healthy. My eyebrows were plucked and shaped into perfect arches. After years of feeling defective and incomplete, defining myself by my inability to get pregnant, I finally felt a sense of wholeness. Not exactly put together, but at least holding all of the pieces.

Inside the house, I had the feeling that Davis and Delia didn't know quite what to say about my appearance, so I let them off the hook: "I clean up pretty well, huh?" I pirouetted around in a circle for full effect.

"You look beautiful, darling," Delia said, hugging me.

"Truly wonderful!" Davis agreed.

I felt wonderful, too. Exactly where I wanted to be—surrounded by family and on my way to China to get Sam. The hole in my heart was closing in on itself.

# Chapter Twelve

On Friday, three weeks before Christmas, Tim and I boarded a jumbo jet en route to Beijing. We would be gone for eighteen days altogether. According to the schedule, we would get Sam on Day 3 of our trip. The travel coordinator told us that ten families from our adoption agency would be retrieving babies from the same orphanage, six of whom were on our flight. Seated next to us in aisle ten were Amy and Tom DePalma. They were from New Jersey and this was their second adoption. Veterans, back for another tour. Their first daughter, Angela, was now four years old and thriving in preschool and ballet. They were back to get her a baby sister, a *mei-mei*.

Amy and I became fast friends. She had Claire's confidence and outspokenness; more than anything, her deftness reminded me of my sister's. The fact that she thought nothing of bringing her four-year-old on a seventeen-hour plane ride, the way she steadied Angela on her lap, rubbed her back, peeled apple slices with a plastic knife, all while carrying on a completely intelligent conversation with me. Within hours, over boxed meals, peanuts, and a plastic glass of Chardonnay, Amy had schooled me on the huge issues such as milk-based formula versus soy, a Baby Bjorn versus a Snugli, Huggies versus Pampers, scabies versus intestinal viruses.

"There is a lot of behavior to be expected," Amy said. "These children don't have the best eye contact, they're choosy about who holds them, they have a tendency to hoard their food. That's normal—well, *typical*, anyway."

"That's all something to look forward to," I said, my original fears rising in me, the worry that my daughter would be the product of her abandonment and unable to love me.

"Just be prepared that most of these kids…They're not on what would be considered a normal trajectory. They're not going to hit age-related milestones. Not after being in an orphanage for a year or more."

*Trajectory. Milestones.* It seemed that there was an entire glossary of adoption words.

"Okay," I said solemnly, sipping at my wine.

"If your daughter has behaviors, she'll outgrow them," Amy said with a wave of her hand. "Other kids have behaviors that are more severe. Some kids bang their heads against the floor, pull clumps of hair out of their head. We had friends who went to get their baby and she was what they call a 'self-soother.' She had taken to gnawing on her hand. When my friends got there, she had a two-inch open wound below her thumb and habitually shoved it into her mouth."

"What happened to her?" I asked. Suddenly, all I could taste of my Chardonnay was the plastic cup.

"Oh, nothing," Amy said casually. "She's fine now. Most of these babies are fine after a while."

"Did you guys run into any of these problems?" I asked, a bit tentatively, not sure that I really wanted to know the answer.

"Well, sure," Amy said. "But Angela bonded with us relatively quickly. And really, that's the most important thing. But there were a few years where we really worried that she had OCD. She didn't like water in her eyes, so I would put goggles on her while I washed her hair. She didn't like a cold glass of milk because of the condensation. Canned fruit was too slippery. Tortilla chips were too rough."

"And now?"

"Now, she's great. She still likes things 'just so,' but certainly not to the point where she can't cope on a daily basis. She eats chips and fruit cups all the time. But she's not completely without quirks. The other day she went around the house to every Oriental rug and straightened the fringes into perfect lines."

"At least she's helping out around the house," I joked.

"Right, right!" Amy said. "The good news is that many of these kids—post-institutionalized kids—do outgrow most of their behavior."

*Post-institutionalized.* Another word to add to my adoption glossary.

"Okay!" I said. "You've now officially scared the living daylights out of me."

Amy placed her hand on my arm. "You might not know it now," she said, "but going into this with some knowledge is the way to go. No one told me any of this stuff and I felt completely helpless. All I wanted was some *instruction*, something I could work with—a handbook, a manual for how to raise my daughter."

"As long as the love is there," I said.

"The love is there," she said. "For sure, the love is there. But be patient, that's all I can say."

When we arrived in Beijing, seventeen hours and many time zones later, we were greeted by Max, our translator/tour guide/adoption liaison/all-around source for everything and anything we might need. Max was a dervish, constantly texting or talking on his cell or shuffling through the papers clamped under his arm. He was tiny—couldn't have weighed much more than a hundred pounds, counting his black leather jacket—but still tossed around giant suitcases like they were nothing. Once our group's luggage had been corralled, he gathered our papers, shuffled us through customs, and then loaded us onto a bus bound for the Jade Garden Hotel, where we would stay for two days before flying south to Sam's province. We watched in wonder as smoke plumed from factories, bike riders jockeyed for position alongside cars, elderly women walked daintily down the road under colorful umbrellas.

In the lobby, Max gathered our group. "Two days in Beijing!" he said. "Go sightseeing," Max urged us. "So much to see! Take a ride on a rickshaw; tour Tiananmen Square, the Forbidden City." We nodded and asked questions about transportation and places to eat, but it was obvious that each of us was feigning interest. We were here to get our daughters and the thought of sightseeing for two days stoked our impatience and jittery anticipation. We'd do it, because these were the standard travel arrangements for foreign adopters, but I doubted that any of us planned to enjoy it too much.

Then Max collected our cash donations for the orphanage so that he could put them in the hotel safe. I was happy to hand over the thick stack of bills and unstrap the money belt from under my shirt, padding as thick as Kevlar.

The next day we boarded a bus and headed to the Great Wall.

"Ready to do some climbing," Tim said enthusiastically. It was a chilly December day, and we were padded in Gore-Tex jackets, hats and gloves, but I was still cold, holding my cup of tea up to my mouth, letting the steam billow around my lips.

"How far?" I wanted to know. The wall seemed to wind on endlessly, like a Chinese dragon slithering into eternity.

"As far as we can go!" he said, grabbing my hand and pulling me to an entrance.

We quickly found out that the steps weren't so much steps as they were gigantic stone slabs, as high as our knees. Each step required significant leg lifting. After about fifty lunge-type steps, I was winded, hot, and tearing off my hat and gloves.

But each time I looked up and out at the lush green mountain ranges and around at the giant crimson flags flapping defiantly against the wind, I felt more energized and alive.

By the time we made it to the first watchtower, I was feeling invincible, the adrenaline pumping through me. We stopped for a break, leaning against the impressive wall, our cheeks shining red from the cold and exertion.

"We're in China!" I hollered, as though it had finally just hit me.

"This is too cool," Tim said.

"I've got to call Claire," I said, pulling out the international cell phone that I had rented for the trip, dialing her number. It was the middle of the night, still yesterday in the States, when she answered, groggy with sleep.

"We're on the Great Wall of China!" I said.

"Where's my new niece?" Claire asked through a yawn.

"Still waiting," I said. "We don't get her 'til Monday. But I'll bet she's excited. She probably has her suitcase packed, next to her crib."

"They're probably having a going-away party for her."

"Definitely," I said. "Balloons, cake, and ice cream."

"An engraved Mont Blanc pen."

"A gift card to Starbucks."

"Don't forget to leave a forwarding address for her," Claire said, still laughing. "A long-lost relative might come looking for her someday."

*Oh yeah*, I thought. *Relatives*. Of course, I'd thought a lot about Sam's birth mother, even occasionally about her birth father. But my mind had never wandered to think about the fact that I was adopting a baby who had her own history, a history that went back thousands of years: aunts, uncles, cousins, grandparents, great-grandparents, all the way through the decades of time. I was adopting a child whose history would be severed, cleanly and irrevocably. I was adopting a baby who would never be able to ask a sister or mother or aunt, "Doesn't high blood pressure run in our family? Didn't Aunt Mae have respiratory issues? Didn't Grandma Wu die of heart disease?" An entire society of babies who would always wonder, *From whom did I get my silly sense of humor, my athletic ability, my proclivity for writing, my affinity for art?* An entire society of babies who were given a "do-over," whether they wanted one or not.

After we descended the steps of the Wall, Tim and I wandered around the village. We ducked into one shop, an art studio of sorts, where a man was painting scrolls in calligraphy. With his exacting yet delicate flourish, he wrote Sam's Chinese name for us—Xu, Long Ling. Then we asked him to make a banner for Maura, too. I then asked him how to say "cousins" in Chinese. In his limited English, he explained that the relationships between people were very important in Chinese culture. That there wasn't just one word for cousin, that it depended on whether that person was from the mother's side or the father's side, whether that person was a male or female. In the end, we deciphered that Maura would be Sam's *biaojie*, but Sam would be Maura's *biaomei*.

On the way back to town, Max had the bus stop at a pearl factory. Many such places were simply tourist traps for eager new parents, but I still bought a variety of pendants and bracelets for Sam and myself; Claire and Maura; Delia and Claire's mother-in-law, Martha; as well as for Sondra at the restaurant.

That night, Tim and I, along with Amy and Tom DePalma, ate a late dinner and then lingered for hours in the soft sofas of the hotel lobby, talking easily about the adult aspects of our lives: our jobs, our families. Angela had fallen asleep draped across her mother and while Amy and I talked, my new friend brushed the hair from her daughter's face, a gentle assurance that she was there. I was still on the outside of motherhood looking in—at a future that had drawn so near it was now only a day away—and yet I still could not accept, or let myself believe, that soon I would be in Amy's position, fingering the silky hair of my beloved daughter. A lifetime of letdowns had left me wary, afraid of wanting those things I coveted most.

The next day, Max corralled us back onto the bus and off we went to the Forbidden City, a museum, a park. After a morning of walking, listening, looking at monuments, and reading plaques, the bus returned us to the hotel. Two hours later, we boarded our next plane and traveled south to Sam's province. Max had trained our group well. We now knew to follow behind him like obedient ducklings, with our paperwork in our backpacks and our passports and visas in their designated pouches, securely dangling inside our shirts. Now pros, we boarded the plane, flew a short two hours in the direction of our daughters, disembarked, and got settled in our new hotel rooms.

When a number of the families congregated for dinner, Tim spoke for the two of us when he said that we'd take a rain check.

In the hotel elevator, I asked Tim why he didn't want to go to dinner.

"I do want to go to dinner," Tim said, reaching for my hand. "Let's venture out on our own."

"Venture out?" I asked. "On our own? Where?"

"I don't know," he said. "Let's wander. Like we used to wander around Europe."

"Well, okay," I said tentatively, feeling as if caution had already replaced my sense of adventure as becoming a mother rounded the corner toward me.

We left the hotel with a stack of cards in our pockets. Max had told us always to carry cards bearing the name and address of the hotel so that if we got into trouble, we could hand the card to a cab driver. We ambled our way down narrow streets that led us to outdoor markets; one entire street was given over to jade vendors who spotlighted their jewels in canopied stalls. We turned down another alley and saw what was for sale: whole goats hanging from hooks, turtles in every size, eels, fish, bins of scorpions. Above us, electrical wires crisscrossed in magnificent tangles.

Outside of the marketplace, we passed a little restaurant, and the smells pouring from the door beckoned us: garlic, chili, aromatic spices. We ducked in. The cook behind the counter, a jolly man with a nearly toothless smile, waved us in. We approached him, saw his giant steaming woks, his hatchet and knives on the board in front of him, a variety of ingredients. The cook gestured to us, pointed to the wok. Tim nodded yes. The cook fanned himself, making a wide-eyed face. We guessed he was asking us if we liked it hot. Tim nodded yes, then put his own hands around his neck and shook his head no, as if to indicate hot, but don't kill us. I sat at a little table by the window. Tim paid and returned with four beers.

"Four?" I asked.

"I think we're going to need them," he said. "I saw the chilies."

In seconds, the woks sizzled and bellowed steam. A minute later, Tim and I had two bowls in front of us, noodles drenched in an oily red broth, the seeds from the chilies floating on top. The fragrance that wafted from each was aromatic, complex. We took a bite. It was the hottest mouthful of food I'd ever tried. Instantly, I started to perspire over my eyes, feel the sting in my ears, the scorch on my lips. I gulped beer, fanned my face, waiting for the pain to subside, and then went back for more. The combination of the bite of the noodles against the smoothness of the broth against the spike of the spice was addictive. It was a masochistic sensation, like warming your frozen hands a minute too long in front of a roaring fire. We swallowed back a swig of beer, dug back into the noodles, wiped our brows, ate some more.

"This is too good," I said.

"I don't know what the hell is in this, but yeah, it's really good," Tim said.

"I feel like it used to be," I said. "Just us, traveling."

"We had fun," Tim said.

"Have I ruined our life these past five years, obsessing over having a baby?"

"Do you think that I'll say yes?" Tim asked with a smile, and took another bite. "And live to tell about it?"

I took Tim's hands, looked him in the eyes. "I'm sorry, Tim. I'm really sorry."

"This feels right, doesn't it?" Tim asked. "Being here in China, getting a baby. It's us. It suits us."

"I really can't wait to see her. I can't wait for her to be ours. It's really happening. We're getting Sam tomorrow!"

Tim and I polished off our bowls of noodles, four beers, and asked the cook to make us more. Though we were stuffed and our heads dizzy with alcohol, it seemed that we both wanted to prolong this tender moment, memorialize in stone the wanderlust feeling of our youth, the fairytale romance that had defined the beginning of our relationship years earlier in the hills of Lyon. This was our send-off into the next chapter of our life.

# Chapter Thirteen

The next morning, Tim and I woke early, showered and dressed, and went down to the restaurant buffet for coffee and a bite to eat. My appetite was nil and my stomach was roiling and my head was thumping from the night before, but Tim's ironclad stomach was ready for more. His chef senses were too curious to let even one eating opportunity pass by, even on a nerve-racking day like today when we would be getting Sam. He piled steamed and glutinous buns, a rice and meat mixture, and some soft egg custard onto his plate. The thought of eating any of it at this moment made me nearly sick.

After breakfast for Tim, and multiple cups of coffee for me, we returned to our room and waited. We knew the babies were in the hotel. Tim had already seen Tom and Amy getting off the elevator with their new baby, one of ten who were transported by bus from the orphanage, three hours away.

We sat nervously on the edge of our bed, tapping our feet and bouncing our knees. We checked the batteries in the camera and video recorder. I double-checked the gift bags. It was customary for the adoptive parents to bear gifts for the orphanage director and her people. A few knickknacks from the nation's capitol to accompany the sizable cash donations we had handed over to Max.

As each minute passed, waves of acid splashed in my stomach. While Tim picked at a leftover muffin, I gnawed on a pack of Rolaids.

"When's Max going to call?" I asked.

"Soon," Tim said. "It's just a matter of waiting our turn."

"I've been waiting for my turn for five years," I said.

"He'll call," Tim assured me.

Finally, the trill of the phone stood us both up straight.

Tim answered, then hung up after a short conversation and nodded at me. "They're ready for us."

My hand and Tim's were gripped together in a tight-knuckled mass as we walked the hall to Room 304.

"Oh my God," I kept repeating, squeezing Tim's hand, my heart hammering in my chest.

"I know, right?" he said, giddy, looking more boyish than ever.

Max opened the door. There was a baby in the arms of a young woman, and an older woman standing near the desk in the corner of the room. Sam, her caregiver, and the orphanage director, I presumed. Sam looked at us, then back at her caregiver, then clutched defiantly to the woman's necklace. Sunlight haloed her shaved head. She had petite features, and though she was bundled like every other baby in thick layers, it was evident that she was tiny. The other babies we'd seen were stout, sturdy little firecrackers; Sam looked as if she were a different breed, something delicate, something to be worshipped. When she pursed her lips, the dimple deepened in her cheek, the dimple that I had been staring at for the last month, my screensaver and salvation.

Clutched in her left hand was a torn piece of satin, like the soft top of a baby blanket that had been ripped off. Was it from the orphanage or from her mother? If so, did it carry her scent?

"Sam," I whispered, lurching in her direction, my arms reaching for her, tears pouring down my face. The caregiver placed her in my shaky arms, and the enormity of her being there, after such a long wait, left me breathless. Once, when I was a child, Claire had pelted me with a volleyball, hitting me square in the chest. There were a few brief moments when I literally couldn't breathe, the *heaviness*. "I thought you were ready," Claire had said. That was how it was now. I thought I was ready, but the panic surging through me was making me think twice. A metallic taste pooled in my mouth. I looked around for Tim, but he was talking to the orphanage director in the corner.

"Hey, little girl," I said, stroking the apples of her cheeks, trying for Claire's cool confidence, trying to find that perfect fit in the nook of my arm, thinking that if I acted comfortable, I would *be* comfortable. But Sam shook her fists at me and lurched for her caregiver, as unhappy as a child could be. I dangled my necklace in front of her like bait, but Sam wasn't biting. She wanted what she knew, and that something wasn't me. I suddenly felt like an imposter, like I was taking something—*someone*—who wasn't mine.

We were once told that the babies were matched up with their adoptive families thanks to the divine wisdom of the "matching ladies." These old women supposedly sat in a room, read prospective parents' applications, and then matched them with the just right baby. This was probably more myth than reality. The matches were most likely generated by computer as part of the bureaucratic behemoth Chinese adoption had become. But I liked the idea of the matching ladies. There was some comfort in the notion that a group of sage old ladies with the experience of many lifetimes had had a hand in the selection of my daughter.

I cradled Sam's little body, a tableau of perfect beauty, staring into her almond-shaped eyes. "It's okay," I told her. "I'm not so bad." Sam looked at me, then at her caregiver, took an enormous breath, and began to squall like I had never heard a baby do before.

My confidence plummeted. For a second, I wondered whether the infertility was a sign that maybe I wasn't made for this.

"Do you want to ask her caregiver any questions?" Max asked.

"Yes," I said, though I couldn't think of one of the questions I had thought up days earlier.

The caregiver told me that she was a good baby, smiled a lot, and ate all her meals.

"She's small," I said. "The referral said that she was twenty-four pounds. This baby weighs much less. Is she okay?"

"She's strong baby," the orphanage director piped in. "Weighs twenty-four, eats her meals."

"Anything else?" Max asked.

"Did her parents leave her anything—a note?"

The orphanage director read from the file that, when Sam was abandoned, she was left in a shopping bag, swaddled in one blanket, with thick newspapers tucked around her little body.

"More questions?" Max asked.

*Will she love me? Will she leave me? Will she fill the hole in my heart?* I wanted to ask, but instead I said, "She's beautiful. Thank you."

Back in our room, we couldn't take our eyes off Sam, our idealized baby personified in flesh. After wanting—*waiting*—for so long, my brain was struggling to process the reality of this moment.

I held her on my lap, gingerly grazing my palm over her stubbly buzz cut, allowing my senses to take in that she was really here.

"Sanitary reasons," Tim said, pointing to Sam's nearly shaved head. "She smells like Ajax."

"What could you be thinking of all this, peanut?"

As if in answer, Sam began to cry. I suspected that she was wet. So, layer by layer, I gently undressed her. All of the Chinese babies were bundled like little Michelin men. By now, we had become used to it, seeing little ones bundled in multiple layers wherever we had gone. Sam's outer layer was a quilted cotton smock with an apple pattern. It covered two wool sweaters, which covered a gray sweatshirt, and finally, a blue Pepsi T-shirt. The orphanage received a large number of donations, including clothing, from the West.

"Feel this!" I held up Sam's diaper. It must have weighed a pound. I filled the bathtub with warm water and lavender bubbles, so sure that a nice bath would soothe her after the long bus ride from the orphanage in the countryside. I had helped Claire bathe Maura a dozen times. I knew how much babies loved the water.

"Maybe we should just hold her a while," Tim suggested.

"She'll love it," I insisted, but Sam recoiled, screaming and crying, as if she were being set into a pot of scalding water. "It's okay, it's okay," I cooed. I sponged her body and head with the sweet smells from home, but Sam didn't relent until I removed her from the tub. While Tim bundled her in a soft hotel towel, and I got myself dried off, the sudden quiet startled my heart. In her father's arms, she was finally contented.

I stared at myself in the mirror: my mouth pressed too tightly together, my eyes held open too wide, my jaw clenched too firmly. When finally I made eye contact with myself and saw me—so scared and unsure—I knew that this was going to be hard. Taking care of Tim and myself, even those months helping Claire care for our dying mother, was *nothing* compared to what it was going to be like to take care of Sam, my new daughter who wanted to be anywhere but in my arms.

I dressed her in the same type of footed pajamas that Maura wore when she was a baby. As I cradled her, I looked into her eyes, expecting to see the rich history of an ancient civilization, the look of a little baby who had endured twelve months without parents, yet was still hopeful. I wanted to see her soul, her personality, something that would reveal her nature to me, but instead, I saw just an endless flow of tears from a baby who was sad for reasons she didn't understand. Her bottom lip jutted out and her cheeks shone red and her fists were balled like a prizefighter's, as if to say, *Who do you think you are?*

I now wondered if the matching ladies—or the computer—had made the right match. As I juggled Sam in my arms, trying to soothe her blistering tears, staring at her beguiling beauty, I knew that she wasn't some pushover who could be coaxed easily into a smile, soothed with a lullaby, or captured with a new necklace. *Thanks for the vote of confidence*, I wanted to yell to those women, *but I'm not really an Advanced Placement type of person! That would be my sister, Claire. Go ahead and give me an average child, one of those jolly, chubby-faced babies with an easy disposition!* Somehow, I knew that Sam was rare, that in her exquisite beauty she would somehow come to resent my lack of it, that her temperament would be too much like my own.

"Remember what Amy said," Tim reminded me. "It takes time. Patience."

⌒

A few hours later, our group congregated in the conference room on the ground floor of the Holiday Inn. We were to meet with the notary, a Chinese official who would ask us questions and then stamp our paperwork, making the adoptions official. From there, papers would be filed and we would wait while Sam's passport and visa were processed. As we walked into the conference room, the first thing I noticed was that all of the babies were still in their orphanage clothes. I found Amy and asked her what was up.

"Oh," she said, pulling back her mouth as if she felt badly for not warning me. "Bath time at the orphanage is dreadful," she said. "A matter of logistics, it's just too difficult to bathe so many babies in a cold-weather environment where heat is scarce. Cold air to hot water to cold air again."

"Oh," I said mournfully, cringing at the wrongness of my decision to bathe Sam right away. How was it that Tim knew better? Where was my store of maternal instincts? Just then, my left ovary twinged, as if the smart-aleck, big mouth couldn't keep from commenting on my incompetency as a mother so far.

When it was our turn, the notary official, a stout man with a whiskery beard, asked us if we wanted to keep the baby we had been given.

"Yes," we said, "of course."

"Is there anything wrong with her that you want to report?" He had his pen poised over his clipboard like the guy at the rent-a-car place, jotting down any dings and dents.

"No," I said defensively, clutching Sam tighter, "She's perfect."

———

That night, Tim and I tried for hours to get Sam to sleep. I walked the halls with her, bouncing her in my arms with a rhythmic jiggle-jiggle-pat-pat dance that I'd seen Claire do a hundred times. Tim sang to her in the rocker. We fed her bottles, spooned her congee, changed her diaper over and over again. We burped her, held her high up on our shoulders, low in our laps, bounced on our knees for horsey. But our new baby was full of panic and dread and uncertainty. Her only instinct was to cry, arch her back, writhe as if she were tethered in chains, and lurch for the exit. It was midnight before Sam finally issued her last battle cry, a whimper that fell flat in mid-roar.

The hotel had devised a makeshift crib out of two upholstered armchairs facing each other, their front legs secured tightly together with rope. But from our bed where the three of us lay, the crib looked miles away. Exhausted, worn to the bone, Tim and I lay on either side of Sam, staring at our new daughter.

"Should we put her in her crib?" Tim asked, the weariness dripping from his voice matching mine.

"I can't move," I said. "And if we touch her, she might wake up."

"And then she'll start crying again," Tim said, finishing my thought.

"This is really, really hard." I thought back to over a year before, when Elle Reese interviewed us and wrote our home study. In that report, we had made a lifetime of promises: to love Sam, to educate her, to provide her with health care, food, clothing, and shelter. But absent, it seemed, from our discussions was the fact that this was going to be hard. That parenting was hard—I now knew, only hours after becoming a mother— was the starting point, the *given*. It was the white on the paper that held the promises and proclamations. If separated and weighed, it would undoubtedly be heavier than the words themselves.

Parenting a baby who had been left and then found and then given again might be even harder.

"But are you happy?" Tim asked. "Or is it too soon to tell?"

"I'm happy," I said. "I'm definitely happy. But one thing is for sure: she didn't get the memo that we were coming."

"It's only the first day," he said, rubbing my back. "We're just another bunch of strangers to her."

"Why did I think she would know us?" I asked, remembering the romantic union I'd imagined, where our lives blended into each other's like the many rivers of her native homeland.

"Starting now," Tim said, "we're all she'll know."

"I wonder what she thinks about that?"

"She probably thinks that we're very strange looking."

I smiled, looked at Sam, the way her fists were still balled and a little line of anger was still pinched between her eyes.

"You better call Claire," Tim said. "The time is right. It should be morning there, now."

I rolled over and reached for the cell phone. Dialed.

"Tell me everything," Claire said eagerly, as if she had been pacing with her phone all morning.

"I can't," I stammered. "Too tired to talk. Every bone in my body is tired. Even my jaw. But I just wanted to let you know that all is well, that Sam is adorable, but I'm pretty sure that she hates me."

"Do you remember when Maura was born?" she asked. "She was pretty hostile, if memory serves."

"Yeah," I recalled. "She was mad."

"Anyway," Claire said. "It'll be good practice for when she's a teenager."

# Chapter Fourteen

The next morning, at breakfast, we served Sam an endless bowl of congee, pieces of a steamed bun, and a soft egg.

"She's ravenous," I said to Tim. "I can't imagine why she's so small."

"She won't have to worry about food anymore," Tim said.

"You hear that, Sammy?" I said, tickling the bottom of her chin. "Mom and Dad will always give you lots of food. What do you think about the fact that both your parents are chefs?"

She looked away, still refusing to make eye contact with either Tim or me, and rolled her hands in the high chair tray of food, enjoying the bounty. *The food's good*, she seemed to say. *But let's not get ahead of ourselves.*

Afterward, Tim and I buckled Sam into a stroller and ventured out. We pushed her through narrow streets lined with vendors selling everything from clay teapots to dried beans to rice, eels and frogs in buckets, a variety of insects. Intermittent smells of laundry and sewage and fried foods filled the air. Hanging laundry and hanging poultry dangled and bobbed above us. Sam was dressed in a snowsuit and wool cap, but even so, an elderly Chinese lady stopped and admonished us for not having Sam bundled in enough layers.

"Yes, ma'am. Yes, ma'am," Tim said as the woman shook her finger at us and yelled and yelled. We promised to dress her more warmly and then walked away and burst into laughter.

When we looked at Sam to see what she thought of all the commotion, she seemed to shrug as if to say, *Yeah, the old ladies are like that here.*

In the afternoon, our group took our babies to the clinic for their physicals. The doctors weighed and measured them; looked in their eyes, ears, and throats; pulled on their limbs; tapped their knees for reflexes; and then unequivocally pronounced every single one of them "perfectly healthy."

"How much does Sam weigh now?" I asked, knowing that she was nothing near the twenty-four pounds they claimed her to be.

"Six and a half kilograms," the doctor said. "Fourteen pounds."

"Why do you think she is so small?"

The doctor shrugged. "Some babies get fed more than others."

A shiver slid down my spine thinking of a bigger, more vocal baby taking Sam's share, like a bully on the playground.

"And, Doctor," I asked, "what does this say?" I pointed to a string of numbers on Sam's report.

"How much she weighed when born," he said.

I tapped Tim's arm, widened my eyes at him. "How much did she weigh?"

"Almost two kilograms. Four pounds," he said.

"Four?" I looked at Tim and our eyes locked. Then I put my mouth on Sam's forehead. Four pounds, less than a bag of flour. Four pounds, two days old, alone outside in the elements, crying for her mother. How could abandonment in this country be two things at once—the ultimate act of benevolence, yet so wrongheaded in its execution?

A few days later, Max loaded us on the bus and we headed to Liu Rong Temple, the Temple of Six Banyan Trees, where Buddhist monks would bless the babies.

We followed Max into the Temple of Tranquility and kneeled in front of three gigantic saffron Buddhas. Then a monk, a thoughtful-looking believer cloaked in a brown robe, started to chant and gently bang a little gong on the altar. Sam, who we had dressed in a traditional Chinese dress, a satiny thing we bought on the street, sat in front of me, transfixed by the monk. When I hoisted her onto my lap, she pulled away. *Too close, woman.*

Once we returned home to the States, we would have Sam baptized. For my mother's sake, because it had been important to her. For Tim's parents, too. And because if any soul deserved to be infused with the grace of God, it was an orphan who had been left on her second day of life. For as much as I grumbled over God's will and what I had had to endure in my life, it was hard not to believe in God on a day like today as I looked around and saw maybe one hundred Chinese baby girls being loved in excess by their new parents who wanted more than anything a child to cherish. We would give Sam the faith we grew up with, for the same reason we would feed, clothe, and educate her: because she was now a member of our family and what was ours, was hers. But as we were lulled by the monks' soothing tones, I couldn't help but think that international adoption alone was proof that many gods were working together to bring these babies home.

After the blessing, Tim wanted to climb the seventeen-story flowering pagoda. Once he walked away, I carried Sam inside, changed her diaper, and fixed her a bottle, which she gulped and gulped, always hungry for more. Now that Sam was drinking an unlimited amount of fortified formula, her cheeks already seemed plumper. In no time, she would be gaining weight. When she was finished with her bottle, she wiggled to get out of my arms, so I set her in the stroller with her piece of satin blanket top and pushed her back outside. With the cool outside air and sun on her face, she fell fast asleep.

Much of the literature on Chinese adoption referred to the "red thread," an invisible string that connected an adoptive baby to adoptive mother, as if there were never any doubt that the two were meant to be together. *Maybe*, I thought. I definitely wanted more than anything to protect her from more hurt. But I couldn't yet admit to feeling that our union was predestined. That that sense of fate hadn't yet infiltrated me didn't surprise me much. The spools of thread in my life were always snagged and tangled, never neatly wound. It would take some time to pick at the knotted ball, to loosen just the right one.

Contrarily, it did make me think. If I hadn't been so resistant to adoption, if the paperwork had been completed and submitted six months, a year, earlier, we would have been matched with a different baby. The thought of that alone made me reach for Sam, as if I knew that she was the one I was meant to get. Only two days into this, I couldn't imagine a baby other than Sam.

"Hmm," I thought, happily satisfied with my epiphany. Maybe I did feel the sense of fate. A red thread as strong as rope.

I looked at Sam, considered our future together. I thought of her when she was older, cooking with Tim and me in the kitchen, traveling overseas, and returning to China to visit her homeland. I smiled at the thought of Sam fifteen years from now, turquoise braces on her teeth. I lifted Sam from her stroller and held her in my lap. In just the last few days, I had learned that she slept soundly, that once she was five minutes into a nap, not even a marching band would rouse her. These were the times when I stole her affection. I nuzzled my face into her sweet-smelling neck, cupped her small hands in mine, and whispered to her: "I know you were given to me and you had no say in it, but I promise you, I'll love you so much that someday you'll choose me on your own."

I made a visor with my hand, looked up at the pagoda for Tim, snapped a photo with my phone. Then I snapped a photo of Sam, asleep in the crook of my arm, contented in her deep slumber. I pulled up Claire's name and texted the photo of Sam to her. I slid the phone back into my coat pocket and then, just as quickly, pulled it out again. I pulled up the photo of Sam, and before I lost my nerve, I sent it to Larry, too.

Then I looked around at the countless Caucasian couples from America and Europe tooling around with their new Chinese babies. I spotted Amy and Tom in the gift shop, little Angela holding tight to her mother's blouse tail, new Maria in Amy's arms.

Then I saw a woman with her two grown daughters. Clearly, one of the daughters must have come to adopt a baby, and she brought her sister and mother with her. It made me wish that Claire were with us on this trip, though she never would have left Maura for so long. I couldn't take my eyes off these women. The resemblance. My heart warmed as I thought of Mom and Claire. I gently placed Sam back in her stroller, pulled a notepad from my backpack, and started a letter to Claire:

Dear Claire,
All of the babies have just been blessed by a monk and now Sam's asleep and Tim's scaling a pagoda. I'm sitting on a bench. It's cold, but the sun is out. Really, it's just a beautiful day. Anyway, there's a woman, a few tables away from me: head of brown wavy hair that looks like it's been inflated with an air pump, eyes so

blue I can see the color from here, and cheeks that rise and fall with her infectious laughter. You can see where I'm going with this. Mom.

This woman reminds me so much of her, but of course, this lady is in her sixties and she's sitting with her two daughters who are clearly in their forties, and this is the thing that strikes me: the mom is the one who is divvying up the picnic of cheese and nuts and fruit, sliding portions onto their plates, securing a napkin underneath so that it doesn't fly away, refilling the glasses of wine. Do you see what I'm saying, Claire? This mom is *feeding* her daughters. Her forty-year-old daughters.

That's a mom, right? Wouldn't Mom have been the same way, still wiping our mouths, offering us the food off her own plate? I was just thinking: you're that way, too, Claire. Maura's lucky to have you as a mom. I really mean this: if I'm half the mom to Sam that you are to Maura, we'll be in good shape.

For some reason, looking at these women made me think of how you used to stop by every Sunday. I was in college and you were in grad school, and even though you were so busy, you'd bring me my "food money" for the week. I remember thinking, why don't you just send it or put it in my account, but of course, once I was older I knew that you were just checking up on me, always slipping an extra carton of milk in my fridge, a loaf of bread in the basket. You'd walk around the apartment and check the locks on my windows, make sure that I had my Mace on my keychain, my cell phone charged.

I can see Tim spiraling down the pagoda now. I wonder what he saw up so high. I can't wait to see you next week. Of course, we'll be home before this letter even makes it to you, assuming I actually find an envelope, a stamp, and a post office. Maybe I'll just give you this in person.

Anyway, you were right. I am dreaming about that day at the spa, sprawled out on a massage table, candles flickering. But this is pretty awesome, too!

See you soon!

Love you! Helen

At dinner, Max surprised us with big news.

"The orphanage director has invited your group to tour the grounds," he said.

Seldom were adoptive parents able to see the inside of the orphanage where their daughters lived, so when Max told us that our group had been invited to take a tour, we jumped at the opportunity. The next day, we boarded a bus and headed for the mountainside. With horns blaring, we bumped our way through the traffic, throngs of bicyclists, pedestrians, and taxicabs until we were outside of the city and heading in the direction of Sam's birthplace. As a group, we gasped as the bus skidded precariously around cliffhanging precipices and dodged farmers leading oxen and a family of four stacked high on a scooter. We held on tightly to our new babies, many of whom, Sam included, were more calmed and lulled by this carnival ride of a trip than they'd been in our arms in the quiet of the hotel room. We passed countless rice paddies, drove alongside the Yangtze River, saw lotus blossoms and water lilies. At one point, our bus drove onto a ferry that crossed the river.

We reached the Children's Welfare Institute four hours later. Sam had fallen asleep and didn't budge from Tim's shoulder when we exited the bus. I was glad about that. Sam had just left this place, entered our lives, and now we were back? It seemed like we were doing our best to confuse these poor children.

The orphanage building was no-nonsense, white cinder block. It easily could have been a prison, a bureaucratic building, a warehouse. I shivered when I realized that, really, it *was* all of those things. We were greeted by the middle-aged orphanage director, Mrs. Lu, whom we had met just a few days ago when she delivered the babies.

"Follow me," she said, walking us through a concrete hallway. "The playroom," she indicated, pointing to a bare room with very few toys. "The kitchen," she pointed to a room with pots and kettles and glass baby bottles stacked neatly next to the sink.

Along one wall was a bench—a potty for the babies—to sit on. Holes were cut out and porcelain chamber pots were underneath. The toddlers wore "split pants" so that clothes needn't be taken off, just pulled aside when necessary. There was a coal stove in middle of the room, which seemed to be the only heat source.

We continued to follow the orphanage director.

"The baby room," she said, pushing through the double doors to an enormous open space of concrete walls and floors.

Two rows of at least a dozen cribs each stood in formation. In each crib, four babies lay on their backs, heavily bundled in quilted bunting, with their arms haloing their heads as if signaling surrender. An additional quilt was placed over each set of babies, with a thin elastic bungee cord holding it in place. I looked up to see what the babies saw. Just a plain ceiling full of meandering cracks and splotches of water stains, a crude sketch of paths leading nowhere. I looked around to see what else the babies saw. No pastels, no nursery-rhyme decorations, no farm-animal mobiles. Nothing to reach for. Nothing to want.

"Brand new," the director said, pointing to the tiniest baby I'd ever seen. *Maybe* she was four pounds. But her furious cry was that of a giant, her little face purplish-red, and her fists cutting through the air like a meteor shower.

"A newborn!" one of the other women said.

"This morning she come," the director said.

In the time that we'd showered, fed Sam congee with pork and a warm bottle of formula, eaten breakfast ourselves, and bumped along on our bus ride, a baby had been born. Born. Abandoned. Found. Appropriated. All in a matter of hours. It was not lost on me that Sam had had that same exact day only a year earlier.

"She wants to be picked up," I said, knowing that I'd overstepped my boundaries. Max had told us to nod politely at just about everything. Compliment everything. Criticize nothing. But I didn't care. This baby needed to be held on her first day of life. "May I?" I asked.

"No, no," the orphanage director said with a wide smile. "She will just want more hold." As if granting a newborn comfort would be the first step toward a spoiled existence. And then she walked away, indicating for us to follow, leaving a day-old baby crying, and many others, months older, to soothe and entertain themselves, day after day.

As we turned the corner, the director pointed out a large room with a window facing the hallway. "Hard to place children," she said. There were a handful of older children sitting on a bench, staring aimlessly. A few others were wild, pressing their faces against the glass, knocking to get our attention. Some were clearly mentally challenged. One was plagued with a pigment problem that left his brown skin splotched with white patches. A few others had cleft lips. One was missing an arm. And then there was a perfectly beautiful toddler, maybe three years old.

"Oh God," I said. I looked up at Tim, who seemed to be holding tighter to Sam than he'd been a minute ago. His face was bright red and his eyes had welled up and all he could do was nod. For the minute that we stood there, my eyes remained fixed on the little toddler girl. It was hard enough to swallow the fact that most of the children in that room would never have parents, but why on earth was this little girl hard to place? Was she the one-hundredth-and-first baby out of one hundred adoptive families? Was being adopted just a game of symbols and chance, like baby mahjong? Was a girl's fate as random as a slip of paper in a fortune cookie? For whatever reason, would that poor baby grow up in an orphanage or be sold to a labor camp, or worse, when she—as easily as Sam—could have been placed with a loving family in the States? I reached up and rubbed Sam's back, wanting her to know that we knew what a miracle it was that she was in our arms. A now familiar pang of guilt stabbed at me, thinking of all the time, money, and insistence I had put into having a baby of my own, when there were thousands to be had right here.

The orphanage people had prepared a nice lunch for us. Tim bravely tried marinated duck tongue, sweet-and-sour chicken feet, and salted bird gizzard. The rest of us gravitated toward a tasty pork and rice dish and chicken-and-corn soup.

"How often do the babies get out of their cribs?" I asked in my sweetest voice, hoping to sound perfectly innocuous.

"One time per day," she answered. "They eat in their cribs and play in their cribs, but their nanny takes them out one time per day."

I looked down at Sam, who seemed, for once, to be happy in my arms, and spooned a scoop of soft egg into her mouth. I put my face to her ear and whispered, "Take your time, baby. I'm not going anywhere."

Afterward, we took pictures of the buildings, the babies who had yet to be adopted and the poor ones who would languish inside for years, and the road leading up to the orphanage where so many of the newborns earned their first official document—a certificate of abandonment.

Hours later, we were back at the Holiday Inn. Sam had fallen asleep as we were walking up to the room. Tim and I—exhausted and dizzy from the bus fumes—took the opportunity to lie down ourselves, to sleep for a few minutes. When we woke two hours later, it was ten o'clock at night, the room was dark, and Sam was wide-eyed, sitting up, and busily playing with her toes—a part of her body that was usually covered up in the orphanage.

We fed Sam, ate some dinner, and watched some television. It was becoming clear that allowing Sam to sleep so late in the day was going to make it nearly impossible to get her down for bedtime. We walked her through the hotel and at eleven thirty, when Sam was still awake and showing no signs of sleepiness, I joined some fellow parents in the hotel hallway, a group of weary moms and dads who had congregated while they tried to get their babies to sleep. I was happy to see Amy swaying against the wall with Maria in her arms. By nearly one o'clock, Amy and I were the only two left. The other parents either had succeeded in lulling their babies to sleep or had moved their efforts into their rooms. Sam was getting close to nodding off, I could tell by her writhing, mad-as-hell, last attempt to get me to cry uncle. Sleep tended to follow this last hurrah. While I jiggled Sam, Amy bounced Maria.

My new friend awed me in the same way Claire did, with her coolness and ease with motherhood. The night before, we had stood in the hallway rocking our babies while Amy threw a ball to her four-year-old, Angela, who was happy as can be to play fetch. I was managing with Sam, but Amy was a natural, the way she measured out the Enfamil one-handed, unscrewed and poured boiling water from the thermos, and punched the nipple through the ring like it was nothing.

After midnight, I was feeling a little punchy and was tired of talking about diapers and rashes and teething and toileting.

"I love your hair," I said, commenting on Amy's short blonde cut. It was spiky and tufty and made you want to give it a scruffy, *Dennis the Menace* rub. "I wish I could wear my hair short," I said, pulling at my tangle of curls.

"You can!" Amy said, shaking her head back and forth. "But first you'll need to take six months of chemo."

"Oh my God!" I said. "I'm such a jerk. I'm so sorry, Amy."

"Oh, *please*," she said. "I'm through with it now."

"Are you better?" I asked, not knowing what to say.

"The doctors say I'm clean," she said out of the side of her mouth. "But believe me, once you've had cancer, you're never completely better."

"When did this happen?"

"This *just* happened. My last treatment was just six weeks ago. This hair you love is brand new! I didn't even know if I'd be able to make the trip. Tommy was prepared to come alone."

"What kind?" I asked, because it was late and Amy didn't seem to mind.

"Breast," she nodded. "Of course. It's as dominant in my family as brown eyes."

Family history. Claire and I were at an increased risk because of Mom's ovarian cancer, a silent killer that rarely announces itself until it's hovering over you with a gun at your head.

Amy proceeded to tell me how she'd found the lump while in the shower soaping up. How she had just *known* that it was cancer because her sister had had the same experience.

"What did the adoption agency say when you told them?" I asked. "Did they care?"

"Oh, I'm sure they would care *plenty*," she said. "But there was no way I was going to say a word. They don't know."

"Why? You think they wouldn't have let you come back for another baby?"

"I have no idea what they would have done. All I know is that I couldn't take the risk. I needed to get a sister for Angela. Especially after having cancer. If something were to happen to me, God forbid, she would need a sister. It was now or never."

I knew what she meant. God, did I *know* what she meant. I wanted to tell her that my mom died of cancer and my sister nearly saved my life, but I didn't want to depress her with talk of dying. It was hard not to tell her that her instincts were right, that losing a mother nearly killed me, but having a sister saved me.

"How do you keep such…" I searched for the right word. "Perspective," I said. "You seem so *together*, so unfazed."

"This is my new reality," she said simply, shrugging. "You adjust to reality very quickly, I've found. I'm here now. And while I'm on this earth, my job is to take care of my girls, plain and simple."

While I was imagining her two little girls growing up without their mother, my mind drifted to Claire, how on the morning of Mom's funeral she brushed my hair back into a ponytail and blotted my cheeks with a cold washcloth. Larry sat across the hallway, sitting on the edge of the bed, his face in his hands. "She loved you so much," Claire had said to me back then, letting me off the hook for months and months of my crappy behavior. "And she knew that you loved her, too."

"Looks like you did it," Amy said, pointing to Sam, who had grown limp with sleep, slouched in the crook of my arm.

# Chapter Fifteen

On our tenth day with Sam as our daughter, she woke in the night with a deep, wet cough that sputtered and spat, like coffee pushing up into a percolator. Her face was beet red and tears coursed down her cheeks. Her hands and feet were as hot as coals. I lifted her, propped her high over my shoulder, and pounded on her back, where it seemed I could almost feel the crackling of wet lungs.

"Let's call Max," Tim said.

"Should we?" I asked. "Or do you think we should call Amy? She might know what to do."

Amy rushed over and listened to Sam. "I'd get her to the hospital," she said. "That doesn't sound too good. Could be pneumonia."

"Okay," we said, walking in circles in our panic.

"Bring your own medicines," Amy said. "Bring your antibiotics, your baby Tylenol, everything you have. Just in case."

Claire and her pediatrician had helped me compile such a first aid kit. Tonight I was grateful for it.

So, in the black of the night, Max ushered us into a taxicab and down the wet slabs of asphalt to an all-night hospital. It was down a road that looked more like an alley, bookended by a video rental shop and a grocery store. While I knew that the hospital wouldn't be modern and well lit like in the States,

I hadn't considered that it would look like this. I almost wondered whether we were better off back at the hotel.

"Tim?" I asked nervously.

"It'll be okay," he said, helping Sam and me out of the taxi. Max trailblazed ahead of us. He talked to the receptionist, slipped her some Chinese money, was given a slip of paper with a symbol on it. Maybe it was a number, like waiting your turn at the deli counter. The waiting room was packed. The row of plastic chairs were filled. Mothers paced with their screaming, coughing, wailing babies. Grandmothers shot us disapproving glares: Sam wasn't bundled; in these women's minds, I was neglecting my new baby.

Max assured us that they would get to her as soon as possible.

I leaned against the wall, swaying back and forth with Sam pulled tightly into my chest. I nuzzled my nose into her shiny buzz cut and breathed in the faint smell of the apple shampoo we'd washed her hair with the night before. She melted into me, dozing off and then waking with a start when a bout of coughing overtook her. As I stared at the receptionist, willing her to call our name, I had the discordant feeling that time was standing still and whizzing by at the same time. Or maybe it was more the feeling of déjà vu—though, clearly, we had never been in this situation before. All those months leading up to the adoption, I had sat in Sam's empty room, imagining the weight of her in my lap, her breath on my neck, her tender arms wrapped around me. And now, here she was, clinging to me in the way—the singular way—that I had been waiting for a child to cling to me all these years. She clung to me as if I were the only person in the world who could make the hurt go away.

Another wave of déjà vu. That's when it occurred to me: even seven thousand miles from home, hospitals all smelled the same.

I looked around the ER. All around the world there were emergencies. Always a kid with a raging ear infection, a toddler with a marble stuck up his nose, a grown man clutching his chest, a child testing the nerves of her brand-new parents.

My mother was in and out of the hospital for nearly a year. The cancer ward, where she spent weeks of her life, was a quiet story of rooms on the third floor. Family members floated in and out like ghosts, tiptoeing through the halls with their flowers and books and balloons. Nurses and doctors slipped in and out, their heads down, scribbling on charts. The whole place just seemed dark and gray, and breathing the air was like trying to get a good breath with a plastic bag over your head. I remember how restless I felt back then, like I just wanted to open all of the curtains and windows, and play something upbeat on my Walkman, like Bobby McFerrin's "Don't Worry, Be Happy." I imagined my mom and all of the other patients miraculously hopping to their feet and dancing in circles like it was all just a mistake that they were there.

The nurses ran the show. They were the ones who worked around the clock, taking vitals, making sure Mom was comfortable, sneaking me sodas from the nurses' lounge. One nurse, Tammy, always had Hershey miniatures in her pocket. She'd see me sitting next to Mom's bed and she'd open her pocket for me. Sometimes Tammy would let me fool with her stethoscope, anything to make the time go by. There was always so much waiting—waiting for the doctor to come, waiting for the next meal, waiting for Mom to get her next chemo treatment. Waiting for it all to be over. One way or another.

My mother's doctor, Dr. Sam Goldberg, checked in once in the morning and once in the afternoon. He had kind eyes, and his bedside manner was so good that there were times when I wondered whether he had a thing for Mom. He'd sit on the edge of her bed and put his hand over hers, and talk to her about the options that were left, the course of treatment he recommended. Mom was such an agreeable patient, the type who accepted her fate as if it were predetermined and any fight or fuss she waged would just be a silly attempt to move mountains. He'd say that there was still hope, and Mom would nod and smile, saying that she knew he was doing his best, that she felt that she was getting excellent care. I remember feeling sick every time she let him off the hook like that, thinking, *Shut up, Mom, let him talk, let him explore every possible option.*

I was a brat back then, thirteen years old and all attitude and self-pity. Claire was so involved in Mom's treatment that she could recite the significance of every blood test and blood count; she could tell you why the chemo wasn't working, why radiation wasn't an option, how it was basically just management of the disease at this point. I knew "management" was just a euphemism for keeping her comfortable until she died.

"Come sit with me," I remember Mom saying, patting the side of the bed.

"I'm fine," I said, slumped in the hard corner chair, my legs hanging over the side.

"Gin rummy?" She pulled the deck of cards from her end table and waved them at me.

"Not in the mood."

"What's new at school?"

"The same."

"What's new with Lisa? Ellen?" she listed my best friends' names.

"They're not my friends anymore," I said in a pitiful voice. "They said it's no fun hanging out with me because I'm always gloomy. You know, because of you." It was a lie; Lisa and Ellen never said that. A shudder of betrayal sent a chill down my back.

"Oh, honey," she said, seeing right through me. "I know you're sad. And I know you're mad, but this is just the way it is. It's just part of life. No one's to blame—not me, not God," she said, defending her one true love.

"How could there be a God?" I said, almost too quietly for her to hear, though I knew that she had heard my defamation. Then I looked out the window that overlooked the parking lot, put on my earphones, and started my music, wondering why I was worrying Mom so. Like she didn't have *enough* to deal with. Maybe I thought that if she had something other than cancer to worry about, she'd fight harder. Maybe the idea of her daughter having no friends was just the fuel she needed to kick herself into remission. Maybe Claire was making it too *easy* for her to let go, with all her proclamations of responsibility and accountability. Her to-do lists. Mom knew Claire would look after me, she knew she'd make me go to college, she knew Claire wouldn't let me end up in the gutter. *Fight, Mom!* I thought. *It's not Claire I want. It's you.*

You don't get back those moments, that's what I know now. I think of what it would have meant to her if I had just crawled into bed and hugged her, cried on her chest, looked her in the eyes and told her how much I loved her. I didn't, though, and she died without having heard the words come from me. My withholding must have caused her great pain. And now I had a daughter of my own, and even though I had only known her for a little more than a week, I already knew that I would be devastated if she ever treated me that way.

"Triage is ready for you," Max said, and led us back. "The nurse will check your daughter."

I looked into Sam's charcoal eyes and cupped my hand around her porcelain face. "We're going to see the nurse, okay?" Sam looked at me, coughed in my face, and then looked away.

We sat on the folding chair next to the triage nurse, who pulled the curtain behind us and wrote on her pad. She took Sam's temperature, height, and weight, and then asked, "What's wrong?"

"She's coughing," I said. "And has a fever."

Max translated in Chinese, prattled on for minutes when it seemed like it shouldn't have been taking that long to say that she had a cough. It made me wonder if he was giving the nurse information about Sam that I hadn't been told. Maybe she had a condition that had not been disclosed to us.

The nurse listened to her chest, called for the doctor. He, too, listened. An X-ray was taken.

"Her lungs are filled with fluid," Max said evenly. "The doctor wants her to stay the night."

"How did her lungs get filled with fluid?" I wanted to know. "Has she had this problem before? Is there something wrong with her lungs?" Were her lungs even fully developed when she was born, a bruising four-pounder?

Max shook his head and the doctor shrugged. Neither knew what had happened or what we should expect. When the babies got sick at the orphanage, they were treated, but rarely was a report written.

I looked expectantly at Tim, and he shrugged as if this was our only option.

"Can we trust these doctors?" I asked Max. "Is this our best route to go?"

Max assured us that he had been here before with many babies, that this hospital was not modern like those in the States, but that the care was good.

The nurse administered the IV and Sam shrieked like she was being flayed. I pressed my entire body weight into her, turned my face in the opposite direction so that she wouldn't see the tears pouring down my face, and held her still while the nurse poked and prodded and taped her tender little arm. I whispered apologies into her ear and swore that it wouldn't always be this bad.

Later, after Sam had forgotten about the IV and was used to the respirator, she twitched and kicked and whimpered until, finally, she gave in to sleep. Her swath of satin blanket was in one hand and mine was wrapped around her other. With Tim positioned at her side, I stepped out into the lobby and called Claire. I explained what was wrong with Sam: the fever, the congested lungs, her birth weight. She took down as much information as I had to give and then hung up to call her pediatrician, who now was also ours. When she called back, she requested Sam's X-ray report and hospital input form, so I walked down the road to a storefront that advertised a fax machine. With a string of international codes, I sent the fax. An hour later, Claire called back. She and the pediatrician had discussed Sam's case. The Chinese doctors were doing what would be done in the States. The course of treatment was good. By the time Claire and I hung up for our last time, it was three o'clock in the morning.

When I went back to Sam's room, I found Tim asleep, his hand covering Sam's.

Dear Max, in his Levi jeans and leather jacket, was still with us, punching on his BlackBerry, solving problems for all of his parents. He sat down next to me, handed me a Coke from the vending machine, and said, "There is an old folktale about a breed of wasps that was said to steal baby bollworms off the mulberry trees, take them to their own nests, and raise them as wasps."

I listened, nodded.

"Sometimes these girls—Chinese girls who get adopted—are called that: children of the mulberry bug."

"So us parents, we're like *abductors*?"

"No, no," he said. "You parents, you're more like saviors. Saving these girls from an unpleasant life."

"That's nice of you, Max," I said. "But I think most of us—well, at least speaking for myself—didn't adopt out of pure benevolence. We just wanted what we couldn't have, you know?"

"Perhaps," Max said. "But there are unintended consequences to everything we do in life. And I happen to believe that parents who adopt not only gain a life, but save one."

I considered his folktale, thought it through. In a way, each of us had been abducted or robbed of something precious. Sam had been taken from the life she'd known and enveloped in mine, through no choice of her own. My mother had been stolen from me when I was far too young. God, it broke my heart to recall all of my mother's promises of forever: "You'll always be mine," "Forever, my love," "'til the end of time." She'd meant them all; she'd believed it. There was no way for her to have known that promises made of gold could so easily melt to nothing. Everything that mattered, it seemed, was out of our control: whether we could bear a child, bestow upon that child a life; whether life, once given, ever truly belonged to us.

The following forty-eight hours passed with a disorienting sense of dislocation. The low light of the fluorescent bulbs gave no indication of whether it was morning or night. At some point, I had lifted Sam into my arms and positioned myself along the length of the hospital bed. When I woke, the light seemed more pronounced, a golden glow, and I was certain that it must be morning. I reached over Sam's tender wing of an arm, still strapped to the IV, and pushed the button on my cell phone. It registered as five in the morning. Only a few hours had passed. Sam had since sunk lower in my lap. Her legs curled between mine; her head rested atop my stomach. A pool of drool puddled around her mouth and through my pants.

Tim was asleep, slouched in the corner chair, his head pitched at an unnatural angle. He would hurt when he woke. I thought of the Advil in my purse.

I tried to close my eyes, to get a little more sleep, but my lids stung as if they were being forced against their will. I ran my finger down Sam's arm. Indignation threaded up my back. Why was Sam sick, damn it? Was she sick *because* we adopted her? Because these days with us had proved to be too taxing for her tender constitution? The many long bus rides, the change in diet, the recirculated heat in the hotel room. Would she have been better off left alone? Or would she have gotten sick anyway? And if she had, who would have cared for her at the orphanage? What if I weren't here yet? What if this bout of sickness had consumed her *last* month? Whose arms would she have snuggled in, Goddamn it? Who would have cared for her in my stead?

I wanted to kick my feet against the hospital bed's metal railing, scream at the top of my lungs, and beat a pillow with my fists. The thought hit me hard: I almost wasn't here for her! I almost missed being a mother to my sick daughter. No more, never again. Sam would never be alone again! As I wrapped this conviction in my fist, I thought of how loosely we all played with our relations. How we took for granted that they'd always be there. Look at Claire and me with our own father. *Estranged.* What were we all waiting for? Damn it all.

"When we get home, peanut," I whispered to Sam, "we're getting this family together once and for all. You and Daddy and me and Aunt Claire and Maura and Uncle Ross and Grandpa Larry."

By the next morning, Sam's fever had broken. As she drenched her sleeper suit and regained her strength, I swabbed her forehead with soft washcloths.

"Good girl," I cried. "Good, strong girl. I knew you'd get better."

The doctor examined her. Her lungs were clearing, her breathing had moderated, and some color had returned to her face. After I fed her a bowl of congee and a bottle of formula, I changed her diaper and held her in my arms.

"You're okay, pumpkin," I whispered in her ear. "You're going to grow up big and strong, don't you worry."

"Look what I found," Tim said, holding up a yellow paperback he had fished out of a basket in the lobby. It was *Curious George Goes to the Hospital*—in English! Tim scooted his chair next to mine and read the book aloud. When we got to the part where George passed out from sniffing ether, Tim and I laughed—real laughs—and hugged Sam tightly.

"When was this book *written*?" Tim asked as he wiped his eyes.

I looked at him and smiled, remembering my Norman Rockwell dream of a family just like this, a family with enough love to have fun even in a Chinese hospital. Enough love to pull the joy out of suffering.

After a while, Sam grew sleepy. Tim urged me to take a walk down the street, to get some fresh air.

"Fresh air?" I said with a smile.

"Well, air, anyway."

I exited the hospital, made a visor with my hand, and looked around. This part of town didn't look as seedy as it had in the middle of the night. There were businesses and storefronts with their doors open, groups of men huddled around a tree smoking cigarettes, mothers pushing strollers with heavily bundled babies. I stretched my arms above my head and arched my back. All sorts of pops and cracks. I leaned over and touched my toes. I wandered down the road, swinging my arms, turning my neck, trying to loosen up.

I cut through a city park and wound my way down a path lined with benches and flowers. Nestled among trees backlit by sunlight, boulders glistening with their natural glitter, and gigantic pots of flowers was a Buddhist temple. Though apprehensive, I inched my way up to the ornately carved red wood door and peeked in. Near the door was a pile of shoes. I slipped mine off and quietly eased my way in. The incense, the candles—the scents of my childhood, only Buddhist, not Catholic; only in China, not the States. At once, the differences seemed irrelevant. The brown-robed monks were going through their prostrations. When they were finished, I kneeled down and put my hands together. The prayers and gongs and recitations and bells. A soothing calm warmed me, like swallowing a spoonful of butternut squash soup, feeling it coat my throat and slide down to my belly.

I stared at the statues of Buddha. I thought of Sam, a child I hadn't known existed until recently, hadn't touched until eleven days ago, and now who occupied my every thought. I squeezed my eyes shut, and at first I saw Sam, but then I saw Mom. I smiled to myself because seeing her was always a rare treat, like slipping into an old-fashioned diner on a rainy day to find a chocolate cake frosted with boiled icing, the kind Mom made for every one of my childhood birthdays. But I also felt a tug of sadness, imagining how she would love being here, her pride in my adopting Sam, her head pulled forward from the weight of her 35 mm camera hanging around her neck, documenting every step of our journey.

Locals and tourists came and went, prayed and offered. I, too, was preparing to leave when I noticed that there was a group of ladies near the front of the temple. I had been watching them bowing and chanting, and now they were lighting incense. They appeared to be in a group and when they kneeled down, they spoke together, reciting the same prayer. They reminded me of Mom. She had been part of a group called the Legion of Mary; it meant that she would say the complete rosary every day. Once a week, she said it aloud with her group, in the front pews of St. Mary's.

With a thumping heart, I inched my way up toward the women, kneeling behind them and putting my hands into prayer position. For the next twenty minutes, while they chanted their prayers in Chinese, I whispered my prayers in English, a metronome of pleases and thank-yous and never-agains and forevers. When the Chinese women finished, they rose quietly, but stirred enough to knock me from my own meditations. One, a kind elderly lady, looked me square in the eyes, reached for my hand, and squeezed it.

She said something to me in Chinese that sounded a lot like, "It was nice having you here, dear."

"Thank you," I said, and a shiver tingled throughout my body.

Afterward, I lit some prayer candles and then went outside into the garden, where I sat on a concrete bench and stared at a statue of Buddha.

I took a deep breath, looked to the sky, and knew that it was time to have a conversation with my mother, my dear sweet mother, whom I hadn't addressed directly in twenty-two years.

"Mom," I said, testing my voice, my ability to actually say her name. "I'm here in China. Are you watching? Do you see that I have a daughter now? Isn't she adorable?" I reached into my purse and rooted around for a tissue but only came up with one of Sam's socks. I remembered how Claire used to stick her hand in a jacket pocket and come up with a binky. This sock made me feel like my sister, like a legitimate mom. I dabbed my eyes with it and swiped it across my nose.

"Mom," I said. "I've thought this a million times and I've felt the shame and regret of it every day of my life, but I've never said it. So I'm going to say it now: *I'm sorry*, Mom. I'm sorry that I wasn't the daughter you needed me to be when you were sick. I'm sure, knowing you, that you'd say, 'Oh, honey, you were sad. It's okay. You did your best.' All that's true, but if there were a way that I could go back, I would have been exactly what you needed. I would have loved you with such honesty there wouldn't have been any doubt in your mind as you left this world. Your heart would have been overflowing. That's what I wish. I'm sorry that I wasn't that way. I'd do anything to hug you and tell you how much I loved you. How much I still love you. I love you, Mom. I really, really love you. And I'm sorry."

By the time I got back to the hospital, Tim was holding Sam, who was cheerful and rested. When she saw me, she smiled and reached in my direction. A sense of pride and propriety filled me. Our red thread seemed to be reinforcing itself with a material that could not be breached.

⌒

After seventeen long days, we said good-bye to Max, our fellow adoptive parents, their beautiful new daughters, and the region of China that bore Sam. Amy and I promised to e-mail each other often. The husbands took photos of us holding Sam and Maria, little Angela between us. Then Amy took one last picture of Tim and me with Sam, and we did the same for her family. When Amy hugged me, I cried because I couldn't have made it through these last weeks without her. She was my surrogate for Claire, a version of my older sister, seven thousand miles from home.

We boarded the Boeing 747, bounced Sam on our laps, and gave her a cookie to chew on during takeoff. When she shrieked from the noise and air pressure of the plane, I pushed her piece of satin blanket top into her little hand, held her tightly against my chest, and promised her that soon we'd be home.

"Do you hurt, baby?" I whispered to her, rubbing the outsides of her ears.

Sam looked up at me, made the briefest eye contact, before looking away, as if to say, *Not as much as I used to.*

When finally we arrived home, the bubble of emotion exited me: I emitted an embarrassingly loud squeak that turned the heads of passersby. Tears poured down my face. The glorious sign read, *The U.S. Customs Service Welcomes You to the United States.* When we cleared customs and made our way down to baggage claim, the tears gushed again at the sight of Claire, my sister who was usually so well composed, crying in anticipation of our arrival. With Maura on her hip and Sam on mine, we clustered in a hug that smeared mascara and lipstick, a huddle of happy, happy tears.

"Look at us," Claire said, wiping her eyes.

"Yeah," I said. "Finally."

# PART THREE

# Chapter Sixteen

Two days later, on Christmas Eve, we gathered at Claire's. Her house was decorated exquisitely, as if Martha Stewart herself had waved a crafty wand. A ten-foot Fraser fir was wrapped in tiny yellow lights, garlands spiraled around the staircase banister, and piney wreaths welcomed our arrival. Bowls of candy adorned each table. Eggnog was chilled. Stockings were hung, especially a new one, freshly embroidered with the name *Samantha*.

Davis and Delia were there, and Martha, Ross's mother, was there, too. Maura was buzzing around with the energy of a kid who had eaten a pound of candy. I sat in front of the tree with Sam. By the way she marveled at the lights, I figured that she'd be happy staring at them for a while. Claire had pulled out packed-away gear from Maura: a bouncing chair, a walker, a Johnny Jump Up. I inserted Sam into the walker and she hung from the harness, mesmerized, reaching for the ornaments.

"What do you think, sweetheart?" I asked, tracing my finger across her cheek. "Do you like the tree?"

I thought of my friend, Amy DePalma, and how she warned me against overstimulating Sam. "These kids need to be eased in to everything!" she told me. "When you get her home, don't let her have a trunk full of toys or her choice of food to eat. I'm serious, Helen," she said. "Strip her room to nothing but the crib. It's what she's used to. Anything more will freak her out."

I nodded and agreed, because if anyone knew, Amy did. But how could we avoid the excess of Christmas? I looked at the tree. It seemed to be buoyed by an island of presents, many of which I knew were for Sam, my daughter from rural China who came with one possession—a strip of satin blanket top.

Though we were at Claire and Ross's, Tim offered to cook. He had picked up a beef tenderloin, which he planned to sear on all sides, warm in the oven, and serve pink and juicy—thick slices of filet mignon. While Sam admired the ornaments and her new cousin, Maura, dancing around her, I went into the kitchen and whipped up a few batches of rosemary biscuits and a piecrust. Tim roasted red peppers for the soup. Claire skinned potatoes.

The night wrapped around me like a warm blanket. The emotion that now bubbled out of me was pure gratitude. To be with Tim, home with Sam, bonded tightly with my sister, nearly filled a hole in me that had existed since Mom died. I thought of Larry, wondered what he was doing at this exact moment. I wondered if he was home alone in his recliner, sipping eggnog, listening to Bing Crosby. He was what was left. The one missing piece. The last inch of the hole to be filled. Maybe by this time next year, we'd have adopted him, too.

Later, we dressed Maura and Sam in matching flannel Christmas pajamas and situated them on the sofa for a photo shoot. Maura took her big-cousin job seriously, holding tightly to her little cousin. Christmas lights twinkled, "Rudolph the Red-Nosed Reindeer" played, cameras winked and whined, all while Sam looked up curiously, offering the occasional smile when Maura tickled her.

Fifty shots later, I finally had the photo that summed up my emotional state, the photo that would stand iconic for this first Christmas with my new daughter: Sam staring dreamily into

Maura's eyes, astonished and amazed, wondering (not unhappily so) how the heck she had ended up here.

When we said good night, I pulled Claire aside. "These last few years…" I stumbled to put into words an apology for my half-decade depression.

"Forget about it," Claire said, waving away my concern.

"I'm happy now," I said. "I'm really happy now."

"Same," Claire said. "And I'm wild about my new niece. She is the cutest thing in history."

"What about Larry?" I asked.

"What about him?"

"I don't know." I shrugged. "Just thinking."

"You keep thinking," she smiled. "I'm going to bed."

The next morning, Delia helped me bathe Sam. Once she was dry and powdered and creamed, we wrestled her into a pair of ruffled-bottom tights and a ruby taffeta Christmas dress. We clutched our sides laughing at the sight of her, her little head, with tufts of black hair sprung in every direction, bobbling above the too-puffy dress. The more we laughed, the more Sam laughed, our little sidekick, solidly in cahoots.

On our way to church, I thought back to the last time I'd been at St. Mary's. It must have been a Christmas or two ago, when Claire had dragged me along with one of her "Christmas and Easter is the least you can do" guilt trips. I had sat in the pew next to Claire and watched the families stroll in. Pregnant mothers in their bulging maternity dresses, holding babies on their hips, others by the hands. Hordes of families with strings of children: three, five, seven, ten. I remember a ladder of girls sitting in front of me in their red-and-green smocked hand-me-down dresses. The littlest was probably three, the oldest in her teens. One of the middle girls looked back at me, shrugged her shoulders as if to ask, *Where's yours?* I swirled my finger at her, indicating that she should turn around. I didn't need a slice from the fertile-Myrtle pie mocking me, too. Today, though, I was one of them. I was finally a member of the one group I had always wanted to join. My empty arms were now full.

Once in the pew, I slid down onto my knees, closed my eyes, and thanked God. Having Sam in my arms after years of disappointment seemed like a true miracle. The idea of adopting once had felt heavy and false, and now it felt light and right, like the mystery of thick sugar and viscous corn syrup combining to create a delicate crown of spun sugar.

After Mass, I kissed Sam good-bye and left her in the care of Tim and his parents. I was on my way to meet Claire at the cemetery to visit Mom's grave.

"Are you sure you don't want us to come along?" Tim asked.

"Definitely," I said. "I won't be gone long. When I get home, we can have lunch, okay?"

Kisses and hugs, and then I was behind the wheel. It took me only a moment to notice that I couldn't help checking the rearview mirror for split-second glances at Sam's car seat. The maternal instincts that I once feared were trapped in my defective ovaries were thrumming, as alert as a school crossing guard.

Half an hour later, I pulled through the wrought iron entrance to Oak Creek Cemetery. I parked and started up the hill that led to Mom's gravesite. As I crested the hill, I saw Claire, on her knees in front of Mom's headstone. I watched as she doubled over, wiped her eyes, and shook her head as in disbelief.

I eased my way up, and careful not to startle her, I said in a soft voice, "Hi, Claire."

"Oh!" she said, standing up, wiping her eyes. "You got here fast."

"Are you okay?" I asked, searching her face.

"Definitely!"

"Why are you crying?"

"Oh, tears of joy," she said. "You know, sometimes you're just overwhelmed with gratitude."

"Claire, seriously," I said. "You're upset. What's going on?"

Claire wiped her face again. "Seriously, Helen, it's Christmas! What on earth would I have to be upset about?"

"Is everything okay with Ross? Maura?"

"Of course," she said. "That was part of this little tear-fest," she said. "Maura wore this black velour dress to Mass this morning with these little high-heeled shoes, and I'm telling you, Helen, it nearly killed me. She looked so grown up. I just kept thinking, 'Here we go...'"

"So you're okay?" I asked. "You're sure?"

"Definitely," she said. "Now let's spend some time with Mom."

<hr/>

Two weeks later, Davis and Delia were packing their suitcase, preparing to go back to North Carolina. I stood in the doorway with Sam on my hip. "Thank you so much for being here," I said. "For helping me with Sam, for stocking the fridge, for all the cleaning and handiwork you've done around the house. It's been a wonderful homecoming."

"We'll stay if you need us, dear," Delia said, reaching for Sam, the new granddaughter she couldn't get enough of.

"I'd love it," I said. "But we'll be fine. We need to get into a routine."

That night, Tim cooked pork chops the way we had learned to do in the French countryside, dredged in flour, slow-cooked in milk, and served over a pile of creamy potatoes. The meal was delicious and we all ate slowly, savoring every morsel of food. We passed Sam around and savored her, too.

The next day, Sam and I waved good-bye to Davis and Delia, and then an hour later to Tim, who was eager to get back to the restaurant.

With Sam in my arms, we walked through the eerily quiet house.

"Now what?" I said.

Sam glanced at me, testing her eye contact, as if to say, *If I weren't here, what would you do?*

"That's the thing, peanut," I said, gently touching my finger to her nose. "Before you came along, I spent a lot of time sulking. I spent a lot of time in bed, watching soap operas and wanting what I couldn't have. And when I ventured out, I often times landed in front of my father's house. Maybe we'll do that later," I said. "Would you like to meet your other grandfather?" I tickled her tummy.

Sam smiled, showing her dimple. I took that as a yes.

"Before all that nonsense," I told her, "I was a chef. A pastry chef, mostly. Dad and I own a restaurant, what do you think of that?"

Sam glanced at me again, pursed her lips.

"Okay, okay," I said. "We need a routine." I looked at the clock—ten o'clock in the morning. Sam was due to eat. I strapped her in the high chair and mixed a bottle of formula. Then I tossed a handful of cooked rice into the fry pan and cracked an egg on top, heated it for just a minute, and set it in the refrigerator to cool. I opened a jar of squash and sat down next to Sam. She took a few bites of the squash, ate the rice and egg in its entirety, and drank most of her bottle. Then I held her and burped her, flipped up flashcards and called out their names, clapped when she smiled. Then I changed her diaper and dressed her in a fresh zipper-suit. When I looked at the clock, it was only eleven. This was going to be a long day.

"Don't worry," I told her. "When you're a little older, we'll do lots of fun things. We'll bake sugar cookies and have tea parties. You'll be the only toddler in town who knows how to make snickerdoodles from scratch.

"And maybe, too," I said, testing the words out loud, "maybe we'll start the paperwork to get you a sister. Wouldn't that be nice? A *mei mei*?"

Sam looked at me as if she recognized the word *sister* and kicked her happy legs.

"But you'd better be nice to her," I said. "Being a big sister is a big responsibility. Your Aunt Claire was a little too bossy, if you ask me."

I sat Sam on her blanket and started a Baby Einstein DVD, drank a cup of coffee, and read a few e-mails on my phone. Amy DePalma had written, sent a few photos of her girls and a link to an adoption website for me to check out. I was just hitting "send" on my reply to her when the door-bell rang, followed by the turn of the key and Claire's singsong, "Yoo-hoo!"

"Hi!" I said, and hugged her. "I'm *so* happy to see you! I'm going out of my mind today with everyone gone. It's so quiet and time is, like, *crawling*! Don't get me wrong," I rambled. "This is what I wanted, but seriously, Claire, I can see how moms lose their freaking minds being at home all day with a baby." I covered my mouth with my hand in case Sam had heard. "I've only had her for a couple of weeks and I already think that I need more kids. I was kind of hoping for enough noise to fill the house," I said. "Is that weird?"

"Of course not," she said. "It sounds like you."

"How so?" I asked, walking into the kitchen to get us a drink.

"You like activity, excitement," Claire said. "You're at your happiest when you're busy, under fire, traveling around, cooking for a crowd, working against the clock."

"What about you?"

"We're different," she said. "I kind of love being home with just Maura. You have to remember, I've been waiting twenty-five years to be in this position—being *still*. I went from taking care of Mom, to taking care of you, to working myself to the bone through college and grad school, then up the ranks at Goldman Sachs. I just want to sit back and enjoy my daughter and husband. But that's just me."

"That's good," I said, considering her point.

"Remember," she said. "I'm six years older than you—an old lady compared to your youthful thirty-six."

"Yeah, you're ancient."

"Anyway, I'm kind of glad that you're bored right now because I might need some additional help from you. With Maura." Claire strained her mouth into an odd smile.

I poured lemonade for us and then led Claire back into the family room. "What are you talking about?" I sat down on the floor next to Sam, hoisting her up higher on her pillow. "Is there a problem at her preschool?"

"Oh, Helen, this is going to be hard on you."

"On me? What's going to be hard on me?"

"Brace yourself, Helen," Claire said.

"Wait! Could you keep an eye on Sam?" I heard the nervousness in my voice. "I've just got to run to the bathroom real quick." I ran upstairs and into my bedroom and then into my bathroom, closed the door, and sat on the toilet seat. My heart thumped as a wave of nausea coursed through my stomach. When I squeezed my eyes shut, a kaleidoscope of colors blurred and resolved into a scattering of dots. *No, no, no.* I opened my eyes, stared at the white wall, and shook my head back and forth as tears rose in my throat.

"Helen." Claire knocked on the door. "Come out, okay?"

I shook my head no.

"Helen, come on."

I stood, opened the door. Sam was on Claire's hip, playing with my sister's earring.

The three of us sat on the bed. Claire reached for my hands.

"What you're about to say"—I was breathless—"it's not good, right?"

"No, it's not good."

We looked at each other, breathed.

"Just say it."

"I've got the cancer, Helen. I've got Mom's cancer. Ovarian."

"They're wrong," I insisted. "There's got to be a mistake. There's no way that you could. You're checked all of the time!"

"I go in every year," Claire said. "But you know there's no real way for them to screen for it."

"Did you get a second opinion? Those stupid doctors are wrong all of the time! Maybe they got your chart mixed up."

Claire hugged me and I hugged her and our bodies shook in jolting sobs. I was shocked but not shocked; part of me had been expecting this bomb to drop every day of my life. And it felt exactly as I had imagined it would, as if I were drowning. When I was maybe ten years old, I jumped into a swimming pool with a T-shirt over my suit. As I drifted downward, my air bubbles floating to the top, I pulled the T-shirt over my head. As I did, the heavy fabric sucked against my face and I was unable to pull my uplifted arms through the armholes. For a few seconds, I was straight-jacketed. That was when I learned that I was in control of only so much, that I'd be fighting forces bigger than myself for my entire life.

"I'm going to fight it," Claire said. "God knows I'll fight it harder than anyone and I will win. I'll be damned if I'm going to leave Maura alone in this world."

"When did you find out?"

"I just found out. It was that pain in my side. I thought it was a muscle pull, but it was actually a *symptom*. The blood they drew the other day was tested and the count was all off. They called me back and did an ultrasound and found a lump."

"But they can't know exactly what it is until they operate," I argued, even though I knew that ovarian cancer was one of the sneakiest thieves in town, robbing you blind before you even noticed it was there. Symptoms could just as easily be from indigestion or a pulled muscle as from the cancer.

"Next week. They'll do a laparotomy and see if the mass is just on the ovary or if it's spread elsewhere."

"Okay," I said, standing up, lifting Sam into my arms, and beginning to pace across the room. "We'll just need to get you the absolute *best* doctors. We'll go to Johns Hopkins. That's the benefit of living in the nation's capitol. We have great doctors. We just need the best, and you'll be okay, right, Claire?"

"My doctors here are good," Claire said. "At this point, it's standard procedure. Maybe down the road..."

"What's Ross say?"

"Ross is in denial, and he seems irritated with me that I didn't recognize the symptoms in light of Mom. Like I should have known what ovarian cancer feels like. But the thing is, there weren't symptoms, just a twist in my side that came and went. It ached like a pulled muscle. Now that I know, I guess I've been a little bloated, but who hasn't had that every now and then?"

"What about Maura?" I asked. "Does she know anything?"

Maura was the type of kid who preferred her mother's arms to television and toys, her mother's mouth on her boo-

boo over a cartoon Band-Aid, her mother's whisper at night over a CD lullaby.

At the sound of her daughter's name, Claire slumped into the pillows on the bed like bread dough that had been punched down. "No, not yet."

I lifted Sam higher on my shoulder, wrapped both arms around her. I looked at Claire and tried to convey with my eyes that I knew she was scared to death at the thought of leaving Maura, but for God's sake, *I* needed her, too.

"What's the plan?" I asked. This was Claire. There was always a plan.

Claire sat up with her back straight and folded her hands in her lap. "The plan is that I'll be busy for a while with surgeries and appointments, probably chemo, then radiation. That's why I need you. I'd like for Maura to spend more time with you and Sam, to create a routine that she begins to count on. She loves you and Tim so much. And she adores being a 'big cousin' to Sam. I know it's a lot to ask, Helen, with you just getting home with Sam. But it would help if Maura spent more time with your family. I don't know how much Ross will be able to do. Yes, he'll tend to all of her needs. But she'll need someone to fill in as mom. You know how much affection she requires."

"I'll do anything. I swear to you, Claire. I will do anything you need."

"If we're lucky, I'll be through the worst part by summer and we can all get on with our lives."

Six months, good. Claire had already defined her goal and set a timeline. With her day planner, a colorful pack of highlighters, and ironclad determination, Claire would set records with her recovery. This was my big sister, after all. The one who stayed when both Mom and Dad left.

After a while, I handed Sam off to Claire and went downstairs into the kitchen and made a batch of peanut butter–chocolate chip cookies. At a time like this, Claire's favorite cookie with a giant glass of milk was all I could think to do. We ate and ate until we were nearly sick.

"Claire," I said carefully. "I know this isn't the right time to bring this up, but then again, maybe it's the perfect time."

"What, Helen?"

"I don't know. It's just…When I was in China and Sam was sick, I saw everything so clearly. We lost Mom because we didn't have a choice, but we lost Dad, too, and we kind of did have a choice. When I was there, I just felt really strongly about trying to get our family back together."

"So this is about Larry?"

"With you being sick…I think that he'd really like to see you, meet his granddaughters. I know he did us wrong. I know he wasn't there. But still—"

"You do what you need to do, Helen," Claire said wearily. "I've got my own battle to fight. If you want to take that—*him*—on, that's going to be up to you."

That night, I lay folded over on Tim's lap while he stroked my hair. The tears streamed down my face and I cried without making a sound. It wasn't fair. It wasn't fair that Claire and I loved each other so much but never had the chance to be together. For one reason or another, we were always just missing each other. When I was in high school, Claire had to be my caregiver rather than my sister: paying the bills, grocery shopping, helping me with my homework. Then I went away to Europe, and when I got back, we were both new brides, ready to start families. But it only worked for Claire, and once again, our paths took different forks. And now finally, *finally*, we were mothers with daughters, with the time, energy, and desire to spend our days together, and Claire turns up with cancer. It was just a minute ago when I had Claire but not Sam, and now I had Sam, and there was a threat of losing Claire. It wasn't fair. I wanted time with her. I wanted picnics at the zoo, family vacations, cousins growing up close. I wanted Claire to squeeze my hand on Sam's first day of kindergarten; I wanted to be the one who steadied Claire as she watched Maura graduate from high school.

"You mentioned that Claire gets checked," Tim said. "When was the last time you got checked?"

"Years ago."

"Why so long?"

"Because the only thing I thought about for the last five years was getting pregnant and having a baby," I admitted. "I mean, sure, the *thought* would occasionally hover over me, but I was so obsessed with infertility I never paid too much attention."

"Now, though. You need to get tested."

"I will. I just went online. It said that over eighty percent of victims—*victims*, like somebody put a fucking gun to their heads—find out in the late stages. By then, it's pretty advanced. That's what happened with Mom."

"If Claire's been getting regular checkups, then she probably will beat the odds," Tim said. "She probably caught it early."

"I'm betting on it," I said. "The smart money has always bet on Claire. If anyone can beat it, she can."

"You need to get checked, Helen," Tim said. "Even if it's mostly useless. Get checked so that you can stay on top of the latest technology. There's bound to be advances in this type of cancer, right?" Tim pulled me into him. "It runs in your family, Helen. We've got to take that seriously."

"You're right," I admitted. "I will." I got up and went into the bathroom to brush my teeth. What I had just told Tim wasn't entirely true. The thought of cancer sometimes more than hovered. Once, I even had made the appointment to have blood drawn to check my predisposition to it, but at the last minute canceled. If I learned that I was predisposed to ovarian cancer, that would confirm my suspicions that Mom's genes and my infertility were connected. I was more afraid of losing hope in my fertility than I'd been anxious to find out about the cancer mutation.

While Tim was locking up the house, I slipped into the family room and picked up the phone. I held it in my hand, leaned over at the waist, and exhaled. With trembling hands, I dialed Larry's number. He answered on the first ring.

"It's Helen," I said.

"Are you home from China?" he asked. "I got the photo you sent of Sam. She's a cutie."

"I'm home, and Sam's great. But that's not why I'm calling."

My eyes filled with tears—exactly what I didn't want to happen. I wanted and needed to be strong, like Claire. I took a deep breath and let the tears free-fall onto my thighs.

"I'm calling because Claire's sick. She has cancer. Ovarian, just like Mom."

"Oh," he groaned. It was the guttural moan of an animal caught in a trap.

My chest grew heavy and I felt a sadness that turned me inside out because I knew how this worked: He would never be able to un-hear my words.

"You and I, we blew it with Mom," I continued. "We weren't there for her when she needed us. I'm not planning on repeating that mistake." I steadied my voice and took another breath. "I know our family didn't survive Mom's death. I was just thinking—hoping, really—that maybe we could come together for Claire."

He cleared his throat and blew his nose. Without seeing, I knew that he was using a handkerchief.

"I'm calling to say this," I continued. "If you want to try to work your way back into this family, I'll do what I can to help you."

"I do," he said, his voice buckling midword. "I do."

"Okay, then," I said. "I'll be in touch."

⌒

That night, tightly nestled around the curve of Tim's back, I fell asleep and dreamed of Claire and me when we were little. We had built a fort out of sofa cushions and sheets. It was summer, and the fabric felt cool against our skin as we parachuted them high above our heads and hooked them under the pillows. Then we lay on our backs on the floor, staring up at the ceiling, the sun casting shadows through the thin fabric. Claire rolled onto me, straddled me, and pinned my hands above my head. She tickled my arms, my stomach, my neck. "You're so mine! You're so mine!" she said in an evil voice, almost a witch's cackle. I laughed and then I cried and then I laughed again. I begged her to stop; I begged her for more. Finally, she rolled onto her back; I could see the rise and fall of her belly out of the corner of my eye. I rolled onto her, tummy to tummy, and this time she wrapped her arms around me. Tightly. She looked into my eyes and said, in the sweetest voice, "You're so mine. You're so mine. You're my little Helen." And she kissed me all over my face. I woke up startled, looked around. I closed my eyes again because I wanted to feel Claire's arms around little girl me for just one more second, but the moment was gone. That's when I realized that I might never feel Claire's arms again. The thought choked me. I sat up straight, grabbed for my throat, and gasped for air.

"It's okay," Tim was saying. "Slow down. Take a nice, slow breath."

I tried, but my throat was clogged. The tears were choking me. My chest burned.

"Let me get a paper bag," Tim said.

"Don't leave!" I gasped, grasping onto his shirt, pulling him to me, burrowing into his chest.

"Slowly, slowly." Tim rubbed my back as he spoke.

Finally, I found some air. I folded into Tim and cried, in free-flowing, jolting sobs. "Oh my God, Tim. What if I lose her? What would I do?" I cried until my chest burned and my throat was raw. Tim held me tightly, and then even tighter. But even his tightest wasn't enough to tame my greatest fear: one way or another, everyone was going to leave me.

# Chapter Seventeen

Perspective. That's what I got, and fast, the second my sister—my lifeline—told me she had cancer, the same cancer that killed our mother. That's how fast the earth shifted beneath my feet. Claire was sick, and it was now my turn to stand up for her like she'd always stood up for me.

But worrying about Claire would need to wait—at least for a few hours. Knocking at my door was Dr. Elle Reese, at nine o'clock on the dot, here to conduct our post-adoption visit. This would count as the first of three such visits. Claire's news had left me shaky all weekend, waking disoriented in the night, crying in the supermarket, sitting in my car staring into space while Sam slept in her car seat. And when I wasn't worried about Claire, I was worrying about this visit. What if Elle found a deficiency in my mothering, something obvious that I had overlooked, like the fact that I had slathered Sam's bread with honey before Claire told me it was sometimes dangerous to babies?

*Get it together*, I told myself. *Sam's doing great and you can worry about Claire later.* Being a mom now meant that my grief had to be scheduled, like a dental appointment. So I woke early, baked a batch of scones, arranged a fruit platter, and brewed coffee. I straightened the family room and cleaned the kitchen. When Sam stirred, I warmed a bottle, which she drank in her crib, still groggy with sleep, gulping with her eyes shut. Then I changed her diaper and dressed her in a cute pair of overalls with a pink-flowered shirt.

I led Elle to the family room. She sat in the upholstered chair across from the sofa. Today she was wearing a dress that resembled an Indian sari, a drape of orange silk fabric splashed with burnt yellows and reds and heavily embroidered with beads and sequins. Her nest of hair was twisted into a knot and secured with a jeweled clip. Her toenails were painted black with gold flecks and she wore thin gold sandals.

"It's good to see you again," Elle said, settling into the chair and crossing her legs. A gold bracelet circled her ankle.

I went to the kitchen and retrieved the tray of coffee, fruit, and pastries. I set it on the ottoman for Elle to help herself. Then I unbuckled Sam from her high chair and brought her in with us, placing her on the Oriental carpet with a basket of educational toys.

"Well, hello, cutie pie," Elle said, reaching for a maraca and shaking it in front of Sam. Elle looked up at me. "How is little Sam?"

I took a deep breath, steadied myself to say all of the right things, worried that one wrong step would have me deemed unfit as a mother and Sam put in the custody of child services. "She's doing really well," I said. "She's learned to sit and walk; she plays competently with all of her age-appropriate educational toys. She gravitates toward the manipulatives. She likes to put squares in squares, circles in circles. Maybe a future engineer? She's very detailed. She likes small objects—well, not too small!" I corrected. "Not so small that they're choking hazards."

Elle smiled. "Relax, Helen," she said. "It looks like Sam is doing great. No need to be so worried."

"Okay," I said.

"What else?" Elle asked. "How's her schedule?"

"Let's see, she takes two naps per day. Eats with me on a regular schedule—three meals, plus snacks in between. She has gained three pounds in the month we've had her. She's grown an inch. She's been checked out by the pediatrician, who has begun repeating all of her immunizations, just in case. She's friendly and smiles a lot. She loves her big cousin, Maura—"

"That's wonderful," Elle interrupted. "I'm sure you're taking wonderful care of her. How is she doing developmentally? Have you noticed any delays or behavior that struck you as odd?"

"Well, sure…" I stammered, wondering whether it was better to say or better to gloss over. "There's some. I mean, she seems to know that I'm Mom and Tim's Dad, but she's not very choosy about who she goes to. It's kind of the 'highest bidder' type of thing. She'll go to the person who has what she wants. Her eye contact is still a little sketchy, but really, no big problems."

"Do any of these issues concern you?"

"Not really," I said honestly. "I chat frequently with one of the moms who we traveled with. She has two girls from China and she has assured me that most of this behavior is fairly normal—well, typical, anyway."

"And how are *you* doing?" Elle asked, locking her X-ray eyes on mine.

"Good!" I said, nodding my head enthusiastically. "Really good."

Elle continued to look at me as if she didn't believe me. "Being a new mother is tough," she said. "Are you faring okay?"

I nodded, stretched my eyes open as wide as I could, and tried to slide the tears back into place.

"Are you okay?" Elle asked, leaning forward.

"My sister has cancer," I blurted, releasing my restrained tears like a slingshot. "We just found out. The same kind of cancer that killed our mother."

"I'm so sorry to hear that," Elle said.

"I'm sure she'll be fine," I said, wiping at my face with my sleeve. "But still, I just got home and it's such a happy time. It's just really unfortunate that..."

"That what?"

"Nothing," I said. "It's selfish on my part."

"Go for it."

"It's unfortunate that I couldn't have it all," I admitted. "That I couldn't have Sam *and* Claire, just like I couldn't have my mother *and* father. Or my mother *and* Claire. It just seems like a pattern. Something good always balanced by something bad."

"Yes, the circle of life is an often cruel reality."

I nodded, wiped my eyes.

"You're scared," Elle said. "The cancer means that you might lose your sister, that your niece might lose her mother."

"That's not an option," I said. "I can't live without Claire."

"You love her a lot."

"It's beyond love," I said. "We're sisters."

"That Claire's sick," Elle went on, "what does it mean to you as Sam's mother?"

I thought of Sam, how sure I was in promising her forever, when in truth I hadn't a bit of control over what the future would bring.

"It means that I'm no more immune from it than Claire was," I admitted. "The ironic thing is, in the months leading up to the adoption, I worried that an adoptive daughter might someday leave *me*. It never occurred to me how devastating it could be to her if I were the one to leave. So, yeah, Claire's cancer makes it real. That I could get it, too. And the thought of leaving Sam too early scares me terribly."

"Being left is a terrible thing," Elle said.

"I want to give Sam the childhood I never had, one that doesn't end at age twelve when a father leaves, or age thirteen when a mother gets sick. I want to be her rock. I never want her to feel scared or alone or uncertain."

"Your father left," Elle said. "What was that like?"

"It was a crazy time. My mother was sick, and she and my father were separated. Then he left during it all."

Elle paused, twisted her ring. "That must have made matters worse that he left at such a difficult time, with your mother being ill."

"It *seems* like that would have made a big difference," I said, remembering how chaotic it was back then, "but you know how those things go. Life doesn't stop for illness. Mom was working. Larry traveled a lot. Claire was in college. I was just starting high school. Normal life, except that Larry had become an outsider. Following his affair, he moved out for a while. During that time, Mom and Claire and I banded together. When Larry came back home, it couldn't have been too much fun for him."

"What was that like?"

"When I saw him recently," I said, "he told me that he used to sit in the driveway and think, 'Who the hell even cares if I come in?' I can totally understand why he felt that way. Our house couldn't have been too inviting to him. Claire, especially, was as cold as ice. That's Claire. If she's on your side, you've got yourself a strong ally. But if you cross her, look out. She considered Larry's infidelity as pure treason. And Mom just kind of moved around him. Her Catholic sensibilities, she'd rather stay married in some awkward limbo than get a divorce.

"Then, just like that, we find out that Mom has ovarian cancer. I remember how we all sat around the kitchen table as she explained it, almost apologetic to Larry, like her being ill was going to inconvenience him in some way. She kept saying stuff like, 'I'm fine. No one needs to do or change anything. Life will go on just as it had yesterday.'

"If you knew my mom," I said, feeling a wave of emotion rising in me, "you'd understand how the cancer was probably easier for her to reconcile than the end of a marriage. At least with cancer you have the statistics screaming at you, 'Don't take it personally!' It taps you on your shoulder whether you're ready or not. But ending a marriage is a conscious choice, one she wasn't willing to make. Not like any of it mattered, once she was sick."

"Were you angry when your father left?" Elle asked.

"Mom and Claire were angry, and I wanted to be like them—to be included in their club—so I played along. But I never hated him. I remembered some good times, and I just wanted those good times *back*. I felt sorry for him, imagining him all alone in some studio-apartment dump, eating cold beans out of the can. I didn't put all the blame on him is what I'm saying. I was only twelve years old the first time he left, so basically, I still had thoughts like, 'If we were nicer to him, maybe he would have stayed.'"

"And now?"

"*Now* is a brand-new time period. I'm a mom. He's an old man. He failed at fatherhood, but he wasn't the worst thing in the world."

Sam started to fuss and that was when I remembered that Elle had come to check up on her, not to hear my life story. "I'm so sorry," I said. "I've unloaded all sorts of my baggage on you. I'm sure that's not your job."

"Actually, it is," she said. "Writing home studies is only part of my work. The rest of my practice is counseling adoptive parents, and believe it or not, that involves all of their baggage."

After Elle left, seemingly satisfied with Sam's care and my mothering, I lifted sleeping Sam from her playpen and settled into the sofa. She wiggled and fussed but settled right back down.

"What about you, peanut?" I whispered, fingering her new wispy hair. "Do you have plans to leave me?" I wondered whether Tim was right, whether I even had the capacity to believe that someone in my life could stay.

The other night, I had had a dream about Sam when she was older. She was in college, a beautiful, confident twenty-something coed, majoring in math or physics or something else that confounded most people, but that, to her, made perfect sense. I saw her dating her future husband, maybe a grad student: smart, enterprising, and Chinese. He took her home to meet his parents. They served her a traditional Chinese dinner, spoke easily in English, then slipped into Mandarin and back to English again, explaining the meaning of the silk scrolls that hung on their wall. They asked her about the province in which she was born. Coincidentally, they had ancestors and friends who were from the same region. They conveyed more to her about her birthplace in one evening than I had been able to impart to her in twenty years. At the end of the night, Sam looked over her shoulder to find me standing in the doorway. She shrugged and then walked to her new boyfriend, a magnet pulling her toward the life she'd been born to live but hadn't been able to, due to circumstance. Just as I had once strode headlong into Tim's family, people who offered to me the security and stability that my childhood had lacked, Sam insinuated herself into this Chinese family's world without looking back.

When I woke in the night and replayed the dream in my mind, I was disturbed that Tim was right, that my mind seemed hardwired for being left. Then I turned onto my side and told myself to see it differently, to see Sam coming home during Christmas break, falling into my lap, curling up beside me on the sofa, and yapping all night long about her first semester of college.

I let that happy image hover, let it sink into my bones, but it wasn't easy. I was resistant, as if allowing myself to hope in such a manner was superstitious and indulgent. It was better to take it one day at a time.

As if Sam were reading my thoughts, she stirred, pushed up onto my chest, and looked at me, as if to say, *That's not going to happen, Mom. I'm not going to leave you, as long as you don't leave me.*

"I'll never leave you," I said.

# Chapter Eighteen

The following Monday morning, Claire was scheduled for surgery. She and Ross dropped off Maura on their way. Claire, dressed smartly in her chinos and cashmere cardigan, kneeled down next to her daughter. "Be good for Aunt Helen, okay?" With wide eyes and a stretched mouth, Maura nodded.

"We're going to have fun, right, Maura?"

Maura began to cry, sensing that her mother was vulnerable. She was whiny and clingy and making it difficult for Claire and Ross to get out the door. You'd think that a four-year-old wouldn't have a clue what going to the hospital meant, her knowledge bank having been filled primarily by *Blue's Clues* and *Dora the Explorer*. But her intuition was right on. You could see the worry in her eyes, and she didn't want to let her mother go.

"Please stay, please stay," she pleaded between heavy sobs, her arms wrapped like vise grips around Claire's neck.

"Sweetie," Claire tried. "I'll be back before you know it. You're going to have so much fun with Aunt Helen and Sam."

"But I want *you!*" Maura wailed. Fighting words. A hot knife cutting through butter.

Claire looked away as I pried Maura off her mother with promises of making a gigantic jaguar bed out of all of the pillows in the room.

"Aunt Helen," Maura gulped, her mouth a centimeter from mine. "I want to go to the hospital with Mommy."

"Hospitals are boring," I said. "There's nothing to do there."

"Mommy always has stuff to do!"

"Yeah, but I've got really cool stuff to do. Just wait and see! In fact, want to have a tea party?"

"Okay," Maura said, "but Aunt Helen, guess what? X-rays are pictures of your bones."

*Phew.* Back to four-year-old talk.

"Call me the second you hear anything!" I said to Claire and Ross.

"Ross will call," Claire said, and then kneeled down to hug Maura. "I love you, honey."

I kissed Claire and hugged her tightly. "You're going to be okay," I said, as strongly as I could, though my chest was already heaving.

"You're very convincing," Claire joked. "We'd better get out of here before I start crying."

With Maura coiled around my neck and Sam toddling around the room testing her new walking skills, we waved to Ross and Claire from the front stoop as they drove away. In the kitchen, I strapped Sam into her high chair and made a pot of tea. Then I set out the miniature tea set—little white porcelain dishes with delicate pink roses. I placed a cookie on Maura's mini plate and one on Sam's tray, filled the creamer with milk, and scooped some sugar into the bowl. Maura and I called each other "Miss" and used our best "May I's" and even stuck out our sophisticated little pinkies. Sam gurgled and smashed her cookie.

When we were finished, I changed Sam's diaper, sent Maura to the potty, and packed the bag.

"Who wants to go to the park?" I asked Maura in my elevated, enthusiastic voice.

"I do, I do!" Maura cheered. "Mom said I could bring my bug net."

The park was Claire's idea, and she had sent along buckets and bug nets. She said that Maura loved to wade in the water in the little stream beyond the playground. We eased our way down to the shallow stream. Sitting on the bench near the pebbled shore was Larry, wearing jeans and a T-shirt. His newspaper was folded by his side. I'd called him the day before and filled him in on Claire. He wanted to see her. "Let's take it slow," I had said.

Maura led the way down to the stream, walking right by Larry as she kicked off her sneakers and plowed into the water.

"Maura," I called casually. "This is Larry. Can you say, 'Hi'?"

"Hi!" Maura hollered.

Larry looked at me expectantly. "This little peach must be Sam."

"Yep," I said.

"Well, I'll be," he said. "She's a beauty. May I?" Larry held out his arms for Sam like a real grandparent would do. Because I didn't know what else to do, I handed her to him. He lifted her high up on his shoulder, just as she liked.

"Have a seat," he said, scooting over to one side of the bench. I did a quick look to see if there was another bench, but there wasn't, so I sat down at the opposite end, with only a few feet separating us.

"How's Claire today?" he asked.

"She's acting real tough," I said. "But we'll see how the surgery goes. Then she'll have chemo. I read about it online last night. It says that everyone tolerates it differently."

"It did a job on your mother. I remember that," he said, shaking his head. "Watching her go through that. Pure hell."

I nodded, remembering Mom locked in the bathroom, the sound of her being so sick, moaning.

We stared at Maura kicking at the shallow stream. Occasionally, she would be splashed, but she didn't seem to care.

"Maura looks a lot like your mother," Larry said.

"Claire and I say that all of the time," I agreed.

We nodded, stared ahead.

"This reminds me of that area behind our old house," Larry said, slinging his arm across the top of the bench, his fingers only a few inches from my shoulder. "Do you remember that at all?"

At the back of our yard, a trailhead wound through the trees. There were plank bridges covering the little streams and a giant log crossing a dry bed where we would play "balance beam." Under mossy rocks, we'd search for frogs.

"I'd take you and your sister back there and you'd try to fish with sticks."

"Yeah," I said, feeling like I was six years old again. "I loved it back there. You showed us the markings on the trees. You said they were from the deer."

"That's right," Larry said, smiling. "You do remember."

*I remember a lot of good times*, I wanted to say. *That's the problem. Trying to figure out why you left when there was so much that was good.*

I glanced at Larry. His mouth was twitching. God, I'd forgotten about all that twitching. I looked again at Maura. It appeared that she was trying to engineer a boat out of a piece of wood. To watch her ingenuity: the furrowed brow, the mouth falling open in concentration, the intensity of the eyes. She was squatting in the water, not at all aware or concerned that the seat of her pants was wet, as she tried to tie a twig mast onto the makeshift boat. She was a carefree child. I hoped that she'd stayed that way, that her mother's illness wouldn't take that from her as I think our mother's illness had taken it from us.

"How are *you* doing?" Larry asked. I hadn't noticed him looking at me, seeing me wipe a tear from the corner of my eye.

"Fine," I said quickly. I stood up and walked a few steps toward the water, fluttering my eyes to stop the tears, wondering how long it had been since I'd cried into my parents' arms. Over two decades, easily. I wondered if there was muscle memory involved in being consoled, like there was in riding a bike or rolling out pie dough. Did the body know instinctively what to do? Or did some skills, even one as primal as being comforted, wither from lack of use? I was once a daughter. We all were—Sam, Claire, me. We just didn't know that it wasn't forever, that we were only daughters for a time.

I strained my eyes to watch Maura catch minnows and water bugs, toss pebbles, sail her boat in the weak current. It was close to noon. Sam would need a bottle; Maura would need lunch.

"Maura," I called. "Five more minutes. We need to go get some lunch, okay?"

"But we still need to make a fishing pole!" Maura yelled, and then went back to the water.

"There's not a day that's gone by that I haven't thought about you girls," Larry said, rubbing Sam's back gently. "The years kept passing, damn it," he said. "So occasionally I would search your names on the computer. I just wanted to know what you and your sister were up to, that's all." His head hung low. "I wasn't trying to pry into your lives."

*Why not?* was the bigger question. Why *not* pry? Why hadn't he shown up at our doors, pushing his way into our lives with bulldozer strength? Why hadn't he insisted on it? That would have been fine with me. At least we would have known that he cared. We didn't need space; we needed our father. Prying into our lives would have been nice.

"I've followed your restaurant," Larry said. "It sure has done well. And I knew that Claire had retired from her investment business, that she had a baby. Someone had done an article on her."

I knew which article he was talking about, a piece written by the chamber of commerce celebrating successful businesswomen.

I shoved down the emotion that was rising in me. "I'd better get these girls some lunch."

"Why don't you let me help Maura make a fishing pole real quick. Is that okay?" He stood and handed Sam to me. "I'll be right back."

Sam nestled into my neck, and I warmed at the already ingrained familiarity of her touch. We watched Larry open his car trunk and then walk back toward us. With a pocketknife and a piece of twine, he proceeded to craft a fishing pole. He knew enough to get down on Maura's level, squatting while he worked, simplifying his language for her. It looked as though he'd been a grandfather-in-waiting, having prepared himself for this exact moment.

While they built the fishing pole, I sat on the bench with Sam and fixed her a bottle, one-handed, just as I had marveled at Amy DePalma doing in China and Claire doing when Maura was small. I was learning to be a mom, but I couldn't help but wonder why my happiness had to come at Claire's expense. Like, God forbid, I should get spoiled from not having pain in my life.

It was only twelve thirty and I was already beat emotionally and mentally weary, like I had just taken a daylong exam. Claire in surgery. Larry at the park with us. Me taking care of my new baby and Maura. The earth was shifting beneath my feet, and not only did I need to hold steady for myself, I had to hold on for everyone else. *Buck up!* I could hear Claire say. I wiped my face, straightened my back, and turned the corners of my mouth up into a smile.

When Larry and Maura had mastered the fishing pole, I said, "We really should get going."

"Thanks for calling me, Helen," Larry said, clapping his hands together to get the dirt off. "Seeing the girls—my *grand-daughters*—has been tremendous. Keep me posted on Claire, will you?"

"I will," I said. "I'll call you later."

"Give me five," he said to Maura, holding out his hand.

Maura smacked it over and over, smitten with Larry, the guy from the park who knew how to make the coolest fishing pole.

Larry leaned across to me, planted a kiss on Sam's head. Then he paused, stared at me and then Sam and Maura, and uttered, "Beautiful." I watched him take a step in the direction of his car.

"Larry!" I called, hoisting Sam higher on my hip. "How do I know?" I asked. "That this is for real? How do I know that I can trust you this time?"

Larry looked away. Then he looked back at me and cleared his throat. His mouth was pulled to the side, and it seemed that his eyes had reddened. "I can tell you this," he said at last. "This hour, today, with you and my granddaughters"—he paused, clearing his throat again—"was the best hour I've had in about twenty years. I'll be damned if I'm going to mess that up."

I looked at him. Nodded. "Okay, then."

He nodded, too, and we stared at each other for what seemed like minutes. "Okay, then," he said, and turned and walked away.

Once Larry was out of my sight, I pressed my palms into my eyes and pushed back a deluge of tears, took a deep breath, and found a cheerful voice. "Come on, Maura!"

"Aunt Helen, guess what?" she said, sitting on the embankment picking specks of dirt and grass from her feet. "Minnows are baby fish and tadpoles are baby frogs, but you can also call them polliwogs."

The pure innocence of her stabbed at my heart. I knew that it wouldn't last long with a mother battling cancer. I knew that a sick mother would draw the sweetness from Maura as surely as rice absorbed the moisture in a saltshaker.

When we got home, I changed Sam's diaper and Maura's wet clothes. I put Nick Jr. on the television, placed Sam in her playpen, and put the kettle on for tea. I looked at the clock again, wondered when Ross was going to call. I checked my cell phone, the home phone, and e-mail. Nothing so far.

Tim had brought some tomato-basil soup home from the restaurant, so I warmed it on the stove while I grilled cheese sandwiches. Maura and I ate while Sam slept. Just as Maura finished and ran off to watch the television, the phone rang.

Ross, finally. Bad news. The cancer was in the right ovary, as well as the fallopian tubes. The surgeon had had no choice but to do a full hysterectomy.

"Does she know?" I asked, grabbing onto the edge of the counter. The room had started to spin.

"Not yet," he said with a hoarse voice. "She's still groggy. Will be for a few hours."

I took a deep breath, closed my eyes, and blew it out slowly. "She's going to be okay," I said, trying to lift my words, offer a little hope.

"You don't know that," Ross said, his voice hardly a whisper. "Your mother wasn't okay."

"That was a long time ago," I said. "The statistics are better now."

"How does anyone make it through this hell?" Now he was crying, unnatural harsh sobs.

"You deal with reality," I said, understanding that I had a role to play. I needed to be strong for Ross. For Maura. For Claire, soon enough. "This is our new reality. We'll deal with it." I sounded like Claire, a graduate of her School of Putting a Strong Face Forward. Though, inside, I was wondering the same thing as Ross: *How the hell will we get through this?*

"Reality sucks."

"I know, Ross." There was a long pause over the phone line. I could hear Ross swallow his tears, gulp for air, exhale his anguish.

"My dad dropped dead of a heart attack when I was five years old," Ross said.

"I know," I said, nodding, thinking of the photo on Martha's mantel: her husband, young, tanned, wearing swim trunks, a son standing on either side of him, Ross in his arms.

"My mom raised me and my brothers alone. Can you fucking imagine?"

"Your mom's awesome," I said, thinking of Martha as a young widow—three young boys.

"I don't remember my dad."

"No. A five-year-old doesn't remember much."

"Maura's not even five yet."

"I know, Ross," I said, my voice breaking. "I know." The implications were heavy, like a tree branch covered in too much snow. Maura—without Claire, not remembering.

"Tell Maura I love her," Ross said. "And tell her that Claire loves her."

"I will," I promised. "Take care of Claire. Call me later."

Before I called Tim to tell him the news, I sipped at my tea and thought it through. Maybe this was *good* news. Better to take out too much than to risk leaving any of the cancer behind, right? Why leave any of the organs that could potentially breed the cancer later? Get them out of there! Give her a clean slate. A fresh start. This was Claire we were talking about. Sure, she'd be sad about the hysterectomy; she'd mourn the loss of her fertility, but she'd get over it. She'd have a new plan by morning.

Feeling resolute with the soundness of my theory, I called Tim.

"I'll be home in half an hour."

"You don't have to," I said quickly. "I'm fine. Really! It's going to be okay. She's going to be okay."

"I'm coming," Tim said. "I'll be there soon."

When Tim walked through the door, he slung his arm around me and pulled me in for a hug.

I embraced him quickly and then pulled away. "What's new at the restaurant?"

"Helen."

"Seriously. What went on today? Sondra? Philippe? Any news?"

"Let's sit down," Tim said, reaching for my elbow.

"I've got laundry in the dryer," I said, sidestepping him.

"Helen!" Tim stood before me like a blockade. "Stop. Let's sit down and talk this through."

"No."

Tim pulled me into a hug, and as my cheek brushed against the soft wool of his sweater, I began to cry. I cried until I couldn't catch my breath.

That night, I sat in the Jacuzzi tub with Maura across from me and Sam in my lap. When Maura laid soap bubbles on Sam's legs, my new daughter squealed. When Sam smiled widely, her two front teeth poked out and her dimples deepened. She was precious. I thought of Claire, how she would never leave

Maura. I thought of Sam's biological mother, how she must have struggled.

I had read accounts of mothers who placed their daughters on the side of the road, maybe in a box that had once held vegetables. I thought of Sam's mother, raw from childbirth, yet walking miles to find the perfect spot to leave Sam to spare her daughter from a worse fate. I imagined her hiding behind a row of bushes, watching as passersby commented on the abandoned baby, the will it must have taken for her to stay still when every instinct in her body must have been to return. How her heart must have lurched. How her insides must have grown dark and hard, as if her heart had turned to stone.

After bath time, when Sam was dried, powdered, and dressed, and Maura was comfortable in her Dora pajamas, Tim put on a movie and we all piled into our bed. I cuddled into Tim's chest and Maura made a pillow of my hip and little Sam snuggled inside the triangle that our legs made. A half an hour later, Maura and Sam had drifted off to sleep. The two girls had inched toward each other, curled into each other like cashews, four little hands balled together like a bouquet. Spikes of Sam's licorice hair and Maura's chestnut hair fanned around their sweet faces, two perfect peaches of cheeks, pouty pink lips.

"How'd it go today with Larry?" Tim asked. Though he had already taken his after-work shower, I could still sense the scent of rosemary on his hands.

"Good," I said, still trying to isolate the feelings with which that encounter had left me. "A little awkward, but having the girls there helped. We kind of just stared at them. We didn't talk that much."

"It's a good start, right?"

"It was nice having him there," I admitted. "He held Sam like it was nothing."

"What's he think about Claire?"

"Reminds him Mom, of course."

"What's next with Claire?"

"Chemo, Ross said. In two weeks."

"You're doing a really good job, you know? With Claire and the girls. They're lucky to have you."

"You didn't know me back when my mom was sick, but I was a real jerk. It's not often that we get second chances, but with Claire being sick now, it's like my chance to make it up to Mom."

My mother died on a Monday. I had gotten up around seven o'clock and walked past her room. She was up already, propped against pillows, a folded newspaper with a crossword puzzle on her lap. Thinking back, I don't think she slept much in those last days.

"Can I get you anything?" I asked her, though I knew that Claire had already been in. An untouched piece of toast and a cup of tea sat next to Mom on the end table.

"A hug would be nice," she smiled. Her skin, as thin as vellum, stretched across her cheekbones.

I bent down to hug her, placing my hands on her shoulders—knotted knobs poking up at her nightgown.

"I love you," she whispered into my ear.

"I know," I responded.

I hated her hospital bed. I hated the smell of the Tiger Balm that Claire rubbed on her back. I hated the cluster of brown plastic medicine bottles on her nightstand.

As I began to stand up, Mom cupped my face in her hands—cold, frail, bird-bone hands. She forced me to look at her. "I love you. I really, really love you."

My cheeks flushed hot, my nose began to tingle, and my mouth darted downward. I tried to say it back, I know I did. I remember the words fighting against the cement in my throat.

But the cement won, and the words never came out. I nodded and left her room.

By that night, Mom had slipped into unconsciousness. Claire was ready. If memory serves, I believe she had a to-do list for that exact moment. The doctors were called. Hospice sent a full-time nurse. My mother was an only child and her parents had already passed on, so there was no other family to call except for a few great aunts and uncles. After Claire made those calls, I watched her from around the corner as she picked up the line, wrapped the spiral phone cord around her finger, and called Larry. "She's unconscious," I heard her say, her voice cracking for the first time. She wiped her face with her sleeve. He must have said something kind, because kindness is Claire's kryptonite, and she just stood there with a wide-open mouth, a silent cry bellowing from within her, and tears streaming down her face. Once she had composed herself, she said. "Okay. Yeah. Come on over."

There was a moment while Mom was unconscious, while we were waiting for Larry and for the doctor to arrive, when Claire was on the phone taking care of the business of dying, and I slipped into Mom's room and climbed into her bed. I did what I hadn't been able to do just a few hours before. I hugged her, as I should have a thousand times in the past, and I whispered to her, "I love you. I really, really love you."

# Chapter Nineteen

The next day, Sam and I drove Maura to school, and then headed to the hospital to see Claire. Larry was waiting for us in the lobby. I had called him earlier that morning. We entered the elevator with hardly a word. When we exited, Larry touched my elbow. "Are you sure this is a good idea? Me coming to see her?"

"I don't know if it's a good idea," I said. "But if not now, when?"

A nurse led us back to Claire's room, where my sister was hooked up to an IV, her poor arms mottled and bruised purple from all of the abuse they'd endured these last few days. Ross was on the phone with his mother. Claire was staring at the television with the sound turned down. A notepad lay across her lap. *What morbid to-do list was my efficient sister working on now?* I wondered.

"What's he doing here?" Claire asked, though her voice sounded weak, like she didn't have enough energy to muster indignation.

"He's our father, Claire," I said softly. "You're sick, and he wants to see you. Let him see you, Claire. Can we just be a family through your sickness, please?"

"How are you, dear?" Larry said, walking tentatively toward her.

"Not so good, apparently," Claire said.

Ross finished his call and stepped over to us. He held his hand out for Larry to shake.

"You remember Larry, right?" I said to Ross, thinking that our wedding was the last time anyone had seen him.

"Thanks for coming," Ross said.

Ross huddled over Claire, kissing her forehead and telling her that he was going to run home to get some of their clothes. He kissed her again, and then left. The three of us looked up at the muted television.

"Seeing you here brings it all back," Larry said. "Your mom, how sick she was." Larry's mouth pulled tightly to the side. "I came to see her at the hospital, toward the end, only days before she went home to die."

"I know," Claire said.

"You never told me that," I said to Claire.

She shrugged. Was there more that I hadn't been told?

"She forgave you, you know," Claire said in little more than a whisper, slowly smoothing the blankets, tucking the edges under her legs. "The sicker she got, the more forgiving she became. She said that we should forgive you, too."

"Through it all, she was one hell of a woman."

"I couldn't do it," Claire said. "And..." She took a long breath, and then another. "I think my grudge distracted me from the grief. Still, I was furious that she forgave you so easily."

"You had every right to be mad."

"I did," Claire said, but there wasn't any heat behind her words. "I still struggle to...understand those years." She looked at him, took another breath, narrowed her eyes. "You and Mom separating, then Mom getting sick, and all of us just falling to pieces."

"Your mother and I—"

"Not that," Claire interrupted. "I can understand you and Mom. What I never understood was how you justified leaving us."

Larry closed his eyes, opened them. "I wanted to come back," he told her. "I tried."

"It was too late," Claire said.

*He wanted to come back when?* I thought, my mind reeling. Before Mom died or after?

"The shame I felt grew bigger every day," he said. "After your mom died, I'd come around. Tell myself that, after everything I had done, I could at least be there for you girls. Each day got harder, though, not easier. The reality that your mother was gone stared me in the face. The hurt I caused her before she was even sick. All I could think was I took her last few years. I was ashamed and finally got to the point where I could barely face you kids. I told myself that you were better off without me. That you didn't want to see me, anyway. But hell, I tried all sorts of things to ease my guilt."

The nurse came in and took Claire's temperature, her blood pressure, and listened to her chest. "I need to take a little more blood," she said apologetically.

"I hardly notice anymore," Claire said, unfolding her arm.

We stared at the television while the nurse took the blood, and then kept staring at it until the room turned dark and Claire grew sleepy. Larry and I slipped out and stood in the bright hallway.

"Do you want to get coffee?" I asked.

We walked down to the cafeteria and filled our cups. He took his black; I poured cream and sugar into mine.

"Your sister doesn't look so good," Larry said as we were walking back through the corridor.

"Well, she just had surgery," I said defensively. "She'll perk back up."

"I think you—*we*—need to prepare ourselves for the worst-case scenario."

I stopped and turned to face Larry. Two doctors in scrubs walked by.

"No way," I said. "Claire is going to be fine." I could feel the heat in my cheeks, the thump of my heartbeat. "She'll turn this around. Times have changed since Mom. Prognoses are better. You don't know Claire like I do. You haven't seen what she's capable of."

"She's a tough gal, I know that."

"Tough doesn't begin to describe her. There's no way in hell she's leaving Maura like Mom left us."

Larry looked at me for a silent moment and then said, "Your mother would have done anything to stay."

"Mom was the best mother in the world, but she was too accepting of the hand she was dealt. Claire's different. She's got the faith, but when it comes to Maura, she'll sell her soul to stick around. She'll beat this, you'll see."

Larry nodded and placed a hand awkwardly on my shoulder. "I hope you're right."

$$\frown$$

Two weeks later, Sam, Maura, and I drove to the Fairfax Hospital campus. As I remembered, there was a playground, conveniently nestled in front of the children's wing. Larry was waiting for us.

"Maura, honey, you remember that I promised you McDonald's for lunch, right?" I asked.

"Aunt Helen, guess what? I want chicken nuggets, french fries, chocolate milk, and a girl toy."

"Great! But do you remember that I said we'd have to make one stop first?"

"You have to see a doctor," Maura said.

"That's right. It'll be quick, and while I'm in seeing the doctor, our friend, Larry, is going to watch you and Sam. You remember Larry, right? He's the one who helped you make the fishing pole at the park a while back."

"That was *so* much fun," Maura gushed.

"Thanks for doing this," I said to Larry, setting Sam down and handing her diaper bag to him. "I really didn't want to give everyone something else to worry about. Especially if there's no reason, right?"

"I'm happy to help," he said.

"Make sure Maura keeps her mittens and hat on," I said, adjusting Sam's earflap hat and snapping her coat. "It's not too bad with the sun out today."

"Take your time," he said. "The girls will be fine."

Once inside, I took the elevator to the third floor and found the office marked Genetic Counseling. I signed in, took a seat in the waiting room, and flipped mindlessly through a *People* magazine.

After a short wait, I was called. A genetic counselor named Michelle completed a family tree of my medical history, an array of branches, some diseased, some not. I told her about Mom, about Claire, about Mom's mom.

"The fact that your mother and sister have both been hit with ovarian cancer puts you at an elevated risk, obviously," she said.

Obviously.

"We'll draw blood. We'll test you for a variety of things, including the mutations of the BRCA1 and BRCA2 genes, either of which would mark you as genetically predisposed toward several different cancers."

"Claire tested positive for those," I told her.

"But you never had the test?"

"I was going to, a few years back, after my sister did it. But I got busy…Well, I guess I changed my mind…chickened out. At the time, I was dealing with infertility. I thought if I came in, the doctor would find something that would confirm my inability to have a child. I was afraid of hearing that—more afraid of that than of finding out about the cancer gene," I admitted.

"The gene is quite indicative," Michelle said. "Women who carry the harmful BRCA1 or BRCA2 mutations are definitely at an increased risk, especially when there's family history."

"That doesn't sound very good for me," I said. "I guess I'll just hope like hell that I don't have the gene."

"Hope. Pray. It can't hurt."

Next, I met with a gynecologist who performed a pelvic exam and ultrasound to look for any ovarian lumps.

"You look good," he said. "But given your history, I'd recommend repeat exams every six months."

"In other words," I said to him, "I'll spend the rest of my life seeing doctors to make sure I'm still well, until the day that I'm not."

"It just means that you need to be extra careful," he said, shaking my hand and leaving the room.

Exactly an hour later, I returned to the playground. Larry was sitting on the bench with his coffee cup, his newspaper still folded at his side, his eyes fixed on the girls. Maura was climbing on an apparatus that resembled a giant molecule, and Sam was sitting in the sand, picking at tiny pebbles, her cheeks as red as roses.

"How'd it go?" I asked, scooping up Sam and pressing her cold cheek against mine.

"Good," he said. "Sam took her bottle and ate some Cheerios," he reported. "Maura fell and skinned her knee a bit, but she got right back up."

I smiled. It was nice hearing Larry talk about the girls.

"What about you? How do things look?"

"The ultrasound was clean," I said. "They drew blood to see if I'm predisposed. It'll take weeks, maybe longer, to find out."

Larry nodded, his mouth twitching. A minute or so passed. I sat down. He offered me a stick of Juicy Fruit. He cleared his throat. "You don't remember my father, your Grandpa Bob. He died when you girls were little. Heart attack. Except for his time in World War II, he never left West Virginia. He was the toughest guy I knew. One time, he cut his leg with a piece of farm equipment. It was deep and needed stitches, but he didn't believe too much in doctors. He gathered what he needed—needle, thread, alcohol. Sewed it up himself, right there at the kitchen table, without saying a damn word.

"As a kid, I worshipped the ground he walked on, but he ruled with an iron fist. The worst thing you could do was disobey him. One time, in the dead of winter, he made me sleep in the garage because I asked him for clarification on a chore I was doing. He said I should've been paying closer attention. Maybe he was right.

"He was tough on me throughout my childhood. Trying to make me a man. By the time I left home, what I felt for him was far from worship. I swore I'd be nothing like him. I had had enough. I married your mom, a loving woman. I thought that she'd be the antidote to my childhood. Then along came you girls. Never in a million years did I think that a farm boy from West Virginia like me would fall so in love with daughters. I did, though. I loved holding you, bathing you. Those were happy times. When you girls were little, you two looked at me like I hung the moon. God damn, I remember how that felt, the way you girls would hang on me, crawl on me. There was a lot of love in our house back then." Larry stopped, looked up at Maura, and sighed.

"Then, hell, I don't know what happened. Your mother was busy at work, volunteering at your schools. Then you girls got older and there was no telling either of you a damn thing. You were both so smart; you seemed to have everything figured out. The more independent you all became, the more I felt my own father judging me for not having more control over my family. I guess a part of me was still trying to win my old man's approval. Shaking him off was harder than I'd thought. You know the rest. I found other ways to make myself feel big again."

Larry stood, walked to the edge of the playground, reached down for a stone, and then threw it into the trees.

I stared at Maura, held Sam's hands in mine. So there it was—Larry's soliloquy. His explanation of why he is the way he is. A childhood that undid him. His failed attempts to stitch himself back together.

I stood, walked to him, patted his shoulder. "I'm glad you're here now."

―⌒―

A week later, only days before Claire was scheduled to start chemo, she was rushed back to the hospital. Ross called to say that her kidneys were failing. Acute renal failure was what the doctor had called it. With failing kidneys, she was no longer eligible to take chemotherapy.

"I'll give her one of mine," I said immediately.

"It doesn't work that way," Ross explained. "Her body isn't strong enough to take a transplant."

"There must be some other option."

"We'll talk to the doctor in a little while."

"I'll be there in fifteen minutes."

"Tell me," Tim said when I hung up.

"I don't know!" I said, throwing my hands in the air. "Either the doctors are idiots or Ross got the information wrong.

According to him, she can't have chemo because her kidneys aren't strong enough. But then he said that they won't let her have a kidney transplant because *she's* not strong enough."

"Helen," Tim said, reaching for me.

"No!" I said. "Someone is wrong. Something's not right. They can't take away all of her options. It's time to get her to Hopkins," I said emphatically. "Time for some doctors who actually have a plan."

"Helen, she's sick," Tim said.

"She's *weak* because she's not eating!" I said, my voice buckling. "You know how she's been lately. She needs a cheeseburger and a chocolate milk shake."

Tim reached for me and pulled me in. I began to calm until I felt *his* chest heave. I looked up at the tears streaming down his face.

I pushed away from him. "Stop it!" I said. "I have a feeling that the doctors are wrong about her kidneys. I mean, Mom didn't have the kidney problem."

"Helen."

"I've got to go."

"I'll be here with Sam. If Ross needs me to come get Maura, just have him call," he said, turning away and wiping his face with the sleeve of his sweatshirt.

The ER was reasonably quiet when I arrived. I had called Larry from the car and he was waiting for me in the lobby.

We tiptoed into Claire's room in case she was asleep, but she was wide awake, staring at the muted television.

"How are you, Claire?" Larry asked.

"It seems that my kidneys are failing," Claire said.

"Take mine," he said.

"She's already had multiple offers," I said. "Apparently, we all want to give her our kidneys."

"If only it were that easy," Claire said, smirking as if it were funny.

"So," I said to Claire, "what's the plan? What are we going to do now?"

Claire just looked at me with raised eyebrows and lips pressed tightly together. For the first time ever, my sister did not have a way out.

For the next four weeks, Claire underwent dialysis. Davis and Delia came up from North Carolina to help with Sam, and Martha came up from Charlottesville to help with Maura. Ross took Claire to dialysis most days, but on the days when I took her, Larry would come, too. Each visit, the icy distance that separated Claire and Larry thawed a little more. Each loosened, opened up, gave a little. More and more, I saw Claire smile in spite of herself. Punishing Larry for his crimes of the past no longer seemed relevant to her.

In the midst of Claire's forgiveness, Larry opened up, filled the hours talking about the old days, stories from when we were little, the games we played, Christmases, and birthdays. For our part, Claire and I brought out photo albums from when we were little, back when we were still a family. We'd laugh and cry over photos of ourselves, so small and young. Then Claire and I took turns sharing photo albums that covered the period that Larry had missed: our graduations, Claire's wedding, Maura's birth, Sam's adoption. It hurt him, I could tell, to see these moments that he had missed, but nonetheless, he wanted to keep looking. He wanted to fill in the blanks.

Once, when there was a break in the conversation, Claire closed the album and set it aside. "I need to clear the air," she said. "Maybe it's more…clear my conscience."

"About what?" I asked.

"There's no easy way to say this," Claire said.

"You have cancer," I said simply. "What can you possibly say that's worse than that?"

"You don't know this, Helen," she started, then stopped, looking at Larry. "Larry wanted to come back. After Mom died. He tried. I asked him not to."

"He *did* come back," I said, remembering how Larry would occasionally stop by to bring the child-support check—at least for a while, it seemed.

"You're not getting what I'm saying," Claire said. "He wanted to come back and *live* with us. He wanted to move into the house. Be our father again."

"Is this true?" I looked to Larry for confirmation.

His mouth pulled to the side.

"We'd all been so hurt losing Mom," Claire said, "it never occurred to me that we could have helped each other."

"We had just lost our mother," I said. "Why would we want to lose our father, too?"

"I was twenty-one years old," Claire stammered. "After the years of taking care of Mom, I felt grown up. I didn't need a father. And I was still furious that he'd left us in the lurch when Mom was sick. You had just turned fifteen, and while maybe I could have conceded that a father figure would have been good for you, I was equally convinced that we were better going it alone. I felt like we all needed to get on with our lives. I thought letting Larry back in would just be dredging up the past. I had no way of knowing whether he would be good for you. How could I trust that he would be? What evidence did I have to support it? What would it have meant if you came to rely on him during your teenage years, and then he left again?"

Larry stood, walked to Claire's bedside, and placed his hand on her shoulder.

"It didn't matter," I said. "I screwed up those years on my own, without anyone's help."

"I'm sorry," Claire said fiercely. "I should have taken the chance. I should have let you be part of the decision. You were capable of more than I gave you credit for."

"Why didn't you come back anyway?" I asked Larry. "What made you listen to Claire?"

Larry gave Claire's shoulder a squeeze and then stepped back, leaned against the wall, shook his head. "That's a tough question, Helen," he said. "I had no legal right to you. Your sister was your guardian, for one. Two, she made valid arguments. She asked me point-blank, 'Can you promise you'll stay? Can you guarantee that you'll never leave again?' The fact was, I never thought that I'd leave in the first place, abandon my family like that, run from my responsibilities, with your mother sick and all. Goddamn, I wouldn't have thought that about myself in a million years! But I did it. So could I make a promise, give her a guarantee? No, I couldn't. I understood why that wasn't good enough."

Larry returned to Claire's bedside, placed a gentle hand on top of hers. "Claire did a hell of a job dealing with everything. We have no right questioning the decisions she made on your behalf."

Claire's body softened immeasurably. When was the last time that she had someone advocating on her behalf, a parent parenting her?

"Hindsight's twenty-twenty," he said. "And there isn't a damn thing any of us can do about the past now. No one has more regrets than I do, but we're here together now. Let's not let that get away from us."

# Chapter Twenty

A week later, Claire was released from the hospital and was back home, on the doctors' theory that she would do just as well there as she would in the hospital. According to the doctors, we were in the same spot with Claire as we had been with our mother for many months: trying to keep her comfortable, strong, and alive, while the doctors considered all, or any, remaining options. They called it "palliative care"—helpful but not curative. I nodded as they spoke, but there was still a part of me that wanted to cry foul. *She'll get better! You'll see.* In my mind, it was truly unfathomable that Claire was terminally ill. The numbers didn't add up; the dissonance was too great. How could Claire die when she had a daughter to raise and I still needed her in my own selfish ways? The numbers were against her, but Claire always came out on top. I was willing to bet the house on Claire versus a 10 percent survival rate.

Claire had asked me to pick up Maura, so when I got to her house, I set Sam on the rug in the family room next to her big cousin to watch Nick Jr. on television. Ross was in the kitchen on a phone call. I waved hello to him, pointed at the girls so that he knew to keep an eye on them, and headed up the stairs to check on Claire.

Her bedroom door was closed. I eased it open just an inch, and there I saw Claire, dressed casually in jeans and a sweater, on her knees next to her bed. Her hair was pulled back in a loose ponytail, thick strands framing her face. Her rosary beads were dripping through her fingers, and she was so mindful she didn't even hear me. I watched her as she worked the beads, fingering each one as a treasured jewel. How did a person like Claire—strong willed, ironclad in her convictions—get such a childlike faith that brought her to her knees each day? Gently, I pulled the door closed and left her alone. It was so obvious that her faith wasn't the memorized version that I'd learned through years of attending CCD to make Mom happy, but rather, the penetrating, every-ounce-of-her-being kind. And for the millionth time in my life, even as Claire battled tragedy, I was envious of what my sister was made of.

Downstairs, I went into the kitchen with Ross.

"How are you doing?" I asked him, once he'd finished his call.

"Crappy," he said. His every emotion had rendered itself down to anger. He looked like he could take down a gang of thugs, one-handed. I eyed the cracked wood of the pantry door. I was willing to guess that his fist fit perfectly in the dent. Not that I could blame him.

"She looks good today," I said cheerfully.

"She's dying," Ross seethed through clenched teeth. "It doesn't matter how she looks."

"You don't know that," I snapped back.

"What are you missing, Helen?" Ross shook his head at me.

"I'm not *missing* anything," I said. "I'm believing in Claire. She's worked hard her entire life and it's always landed her on top."

"Hard work's not going to beat the cancer," Ross said, walking past me and heading out to the back deck, where I watched him pick up a stick and hurl it into the yard.

Other than Claire, who planned for every contingency, no one had said what Ross had just said. No one had said—*explicitly*—that Claire was dying. Leaving it unsaid was what gave us hope. Saying it was just mean-spirited.

"I'm going to go check on her," I said to no one, furious at Ross's disloyalty. I buckled Sam into her bouncy chair for safe-keeping and then marched up Claire's stairs and into her room.

"Oh, good. You're here," Claire said, holding a tablet in her lap. "I need to talk to you about something."

"What?" I said impatiently.

She blinked at me. "What's wrong with you?"

"Nothing, Claire. What is it? What do you want to talk about now?"

I didn't know what Claire was going to say and I didn't want to know! I was so *sick* of serious conversations! In the past month, *just in case*, Claire had gone over her will with me, item by item. If Claire died and something happened to Ross, Tim and I would become Maura's guardians. Claire had shown me a cautionary letter she'd written to Maura: *Always wear your seatbelt! Never walk to your car alone! Always jog with a partner! Never forget how much I love you!* She'd gone through her jewelry, her artwork, the contents of her desk and dresser. She'd discussed funeral arrangements, cemetery plots, and the possibility of a memorial service—open casket versus closed. Closed, of course, for Maura's sake. What the hell was she going to bring up now?

"We can talk another time," Claire said.

"No, I'm fine," I said. "Sorry. What is it?"

"Well," she said. "It's a gift. I want to give something to you."

"Oh. Sorry." I wondered if she wanted to give me last year's wardrobe, her never-ending attempt to get me to wear khakis and twin sets.

"This might sound weird," she said. "But I want to give you my eggs, if you want them."

"Your *eggs*?" Because I was trained as a chef, my mind went to her refrigerator, wondering why she was mentally cleaning out the fridge.

"My *eggs*," Claire said, pointing to the area below her abdomen. "Before I had the surgery, just in case they needed to do a full hysterectomy, like they did, I asked them to freeze my eggs. My right ovary was no good—full of cancer—but my left ovary was clean. It was the *only* thing that was clean. They aspirated, cleaned, and froze the eggs that were inside. At the time, I was hoping that they'd be preserved for me and Ross, in case we were able to try again. But it looks like my chances are up. If you ever wanted to try to make a baby with my eggs, I would be honored."

"You want to give me your eggs?" I asked incredulously.

"Yes."

"That means that you're giving up? Throwing in the towel?"

"Helen, I'm doing everything they tell me to do. But if it's not enough..."

"I can't believe you're going to quit!" I yelled. "You've never quit before in your life. And now, *now*, you're giving up?" My knees buckled and I sat on the edge of her bed. "How can there not be any fight left in you?" I demanded. "People beat cancer all of the time."

Claire looked at me, her brow furrowed as if to remind me that, yes, that might be true, but people die from cancer all of the time, too.

Later that day, at home, I sat at the table with Sam and Maura. Sam was strapped into her high chair, smearing finger paint on her tray, and Maura was painting with too-wet watercolors, soaking her page with a swirl of a sunset. For lunch, I fixed the girls seashell pasta with butter and parmesan. Afterward, I set Sam in her crib for a nap and Maura in front of the television to watch a Disney movie.

On the edge of my bed, I pulled open the drawer of the side table. I placed the twenty-page report in my lap—our home study, the comprehensive examination written by Dr. Elle

Reese in the months leading up to the adoption. I opened the first page. It read:

> *Tim and Helen Francis are a loving couple who wish more than anything to adopt a daughter from China. They live in a comfortable home in northwest Washington, DC, in a neighborhood lined with trees and mature landscaping. The Francises would like two children. Mrs. Francis has a sister with whom she is especially close. She feels that the sister relationship is a vital one, one that she would like to pass on to her adopted daughter. The Francises plan to spend some quality time with their first daughter before applying to adopt a second one.*

I closed the home study, squeezed my eyes shut, and lay back onto the bed. *Claire*, I whispered, *please*.

---

The next month, Claire was back in the hospital. Her lungs were filled with fluid. After I dropped Maura at school, Sam and I pulled into the hospital parking lot to find that Larry's LeSabre was already there. As I rounded the corner to enter Claire's room, I stopped short and peeked in. Larry was sitting at Claire's bedside, holding her hand and weeping. I pulled myself back out into the hallway, glued my back against the wall, held Sam tightly against my chest. I breathed and processed the image that I had just witnessed, a father coming home.

The next day, I kneeled in a pew at St. Mary's. I lifted my face from my hands and looked up at the Jesus statue. What was it that Mom saw, that Claire saw, as they sat in these pews, that I wasn't able to see? Why did they hold the faith so tenderly, so reverently, when I only saw the evidence that pointed in the direction of no God?

*Jesus, God, Mary—any of you?* I wanted to scream. *Help me!* I looked again at the Jesus statue, studied the nails in his palms, the stain of blood, his upward gaze. A shiver snaked around my neck and down my arms. *That's it!* The missing piece. *A miracle!* That's what *could* happen. That was what was left.

*Please, God. Please.* I prayed to God to intervene on Claire's behalf, to save my sister. After communion, I kneeled down again and said the prayers that tumbled easily out of my mouth: the Lord's Prayer, the Glory Be, and the Apostles' Creed. A gentle calm pulsed through my body—the hope that help was on the way. And then, for good measure, I said a decade of Hail Marys, because if anyone understood the fierce love of a mother, it was the Holy Queen herself.

Like every day, Sam and I picked up Maura after school and drove to the hospital to visit Claire. Once parked, I turned around to see that Sam had fallen asleep in her car seat, her fists unfurled, no longer clenched with anxiety.

"Maura, honey? You ready to go see Mom?"

"I don't want to," Maura pouted defiantly.

"But Mommy wants to see you. She loves you. I need you to be a big girl, okay?"

"Mommy's skin feels weird and she looks different."

Maura was changing as she struggled with her mother's illness. Her open, welcoming, trusting face now looked grumpy and anxious. A scowl often played across it, and her cheeks no longer pushed up into a perpetual smile. Just as I'd been repelled by my sick mother sitting feebly in her hospital bed, Maura was working through her own process, as only a four-year-old could. She yelled at Claire, refused to sit in bed with her, turned away from hugs and kisses. Claire kept a stiff upper lip, but we all knew that it was killing her. The cancer may have been ravaging her health, but her daughter's rejection was breaking her heart.

"She's still Mommy," I said softly. "Now, come on. Let's go up there with big smiles on our faces—how about silly faces?" I squished my face and stuck out my tongue. "Let's go give her a big hug and kiss and tell her that we love her."

"What about my birthday?" Maura asked quietly.

Oh dear. Of course, her fifth birthday, only two weeks away.

Maura's chest heaved, her mouth darted downward, and her cheeks flushed red. I slipped out of my seat and opened the back door, sliding in next to her. I scooped her out of her booster and into my lap, hugging her tightly. Her wet mouth pushed into my neck and her hands clasped behind my head. "I want my old mommy back," she cried. I held her, rocked her, until the gulping, choking cries subsided. I wanted to apologize. I wanted to tell her that her mother and I, both, were selfish. That we had brought daughters into our lives without the guarantee that we could live to see them grow up. All evidence had pointed to the contrary, and we'd plowed ahead anyway.

"It's okay, it's okay," I lied, knowing that it was far from okay. I knew exactly how Maura felt, the jab and twist of the knife every time I thought about losing Claire. "We don't have to go right now. How about we go to the cafeteria first for an ice cream? Let's start celebrating your birthday *right now*. We'll go see Mom in a little while, okay?"

Maura nodded, stretched her eyes wide, and sniffed. Sam stirred as I lifted her from the seat. "Ice cream?" I said to my sleepy baby. In the cafeteria, the girls chose their treats and ate them quietly. Afterward, I washed their hands and faces, and loaded them onto the elevator. Maura pushed the button. As we walked into Claire's room, I saw Father O'Meara praying beside her.

"Hi, everyone!" Claire said in the overly enthusiastic falsetto she now used for Maura's benefit. "Come here, sweetheart." She waved to Maura, patting the bed, but Maura inched instead toward the sofa, a magnet pulling her in the opposite direction of her mother.

Claire was wearing flannel pajama bottoms and a sweatshirt, a purple knit cap on her head, and two pairs of wool socks on her feet. She was cold all of the time.

"We were just saying some prayers," she said. "Would you guys like to join us? Maura, would you like to show Father O'Meara how nicely you say the Our Father?"

Maura shook her head no, while a wave of panic surged through me. All of a sudden, I felt as anxious and childlike as Maura. The fact that Father O'Meara was here wasn't good. My brain felt mossy and thick. I needed to get some air.

"Take your time," I said to Claire and Father. "I'll take the girls outside to the courtyard and we'll check back with you in a little while."

"Don't be silly!" Claire chimed. "Stay. I want to hear about last night's sleepover."

Ever since Claire had returned to the hospital, Maura had been sleeping at our house. Sam—as a distraction, as a playmate—helped considerably to ease Maura's grief. *Run, hop, twirl*, I urged Maura, just keep moving so the hurt can't catch you.

"We'll be back. I promise." I hoisted Sam higher on my hip, grabbed for Maura's hand, and zoomed down the corridor, the narrow hallway closing in on me.

The automatic doors opened to the courtyard, blasting us with cool air. Maura collected acorns and pine needles while I hugged Sam tightly, resting my chin on the top of her head, thinking it through. Maybe Father O'Meara visited Claire all of the time. Maybe this time wasn't necessarily significant. Maybe he was there for reasons *other* than to perform the sacrament of anointing the sick, offering Claire her last rites. *Definitely*, I thought. He wasn't there for that; there was no way that he was there for that.

Half an hour later, Father O'Meara found us in the courtyard.

"How are you doing?" he asked me.

"I'm fine, thanks," I said, hearing the unintended curtness in my tone.

"This is a very difficult time," he said.

"We'll get through it."

He placed a gentle hand on my shoulder. The sleeve of his cassock, the white of his collar. "It's time to say good-bye to your sister," he said.

I stepped back, watched his hand free fall off my shoulder. "No," I said. "I'm not—"

"Claire has accepted—"

"No she hasn't," I argued.

Father nodded, bowed his head.

"Thanks for coming, Father," I stammered. "But I'm fine. Claire will be fine, too."

"If you want to talk—"

"It's getting chilly. I need to get these girls inside," I said, scooping up Sam and reaching for Maura.

I had no plans to say good-bye to Claire. My only plan was to love her as if each day were her last, take care of her daughter as she would do herself, and wait for the miracle to come. Whether my sister lived another day or another five years, she wouldn't have a doubt that my heart bled for her.

Five weeks later, in a hospital room just like Mom's, Claire slipped into a coma. To look at her, she looked nothing like the sister I knew. The waxy, white skin, the lifeless eyes, the frail bones. Yet every time I looked away and then looked back at her, the *glimpse* I caught—that split-second image of her that my mind would capture—registered as familiar. *I see you in there*, my mind would say. What was it? The purse of her lips? The cheekbones perched just high enough to frame her face in a perfect heart?

"She's on life support," Ross said. He'd appeared in the doorway. "There's no brain activity. The doctor said that we need to decide when to…you know."

"Turn off the machines?" I said.

"That's what's left," he said. "Machines. Claire's already gone." His voice broke on the word *gone*. He walked to the window and pounded his fist against the wall. Ross had been pounding his fist against a lot of walls lately.

I nodded. I needed to play this one cool with Ross. He was hurting, and each of us wanted different things here. "There's no hurry, right?"

"What's the point in keeping her alive?" Ross wanted to know. "She's already gone."

"I know," I agreed. "I just need to sit with her for a while." I scooted next to my sister territorially and stroked her frail hand.

"I need for this to be over," Ross said. "I want to turn off the machines sooner rather than later. Maura has already said good-bye. There's no way I'm letting her see her mother this way."

I nodded. Ross needed me to be sympathetic. He needed me to not hurt him more than he was hurting already. But I needed something, too. I needed more time with Claire, and I didn't care—seriously, I did not care one bit at this point—whether she was brain-dead or not. I wasn't ready to let her go; I wasn't ready to never touch her again.

"That's not Claire anymore," Ross said. "My wife, Maura's mother—she's gone."

I nodded. "I know, Ross. I know," I said as compassionately as I could. I squeezed Claire's hand more tightly and looked at Ross. "Can we just not make the decision today?"

"I don't want to see her like this."

"I'm begging you, Ross," I pleaded. "Please. Just not today."

Ross turned and left without saying good-bye.

I stayed by Claire's side for two more days. I slept in her bed, applied lip salve to her cracked lips, and rubbed lotion into her hands. I brushed her hair and dotted cream rouge on her cheeks. I massaged Tiger Balm into her back, in case it hurt her the way our mother's had. On the last day of April, when it was certain that the miracle I had prayed for hadn't come, the doctors turned off the machines, and I covered her body with mine until the last breath had left her.

———

Two days later, on the morning of Claire's funeral, just as Sam and I were stepping out of the bathtub, the phone rang. The caller identification informed me that it was the Genetic Counseling office of Fairfax Hospital. I exhaled a stream of breath and answered it, holding tight to Sam and the towel wrapped around us.

"Mrs. Francis, this is Michelle from the Genetics office. I'm calling to let you know that we got back the results of your blood test."

For a split second, I wanted her to say that I was predisposed. I wanted her to say that I would share Claire's fate. For a split second, I wanted her to hand me a one-way ticket to seeing my sister again.

"And?" I asked.

"Good news. The cancer gene did not show up in your blood work."

"Oh, thank God," I said, and started to cry because what I had thought a second before wasn't true. As much as I wanted to see Claire again, I wanted to stay here even more. One of us needed to be here for Sam and Maura. I hugged Sam tightly in her towel bundle.

"So, again, good news," Michelle said. "But still, please remember to make your follow-up visit in six months."

"That's great," I said, rubbing Sam's back. "Thank you for the good news. Um…"

"Do you have any questions?" she asked.

"No," I hesitated. "It's just that…"

"What is it?"

"My sister died," I said, though I wasn't exactly sure why. Maybe I wanted to test-drive the words, see if I could form a sentence out of my pain. "Her funeral is this morning."

"Oh, Mrs. Francis," Michelle said. "I'm terribly sorry."

"I don't want to get it," I said, sounding like a six-year-old worried about catching chicken pox.

"Some women with extensive family history get hysterectomies to reduce their chances," she said. "I'm not advocating it, I'm just saying."

"Thanks, Michelle," I said. "For listening."

# Chapter Twenty-One

We buried Claire on a crisp May morning. Father O'Meara presided over the service. A friend of Claire's from college—Sarah, who I remembered from Claire and Ross's wedding—sang "Ave Maria." Claire would have loved to hear her friend sing, I thought, listening to the haunting, pure tones of the song that meant so much to my sister. But Claire was gone, dead. She couldn't hear it. But that was just me and my lack of faith. If Mom were here, she would have seen it differently. She would have believed that Claire was able to hear the timbre of her friend's voice, see Maura straddling her father's lap, feel the love of those who congregated to remember her.

After the service, we drove to the cemetery. Tim drove and Larry sat next to him in the passenger's seat. I sat in the back-seat, with Sam in her car seat on one side and Maura adhered to me on the other. I had whispered to her earlier that it would be nice for her to go with her father, but she clung tightly to me and shook her head no. Ross said that it was fine, that he wanted her to do what was most comfortable. His brothers were with him; Martha was at his side. We were all statues, buckling under the weight of it; we all needed our scaffolding to hold us up.

At the cemetery, we climbed the hill to the manicured plot. My mind felt fuzzy and unreliable. The surroundings seemed exceptionally vivid. The sky was strangely blue, as in a child's painting. Cotton-ball clouds scattered above us. The hillside was too perfectly sloped, as if Maura had drawn it: a steady line, an exaggerated hump, more steady line. The gladiolus that draped my sister's casket were perfectly shaped trumpets, their colors almost too vibrant. It occurred to me that my senses were piqued, heightened perhaps to compensate for the grief tunneling through my body, digging in, taking root. *I'll be here for a while*, the angry pain seemed to be saying. *Distract yourself with the lovely flowers.*

We stood before the casket—Tim, me, Sam in my arms; Ross, now holding Maura; the grandparents. I was there, but my awareness was skewed as I stared at the grave, the casket. *That's Mom*, I thought as a wave of a fourteen-year-old's insecurity and need pulsed through me. *That's Claire*, my adult mind reminded me. You're all that's left. You're the mom now.

Somehow, we made it home, back to our house. Though Claire's house would have accommodated the crowd better, Ross asked if we could come to ours. He was sure that Claire wouldn't have wanted people at their house in the shape that it was in, messier than normal, a hospital bed in the family room, prescription bottles everywhere. She had been so proud of her decorating and housekeeping.

Our house had the feeling of somehow being whipped, frenzied. Delia and Martha zipped around, tending to the girls, answering the phone, accepting flowers, preparing food. I was aware of Davis playing cards with Maura. *Go fish*, her helium-balloon voice said. Then later, there was Larry, scooping up Sam and taking Maura by the hand into the backyard to show them a bird's nest perched in the crook of a tree, housing three new hatchlings. Maura brightened at the sight of them, her eyes widening. That's what I remember, that Larry was the first to make Maura smile.

The guests left and the sky grew dark. Maura asked for pillows. She was on the floor, watching a movie. I went upstairs
to Sam's room, sat on the bed, and a wave of sadness overtook
me with such ferocity that I had to lie down and cry into the
sheets. Later, Tim said that he'd come up to check on me, only
to find me asleep. By his clock, I slept for twelve hours.

We all, collectively, made it through the next week. *The
week after*. The first week without Claire. It was a cobbled effort
where everyone pitched in, worked, and contributed until they
reached their breaking point, then withdrew until they were
ready to join in again.

In the mornings, Sam and Maura and I would watch kid
television for hours, we'd read a mountain of books, we'd eat
dry cereal from the box. Maura would color, Sam would scribble, and together, they'd piece together puzzles or stack LEGOs.
It astonished me to watch the two of them. I had just assumed
that the age difference between Sam and Maura would be too
big for them to get along. I had just assumed that a one-year-
old and a five-year-old would be in completely different spaces,
mentally, physically, academically. But while it was true that
Maura *was* in a completely different space, her added maturity didn't preclude her from playing with Sam. They enjoyed
the same things, just in different, age-appropriate, ways: Tim's
Matchbox cars, stuffed animals, and arts and crafts. They were
happy companions. It was an odd thing, how we were nourishing each other, how I was bonding with Sam, how Sam was
finding a companion in Maura, how Maura was accumulating
the affection she so desperately needed to restore to her life.

As they played, I'd sit at my computer, checking e-mail.
Amy DePalma wrote daily. Her oldest sister's breast cancer
had recurred. It didn't look good. But in Amy's usual fashion,
she had found peace. She was like Claire in that way, which
was a trait in both of them that I still didn't understand. Claire

was the most principled person I'd ever known, the type who would fight a ten-dollar parking ticket given erroneously, just to right a wrong. Amy, too. At the airport in China, she had argued with a Chinese official who claimed that her suitcase was overweight, when Amy knew that it wasn't. She ended up with her suitcase on the plane and a twenty-dollar voucher for snacks. How, then, did these two women, who stood for everything and put up with nothing, accept cancers as if they were fated in the stars? Of course, I knew. It was their faith. I just wasn't there yet.

Each day, around lunchtime, we'd go downstairs. Delia would fix whatever the girls wanted: grilled cheese, peanut butter and jelly, soup. Then I'd let Delia and Davis, or Martha, or Larry, or Tim, or Ross take the girls outside for a while, just to get some fresh air. Ross tried, but he was struggling. He would play a game with Maura and she would smile or laugh; then his eyes would fill and he'd have to excuse himself. I'd watch him walk away, suck in the air, throw sticks into the woods.

At one point—it must have been Wednesday or Thursday—I looked out the window to see Larry sawing down a dead tree in our front yard, Tim standing next to him holding a beer, Maura riding a scooter on the driveway, Sam toddling behind her, Martha and Delia pulling weeds from the beds. Only months ago, I was a girl with a scrawny family tree. Now in the midst of losing another branch, it was regenerating.

While the girls spent time with their relatives, I'd go upstairs alone, turn on the shower, and stand under the water. I'd make it hotter than was comfortable and let it beat down on me, turning my skin red, curling my toes, while I cried until I was doubled over and coughing. I'd sink to my knees, pull at the hair on my head, and pound my fists on the tile floor. That would be enough to get me through the rest of the day, a temporary patch that would allow me to put on a brave face for Maura and Sam.

I no longer asked Maura where she wanted to sleep. It was clear that she needed me to provide what was now missing from her life—a warm, maternal body. Maura would sleep in my arms, and Sam, now used to having her older cousin around, slept next to her. Each morning I would find the two asleep, touching *somehow*—a tangle of legs, an overlap of arms, two mouths puckered, only a centimeter apart. The girls were comforting each other; they just didn't know it. They didn't know that they were one and the same, that each in her own way had been left.

That was when I realized that a miracle *had* occurred. What I had assumed to be more bad luck on my part—coming home with Sam the same month that Claire was diagnosed with cancer—hadn't been bad luck at all. It had been a blessing. A miracle. Maura needed Sam at this exact moment in her life, and undoubtedly, Sam had needed Maura for the entirety of hers. The realization hit me hard in my chest, and for a moment, I struggled to find the breath to fill my lungs. I was covered in a blanket of sorrow, but now I could see that there were threads of goodness and divinity woven through it.

But the divinity wasn't always so clear.

This morning, Maura stirred, wiped the sleep from her eyes, and propped herself up on her elbows.

"Hi, Aunt Helen," she said, yawning and stretching.

"Hi, sweetheart." I kissed her forehead.

"I love you," she said in a perky voice.

"I love you, too."

She looked at me intently and furrowed her brow. "Why am I in your...oh, yeah." Her cheerful expression slid away as easy as the sand in her Etch A Sketch did. Her mouth turned downward and her eyes drooped.

"Oh, pumpkin," I said and hugged her tightly.

"I want my mommy!" she cried.

"I know you do," I said, pulling her into me and stroking her hair, because other than my set of hugging arms, I had nothing else to offer.

On Sunday night, a week after Claire's death, Tim cooked prime rib. Ross's brothers had already gone home, but Martha, Davis, Delia, Larry, and Ross were still hanging around, helping with the girls and household chores. After dinner, we all lingered at the table, nursing our glasses of wine. Delia took Sam and Maura into the family room to play.

Ross looked up as if he were about to say something. His face had aged in the last few months. Gray hairs now edged his hairline; thin lines were embroidered at the corners of his sad eyes. He shifted in his seat, took a swig of wine. "Here's the thing"—another sip of wine—"I don't want to go back home." He was staring right at me. "This past week. In that house. Without Claire. I hate it. I just don't want to."

"You can stay with us," I said, and looked to Tim, who was nodding in agreement.

"I'm glad to hear you say that," Ross said. "And thank you both for letting us congregate at your house all week. I've decided to put our house on the market, and if it's okay with you, I'd like to make an offer on the blue house across the street from here, from you guys. We'd be neighbors, if that's okay." He looked at me and then at Tim.

"Yes, Ross!" I said. "I think that's a great idea. That way I could help out with Maura, and she and Sam could continue on as they've been." Ross needed time to heal; he needed time to mourn. He simply wasn't ready to be a single dad to Maura yet.

"I can't do this without you, Helen." His voice cracked. He looked down, covered his eyes. His shoulders convulsed with the rhythm of his crying. He wiped his eyes. "I love Maura more than anything, but I can't do this alone."

# Chapter Twenty-Two

A week later, we said good-bye to Davis and Delia, who were returning to North Carolina, and to Martha, who was heading back to Charlottesville, but only temporarily. She planned to move up to live with Ross, to help with Maura. Tim returned to the restaurant, and Ross went back to his office. Daily activity had resumed for them, but Sam, Maura, and I hadn't yet found a good reason to leave our cozy nest of flannel pajamas, blankets and pillows, and bread products. We had what we needed. Each night, Tim brought home leftovers from the restaurant, a hearty supply of protein and vegetables to counteract the obscene amount of dough we were producing each day. With Sam strapped into her high chair and Maura perched on a bar stool, we baked dozens of cookies and loaves of bread, which we would slice hot and slather with butter and jam. When we ran out of all-purpose flour, we opened a fresh bag of silky cake flour and started in on a variety of muffins. This morning's batch we named "triple berry."

There was a knock at the door. I looked down at my pajamas, reached for my greasy ponytail, ran my tongue over my fuzzy teeth. I padded my way to the door with a blanket draped around my shoulders, and saw Larry standing outside. I opened the door.

"Can I come in?" he asked.

"Of course."

"How are you?" he asked as he followed me into the living room.

"I don't know," I said, closing my eyes, trying to find the words to explain what this was like—two girls to care for without the safety net of my sister.

"How are our baby birds?"

"The baby birds that appeared out of thin air," I said. "You'll have to tell me someday how you managed that."

Larry shrugged, smiled.

"They flew the coop," I said. "This morning. Just like that. No note."

Larry nodded. "It was about time for them to leave."

"You want to take off your coat?"

"Let me just grab something from outside. Are the girls here?"

"Yeah, they're in the family room."

Larry went back outside and returned with a box in his arms, then followed me into the family room.

"Girls, Grandpa Larry's here." At some point in Claire's sickness, we had started to refer to him as Grandpa Larry.

The girls were sprawled across the floor with a variety of pillows. Larry squatted down beside them. He placed the box on the floor in front of them and opened it. Inside was a pudgy brown puppy.

Maura clamored to touch it. "He's so cute!" she squealed. "May I hold him?" Her hand was already stroking the soft fur.

"Sit Indian style," Larry said.

"It's now called 'crisscross applesauce,'" I said. "Political correctness."

"Okay, then. Sit crisscross applesauce and make a cup out of your hands."

Maura did as she was told and Sam imitated her cousin. They sat close enough for their legs to rest against each other's.

Larry placed the puppy in Maura's lap, where he went to work licking her hands. Then she put her cheek to him, and he kissed her face. I knelt down next to her and inhaled the sweet puppy breath. The puppy dashed back and forth between Maura and Sam, licking and snuffling and digging into their cupped hands.

"I love him," Maura cooed. "He's the cutest dog I've ever seen. Is he your new dog? What's his name? What kind is he?"

"This here is a chocolate Labrador, because he's as brown as chocolate and almost as sweet. And yes, he's my new dog."

The girls were enchanted. For all the bonehead moves Larry had made as a father, this was a brilliant move on his part as a grandfather. I swallowed hard to quell the emotion that was rising in my throat. It was pure joy to see Maura happy again, to see that broad smile covering her face. And Sam was beaming, too.

"Would you like a cup of coffee?" I asked.

"Hold on to him," Larry told the girls as he followed me into the kitchen.

I filled the coffee pot with water and measured the beans.

"He's for Maura," Larry said. "If you say it's okay. If not, I'm happy to keep him and bring him over to visit. I just thought that she might like a puppy to cheer her up."

I looked into the family room, where both girls were belly laughing as the little puppy nibbled on their fingers. "I think you thought right. I'll have to check with Ross, of course. At some point, he'll be coming around to claim his daughter," I said. "But if not at their house, I'm sure Tim wouldn't mind if we kept him here. Looks like Sam loves him, too."

When the coffee pot beeped, we brought our mugs into the family room.

"What's his name?" Maura asked.

"He doesn't have one," Larry said. "I was hoping that you'd help me name him."

Maura twisted her mouth to the side. "Hershey! Like Hershey's Chocolate."

"That's good," I said.

"No, how about Kisses? Like Hershey's Kisses?" Maura cheered.

"Another good one." I looked at Sam, who was crawling around on all fours, imitating the puppy.

"Maybe Brownie!" Maura clapped her hands. "My favorite!"

"Those are all good names," I said, petting the puppy's velvety coat. "I can see him with any of those names."

Sam smiled and gurgled and tried to make a barking sound, which came out sounding like, "Chip, chip!"

"Did Sam say Chip?" Maura asked.

"It sounded like it," I said.

"Because that's a *real* name, but it's also like chocolate chip."

"Do you want to name him Chip?" I asked Maura.

"Yes!" Maura squealed. "Is that okay, Grandpa Larry? Could your dog be named Chip?"

"That's a great name," Larry agreed. "But here's the thing… I'm kind of busy at home and I was wondering whether you and Sam would mind taking care of Chip for me. Do you think I could leave him here?"

Maura jumped into Larry's arms, giving him the biggest hug she could manage, and then into mine. Then she sat down again—crisscross applesauce—and stroked Chip's ears as the puppy nestled in Sam's lap. Both girls beamed the widest smiles—a shared sentiment. They almost looked alike.

# Chapter Twenty-Three

Summer came and went like the blur of heat on black asphalt—
a mirage of refracted heat and coolness that confused the eye,
fuzzed my head with an uncertain thought of *wait*, the sense
that I needed to slow down and let the truth settle. Most days, it
was Sam who kept me grounded. Her warm and moist breath
would knock me from those moments when I felt hazy and
unsure that this all was truly happening.

But time marched on in its efficient manner—birthdays,
holidays, and special occasions. More fanfare to confuse and
distract: Look at the cake, the presents, the balloons! We tried.
*We* being me, Tim and Ross, and the grandparents who were
now dedicated to the raising of these girls—Martha, Larry,
Davis, and Delia. In our combined and individual attempts,
we tried to give Maura normalcy, to be everything that Sam
deserved after being newly adopted. But none of us knew
what normal was in a time of crisis, so we overcompensated,
overstimulated, over-everything'd. We treated them too often
with cookies, candy, and ice cream, occupied their every waking minute with field trips and activities, and always, *always*,
had smiles on our faces. *Keep them busy*, our thought process
seemed to say. *Keep them smiling*, we rationalized, so that Sam
thrives and Maura forgets that there is a pit of sadness in her
stomach.

At the end of each frenzied day, a calm would soothe us like a cool breeze. After Chip had been fed and walked, after the girls were bathed and dressed in pajamas, we'd go downstairs and let Chip out of his crate and he'd race around the house while the girls squealed with pleasure. Then Sam and Maura would find their spots on the floor with pillows and Chip would circle and flop into their laps. I'd read to the girls while they petted their puppy's velvety ears, took turns with him in their laps. Eventually, Sam would rub at her eyes, tug at her ears, and inch her way into my lap. Her choosing me, the rightness of the fit, choked me nearly every night. My little orphan from China, who I feared would leave, was growing roots. As Sam fell asleep in my arms, her koala-bear hands gripping my nightgown, I'd switch to a slightly older book for Maura, who was just getting interested in short chapter books. She'd lie back on the floor with Chip and listen rather than look. Her face would soften, the furrow between her brows would unknit, her fists would unfurl, and a gladness would pour over me, bringing such satisfaction, such gratitude, because I knew that, for at least a moment, she wasn't thinking about her mother.

As planned, Ross had bought the blue house with yellow shutters across the street and Martha had moved in with them. We had made a big deal of decorating Maura's new room, painting it lime green, plugging nightlights into every socket, and blanketing her bed with stuffed animals. Though Maura still spent most of her days with Sam and me, she gradually began sleeping in her own room, in her own house. Around eight o'clock each night, Martha would come to retrieve her.

Most nights, Ross was still at work by the time Maura went to sleep. Each day, father and daughter seemed to be pulling farther apart. "It's like looking at Claire," Ross had said one day with Maura. Her likeness to her mother was causing him great pain; it was a reminder of what he had just lost. If there were steps to work through, Ross was stuck in anger. Acceptance might have been nearby, but he had no intention of going there—no more than into Claire's boxed-up clothes and belongings.

I wanted to tell Ross that he was playing it wrong, that he and Maura needed to grow closer, not farther apart. I wanted to tell him that I knew because I lived it, that I'd needed my dad, but we'd all been hurting too much to help each other. I wanted to tell him to try harder. That he was the adult. That it was his job to step up to the plate and take charge. That he should pry, push, and nudge his way into Maura's life because she needed him more than he'll ever know.

Fall came and Maura tentatively started prekindergarten. Maybe she should have moved on to kindergarten, but after the year she had been through, the adults in her life, in agreement with her teachers, decided that another year of prekindergarten would be a smoother transition, considering—considering how anxious Maura had grown in these past months, how insecurity and a sense of doom had snuck up on her like a vine coiling around her neck, unnoticeably at first, then all at once, so tightly that it threatened to strangle her.

Maura, a child who had been so carefree and sunny not so long ago, had become shy, skittish, and anxious. She was uncertain of things that she used to take as givens. Her emotions had become erratic, her loyalties switched at a moment's notice: one moment she was ravenous for comfort, curling her entire body in my lap territorially, and then slithering off to her grandmother; the next moment, refusing to go to anyone. She was a kid who had believed in forever, who'd taken as golden the rule that her mother would never leave. But her mother had left, and now she wondered why she should believe that the sky wouldn't fall, too.

And Sam was moving in the opposite direction. Just as I had taken on some of Claire's attributes (or at least hoped that I had), Sam seemed to be absorbing her cousin's old, open personality: Sam, the anxious child from China, trapped under the rubble of her shaky beginnings, was loosening, letting go, learning to trust. So different from the daughter I was handed not even a year ago.

Though Claire had wanted Maura to attend a different school, I—with Ross's approval—had decided to keep her at St. Mary's. I had read that grieving children responded best to structured settings and predictable routines, and St. Mary's seemed to stick to a schedule: circle time, arts and crafts, a Hail Mary at eleven o'clock, and then lunch, followed by music and playground. On Mondays and Thursdays, Maura would be pulled out of class for half an hour to talk to the counselor, Ms. Julia.

On the first morning of school, Sam and I walked Maura into her classroom, found her chair and cubby, and got her organized. Maura looked upset. The corners of her little mouth were darting downward as if she were ready to crack.

"What's wrong?" I asked, kneeling down and brushing the hair from her face.

"My chair is supposed to be green, and this one is blue." Maura pointed at the chair as if it had done something wrong.

"Well, honey, a lot of things are going to be different this year. You have a new teacher, a new chair. You like blue, right?" I patted the chair to show her that it was a good one.

"I can't find the markers," Maura added with a scowl.

"Let's go look for them." We stepped away from Sam, who was busy stacking cardboard bricks in the corner of the room, showing the teachers that she was ready to be in school, too.

"Last year, the markers were in empty oatmeal containers," Maura said, eyeing this year's container, a giant plastic bin in which crayons and pencils were mixed. Comingling of writing utensils—a potential problem. Maura flicked at the crayon nubs as if they were riffraff in the wrong part of town.

"You can do this!" I said, squatting down to make eye contact, summoning the coach in me. "You're a big girl and you're in prekindergarten!"

"I was in prekindergarten last year."

"Well, yeah," I agreed. "But that just means that you'll know what's going on. You'll have to help out some of the other kids, okay?"

Maura thought about that. "Like be a big sister? Like I am to Sam?"

"Exactly! You show the new kids what to do."

"What does kindergarten mean?"

"Well," I said, "I believe kindergarten means 'children garden.' It's like a place where kids can grow. Does that make sense?"

"That's silly," Maura said, her eyes widening, "because kids don't grow in gardens. But they do grow."

"It is silly, isn't it?" I said, flinging my arms around her, so happy to see her smile. I gave her a final kiss and a squeeze and promised her that Sam and I would be back for her at one o'clock.

"You *promise*?" Maura said.

"Maura, I *promise*."

On our way out, we found Ross standing in the parking lot, pulling at his hair as he looked up to the sky.

"Hey," I said.

"Hey."

"I thought you had an early-morning meeting." My tone wasn't too forgiving. I hadn't been too subtle in expressing my displeasure when Ross had told me that he wouldn't be able to drive Maura to school on her first day.

"I did…I do," he said, smoothing his silk tie. "I told them I needed to take a half-hour break."

"Good."

"But you already got her settled?"

"I did, but go in anyway," I urged. "She would love to see you."

"I don't want to disrupt the class, if she's already settled."

"They haven't started yet. Go. See her."

Ross nodded hesitantly, looked in the direction of the school.

"Ross, listen. I know you're hurting."

Tears sprang to his eyes.

I reached out and touched his arm. "And I don't know how to say this to you without hurting you more, but Maura needs you in a way that you can't even understand. You know that I will care for her, love her, cherish her as if she were my own, but you need to stay close to her. You need to scoop her into your arms, kiss her on the mouth, and sleep by her side. I'm telling you, Ross…You cannot let the distance between the two of you grow even one more inch. You've got to stay close to her. She's got to know that her father is still here."

"It hurts so fucking bad," he said, covering his eyes, rubbing them hard.

"Claire and I needed our dad, Ross, and he wasn't there. You've got to trust me when I tell you that you'll regret making the same mistake."

Ross turned, clenching his jaw while tears poured down his face. When he opened his mouth, cries bellowed out like a baby's. I wrapped my one arm around him, while Sam buried her face in the cave of our hug.

"I love her so much," he said.

"Everyone knows that but her, Ross, and she's the one who needs to know."

Ross nodded, kept holding on.

"She's going to be so excited to see you," I said. "Go. Go now."

⌒

Each morning, after Sam and I dropped Maura at school, we'd walk across the parking lot to the church for morning Mass. The half-hour service each morning had become meaningful to me in a way I hadn't yet figured out. But then again, I wasn't clear on how most things worked: how the planets aligned, how the sun moved the waves, how birds knew when to fly south in the winter. So why did I need to understand the grace of God to believe in it? I still had my doubts, the doubts that had grown in me like a wildfire when Mom got sick. I still had my fury: What kind of God would take a mother from a daughter who needed her so badly? First Mom, now Claire. Even back when I was a kid, as Mom fought for her life, she'd tried to explain to me that God's will was a mystery, not always easily understood. And while my doubts were still a part of me, I couldn't deny that, in some way, on some level, I *felt* Claire and Mom. Still with me, undeniably so. And if I could still feel them, I reasoned, in at least that way they were not truly gone. What then was the truth about death and dying? Really, just maybe, it wasn't so hard. Maybe it was all just a matter of faith. Those who had it were in the clear—for dealing, for understanding, for rationalizing. Those who didn't were the ones who struggled. My resistance was still there, but I was veering in the right direction.

There were other moments, plenty of them, when, clearly, I didn't have it. Moments when my perspective was anything but divine, when my thoughts grew dark and murky, and finding meaning in any of the pain seemed a fool's game. I hurt too much.

From St. Mary's, Sam and I headed down to Harvest. We had hired a part-time college student, Abby, to watch Sam for three hours each day. In those hours, Abby would wheel Sam to the park in her stroller, take her out to lunch, scribble pictures with crayons. Other than that, Sam was with me. By now, I had read plenty of resources on adopted children, and one point was clear: it was vital that Sam viewed me as her primary caregiver until a strong bond was established. I knew what it was like to miss, want, and need my mother. I never wanted Sam to feel that way.

In my mornings without Sam, I would stand behind the stainless steel table, working through the motions that many would find monotonous: the cutting, the measuring, the stirring, the kneading. But I found deep pleasure in the repetition, the assurance that there were a few things in life that I could control. Margot—the other pastry chef—and I were now job-sharing. Allowing me to be a full-time mom to Sam and an attentive aunt to Maura.

Tim had made a commitment, too, the day Claire died. He decided to let Philippe run and close the kitchen from Sunday through Wednesday. This way, he would be home with the family on four nights out of seven. And Larry was part of the gang now, too. He came over a few times a week. He and Maura were training Chip. Sit, come, stay. Larry would buckle Sam in the stroller and walk with Maura and Chip around the block, throw him a tennis ball in the backyard, and give him baths with the hose. The girls would take turns brushing him, rewarding him with biscuits. Eventually, I would put Sam down for a nap and set Maura in front of the television, and Larry and I would sit and drink coffee. Sometimes he'd talk about Mom; often we'd talk about Claire. I'd watch as his face would soften and a smile would turn up the sides of his mouth. He provided for me the one thing that Claire never could: he allowed me to talk about Mom, and now Claire. I had suspected all along that Larry and I were alike, that we were fellow wallowers in the past. We were good for each other that way.

Sam was out with Abby one morning when my cell phone rang. On the phone was Mrs. Murphy, Maura's substitute teacher. Her regular teacher had sprained her ankle and was on leave for the next three weeks.

"Is everything okay?" I asked. "Is Maura okay?"

"Everyone is fine," Mrs. Murphy assured me. "I was just hoping to grab a few minutes with you before pickup today. Would that be okay?"

The kids were on the playground when Sam and I showed up at school. Sam found the cardboard bricks in the corner of the classroom, while I perched on a little plastic chair with Mrs. Murphy, feeling like a giant.

"It was such a gorgeous day today," she began, "I decided to take the kids outside to eat their lunch on the hill while we did our music lesson. 'Grab your lunch boxes and rhythm sticks,' I told the kids, and we marched outside. After a while, I noticed that Maura wasn't eating her lunch *or* playing her rhythm sticks. When I asked her what was wrong, she just looked down and wouldn't answer me. You can see why I was concerned."

I pointed to the blackboard, where there were fat, colorful arrows—a pictoral flow chart of the day—clearly indicating the schedule. After "Arts and Crafts" was "Lunch." After "Lunch" was "Music." My heart was thumping. I wanted to throttle this woman. I thought of poor Maura, how she must have felt so betrayed by the schedule.

"Maura just lost her mother," I said, trying to steady my voice. "I figured that someone might have told you that. So for her, now, predictability is very important. In *her* mind, the day didn't go according to plan," I said, pointing at the flow chart. "That is what she expected," I said, pointing to the arrows.

"She needs to know exactly what to expect. As long as you stick to the routine, she'll be fine. But being spontaneous doesn't work for her. She's a kid who doesn't need more surprises, even small ones like a change in the schedule." My stomach twisted in a knot.

"I see," she said, though her voice was strained.

"I'm sure she'll loosen up over time," I said, wanting to be sure that I didn't make this into something bigger than it was. "I'm just saying that the reason why she didn't eat her lunch is because, according to the schedule, lunch comes after arts and crafts, but before music."

"Okay," she said quickly, as though I'd hurt her feelings. "I think I understand."

*Come on, lady!* I wanted to say. *She's a kid. Just tell me that you can stick to the schedule.*

I softened my voice considerably. "Did she meet with Ms. Julia today? Maybe she has some thoughts on this issue."

That night, I sat on the edge of the tub, helping Sam and Maura wash and shampoo. Maura used to love baths, but now bubbles bothered her—the fact that she could never completely get them all off before she left the tub.

"I talked to Mrs. Murphy today," I said to Maura. "She said that you didn't eat your lunch."

Maura shrugged.

"Did something happen at school today that upset you?"

Maura shook her head.

"I told her that you probably weren't used to eating outside," I said, offering Maura an out. "Plus, you were supposed to have lunch, *then* music, right? Not at the same time!" I said it in a silly voice with a slap to my forehead. "How can you eat lunch *and* play music at the same time, right?"

"We have to make a family tree," Maura said.

"Oh, honey," I said.

"There's a spot for a mom, but I don't have one."

"You can still put a picture of Mom in it, honey."

"That's okay," she said. "I'm going to leave it blank."

Sam looked at me, splashed, and chanted, "Mama, Mama!"

"Well, honey," I said. "That's up to you. Whatever makes you feel the most comfortable, but I think it would be nice to put a picture of Mom in the spot."

"I'm going to leave it blank," Maura repeated, looking away, pouring cups of water over her arm, which was covered with stubborn bubbles.

I used my hand to wash away the bubbles on her shoulders. "Did you meet with Ms. Julia today?" I asked, knowing that Tuesdays and Thursdays were the days she visited the school counselor.

"Uh-huh," she said, nodding.

"What'd you two talk about?"

"I said that I wanted Mommy to come to school with me," Maura said.

"And what did Ms. Julia say?"

"She said that Mommy *does* go to school with me because she's my angel." Maura looked at me skeptically, gauging my reaction. The old Maura would have bought this, hook, line, and sinker. The new Maura had her doubts about everything.

"I believe that's true, Maura," I said, bobbing my head up and down, putting my weight behind the Catholic school's unequivocal rules of life and death. Rules where there was no wiggle room, no gray to contemplate, just black-and-white beliefs.

"I hope so," Maura said solemnly. She poured another cup of water over her arm. All of a sudden, light flooded her eyes and her mouth turned upward. "Maybe I could put a picture of Mom on the family tree," she said excitedly, "and draw angel wings around it."

"You could do that, honey," I said, pulling a strand of hair from her face. "You could definitely do that."

After bath time, Sam and I walked Maura across the street, just as the sun set in a fiery ball of vermillion on the horizon. Martha scooped her granddaughter into her arms. Eight o'clock at night and her father was still at work.

"Mawa!" Sam called, reaching for her cousin.

"I know, pumpkin," I said. "You love Maura. We'll see her tomorrow."

"Mawa," Sam repeated, burying her face into my neck.

As Sam and I crossed the street again, the sunset to our backs, and entered our house that was now firmly a home, a sudden jolt of electricity surged through me. An idea—*the* idea, a recurring thought, an ember that would not be extinguished—kindled again. But now, the idea was accompanied by a solid assuredness, a rightness, and a plan.

"What's with you?" Tim asked when he got home, a smile covering his face.

"Oh, nothing!" I said. "Well, *something*," I admitted. "I'll tell you after I put Sam down." In Sam's room, I sat on the bed and read her a stack of books, tidied her room, and then tucked her in her crib. I leaned down and put my face near hers. "Mommy and Daddy love you, peanut," I said. "Up to the sky and around the stars and through the clouds. We love you and we will forever and always."

"Moon," Sam said, uttering another beautiful word to which she had heard me claim that my love was big enough to fly.

"That's right!" I nodded my head exaggeratedly with a gigantic grin. "We love you to the moon, too."

While Tim showered, I sat in the corner chair in our bed-room and watched my knee bounce. When Tim turned off the water and exited in a billow of steam, I popped up and stood in front of him.

"I've been thinking," I said, hearing the shakiness in my voice.

"About?" Tim asked, going to his dresser for clothes.

"Stuff," I said, following him.

"What kind of stuff?"

"I can't just say it." I went to the bed, sat down, then stood again. "I need to preface it with some remarks."

"Some remarks," Tim repeated. "Will there be a Power-Point presentation?"

"Stop. This is hard to say."

"Just say it," Tim said, smiling.

"Okay," I began. "Here we are, only five months after Claire's death, and don't get me wrong, it's hell. I still wake up every day and feel sick when I remember that she's gone. But in relative terms, I have to admit, there are some things that I like about our new situation. I like Ross and Martha living across the street. I like that Sam is like Maura's little sidekick. I like having my wayward father back in our lives."

"It's okay to be happy," Tim said. "Claire wouldn't want it any other way."

"Of course," I agreed. "I just wish that it hadn't taken her death to set all of this in motion. I wish *she* were living across the street."

"I know, sweetheart."

"You would think, with Claire dying, that I would feel less grounded than ever," I said. "I mean, how can you count on anything when something like that can happen, right?"

"You've had more than your share of heartache."

"Mom and Claire—cut down in the prime of their lives," I said. "How could any of us—me, especially—not think that this could all end tomorrow? But I don't feel that way anymore. I see now, having been hit over the head twice with the same pan, how precious life is."

"I get that."

"It's like *I* finally get it. Sickness and accidents steal lives all the time, but that doesn't mean that we shouldn't live. Look at Mom and Claire—motherhood wasn't about an entire lifetime for them, but I know they wouldn't have traded it for anything."

I took his hands and looked him straight in the eyes. "I have a plan. There are two parts." My heart hammered and skipped.

"A plan with two parts?" Tim raised his eyebrows. "What's Part One?"

"Part One is…" I looked at Tim and then covered my face with my hands as if I were a child. I hadn't felt this charged up since the first time I held Sam's referral photo. I opened my hands and said, "I want to use Claire's frozen eggs and have another baby."

"You do?" A smile played over Tim's face.

"I do. I want to add to this family. I want Sam to have a sister. I don't want to deny her that. I love how she and Maura have been together, and I pray that Maura will always be right here, but we can't guarantee that. Someday Ross might remarry. He might move away. He and his new wife might have more children. Sam needs a sibling. She needs a sister."

I sat down on the bed, laid my head back onto the crisp pillow, closed my eyes, imagining a Christmas portrait of three-year-old Sam holding a newborn with Claire's eyes.

"You do know that these babies," Tim said, "they come in girls *and* boys."

"It'll be a girl."

"What will Ross say?"

"I'll—we'll need to talk to him. I would never do it without his blessing."

"Do I dare ask what Part Two of this plan is?"

"Part Two is that, after we have the baby..." I looked at him and a tear slid free from my eye. "I want to have a full hysterectomy to reduce my chances of getting the cancer."

Tim sat down and wrapped his arms around me. He kissed the top of my head and sighed. "That's the best plan I've ever heard. Because, Helen, I couldn't stand losing you."

"I'm not going anywhere," I said, kissing his stubbled cheek.

"Damn straight you're not." He kissed me back. "You're not leaving me with a houseful of girls to raise alone."

# Chapter Twenty-Four

A month later, Tim and I sat in Dr. Patel's familiar office at the fertility clinic.

"Prior to your sister's hysterectomy, fifteen good eggs were aspirated and frozen from her good ovary," the doctor said. "Enough eggs to try in vitro fertilization twice, if need be."

Tim squeezed my hand as I nodded.

"The process of freezing eggs," Dr. Patel went on, "isn't as dependably successful as freezing embryos, but it does work."

"It's worth a try," I said.

Claire's eggs had been tested and treated, and now awaited Tim's contribution, which, too, would be tested and scrubbed. Once fertilization occurred, we would wait three days, as the single cells split, and split again. Then four embryos would be injected via a very thin tube into my uterus. Once again, a Darwinian fight would ensue, and only the winner—or possibly, winners—would survive. After ten days, we would find out if any had implanted.

"The success rate for women your age, Helen, is about twenty-five percent, so that's something that we need to be realistic about."

"We understand that there are no guarantees," I said. But, I thought, the chance of finding Sam was more than one in 1.3 billion people in China, and here we were with her.

"And miscarriage," Dr. Patel went on.

"We also understand that there is a chance of miscarriage."

"On the flip side," Dr. Patel said, "there is also a chance that more than one embryo will be viable."

"We understand that, too," we said, laughing nervously at the thought of twins or triplets in addition to Sam.

We thanked the doctor, told him that we'd make an appointment, but that there was one last thing we needed to do.

A few weeks later, Tim and I sat down with Ross, proposed to him the idea of using Claire's eggs. He cried when he said that he thought it would be a great gift to Claire. He wished us luck and hugged us both.

On what would have been Claire's forty-third birthday, we returned to the clinic. I was sedated lightly and the embryos were placed in my uterus—life made of my sister and my husband, blessed by Ross, and carried by me. For the first time ever, I was holding up Claire.

"If it works, it works," Tim said, trying to keep me level-headed.

"It's worth a try," I said. "And if it doesn't, we'll head right back to China for another. We might want to do that anyway, someday."

"Come back in ten days," Dr. Patel said when he returned to the exam room. "We'll take a look and go from there."

There was a chance that this wouldn't work, but at least for this moment in time, I was pregnant with four embryos.

I spent the next ten days playing quietly with Sam, molding Play-Doh, strolling through the yard, picking flowers and examining leaves, reading stacks of books, and watching videos. Each day at one o'clock, we'd drive down the road to pick up Maura at school. The three of us would nap together on my bed. Afterward, we'd each drink a glass of milk and snack on cheese and crackers.

Ten days later, Tim and I returned to the clinic. In the waiting room, I picked up an album filled with photos of newborn babies. Sam played in the corner, stacking blocks and lining up cars.

"Sam, look at this," I said, calling her over. I pointed to the photo album of newborn babies. Sam toddled over and pointed to a squinty-eyed Buddha baby who had a good three chins. "That little boy's name is Brandon Michael O'Donnell. When he was born, he weighed nine pounds and three ounces."

Sam smacked the photos with her happy hands.

When we were called into the examining room, we assumed our positions. I lay back on the exam table; Tim sat on the chair next to me with Sam on his lap. Tim looked at me with his cautionary eyes—the ones that reminded me that we only had a 25 percent chance that this would work, the ones that worried that my hopes were too high. I nodded my acknowledgement, conveyed to him that he shouldn't worry. I was no longer the girl I once was. I was ready to take a risk, fall, and get back up again.

The doctor squirted gel onto my abdomen and pressed the ultrasound wand until he found what he was looking for. That's when we heard it, the breathy, whooshing aria via Doppler: whirl, whirl, whirl, whirl.

"Ah, the heartbeat," Dr. Patel said.

When I turned my head to look at Tim, tears sprang loose because, for once, being in the odds meant that I had hit the jackpot. I had spent my life on the tail of every bell curve: a mother who died, a father who left, a struggle with infertility, a sister taken much too early. What were the odds of all of that heartache befalling one person? And what were the chances of that same person hearing this heartbeat?

"Good news," the doctor said, staring at the black-and-white sonogram. "One embryo has implanted."

"One," I repeated, though I secretly had wished that there were maybe two, just in case one lost its grip.

"We're not out of the woods," the doctor said. "Take it easy. Let's look again in a week."

A week passed, then a month, then the first trimester. With each ultrasound, the little bean grew, and before we knew it, we were at fourteen weeks and back in Dr. Patel's office. His ultrasound technician, Carly, squirted gel on my belly and roamed around my abdomen with her wand. She called out organs as she found them, identified the chambers of the heart, measured the circumference of the baby's beautifully round head, counted ten fingers and ten toes.

"Carly, come on," I said. "You're killing me."

"Oh!" Carly said, feigning surprise. "Did you want to know the sex of your baby?"

Carly rolled and pressed the transducer wand to the exact spot between the baby's legs. "Surprise, surprise, you've got a girl."

"Did you hear that, Sam? You got a sister!" I said.

Sam clapped her hands, recognizing the word *sister* as something good.

At eighteen weeks of pregnancy, we went in for a 3-D ultrasound. It was offered to us mostly for fun: Dr. Patel had just updated his equipment, purchasing the latest technology. Once I was situated in the ultrasound chair, Carly came in and turned on the machine. It caught Sam's attention, stopping her from what she was doing, pulling on Tim's bottom lip and belly laughing. She stared alternately at my stomach and the ultrasound machine as Carly squirted gel and rolled the wand.

And then an image like nothing I had ever seen before appeared on the screen. Not black-and-white, like the other ultrasound, but more golden, glowing. It was like looking into a cat's-eye marble. There she was, our baby, a perfect bundle curled into the shape of a comma, with her hands at her face and her thumb in her mouth.

"Sam, do you see her?" I looked over at Sam, whose mouth had parted and eyes were transfixed.

And you really *could* see her: the purse of her lips, the cutest profile in all of history, and...Was that a dimple in her chin? And cheekbones that formed her little face into the shape of a perfect heart (thank you, Claire), and the sweetest arms, like two little satin ribbons flowing down from her shoulders and ending in slender, piano-playing fingers.

Carly printed an entire sheet of ultrasound photographs. She printed a few extra to give to Sam, who studied them as if she were charting stars on an astronomical map.

"I don't suppose Sam's birth mother ever had an ultrasound like this," Carly said.

"I think if Sam's birth mother had had an ultrasound, it would have been because she was forced to, to see the gender of the baby. And in Sam's case, that probably wouldn't have ended well."

"She's lucky to have you and Tim," Carly said. Many people had said that over the last year, that Sam was the lucky one. And I suppose, in terms of her survival, the lucky part was that she was abandoned somewhere where she would be found. But it never settled in me that we had done something particularly altruistic. I was the first to admit that my motives were selfish. I wanted a baby, a baby to love, a baby to love me. It had worked out. One side hadn't received more than the other had. As far as I was concerned, we had struck a good deal.

After lunch, we dropped Tim at Harvest and then drove to St. Mary's just in time to pick up Maura after school. I spotted my niece on the sidewalk, talking animatedly to a classmate, so cute in her denim capris and green tunic. Next year she would wear a uniform—a blue-and-green-plaid jumper with patent leather Mary Janes.

"Great day, Mother!" Mrs. Morrissey said as we approached the curb. The director of the school had been in the education field since the seventies and addressed all the moms as "Mother" and all the dads as "Father." The distinction that I was Maura's aunt did not discourage her.

"She looks good today," I said. "Like the old Maura."

"I heard that she was asked to sing a solo in the Thanksgiving celebration," Mrs. Morrissey said. "Maybe that had something to do with it."

"Oh! Great, okay."

Maura was already talking before her seat belt was buckled. "Aunt Helen, guess what?"

"What, honey? Tell me."

"I get to sing a solo at Thanksgiving! The first verse of 'America.'"

"Oh, Maura, honey, that is the best news ever," I said, thinking that Maura singing a solo was just what she needed to counteract the anxiety that seemed to be shrouding her once outgoing personality. "*My country, 'tis of thee...*" Maura sang.

"*Sweet land of liberty...*" I joined in.

I looked in the rearview mirror, saw Maura's cheeks perched high atop a smile, the happy girl she used to be. Maybe today, I pondered, she didn't think about Claire. *Was that the goal?* I wondered. For Maura to forget her mother so that she could be happy? So that the sadness would disappear? As much as I wanted her to remember her mother, because it was only fair to Claire, and because, truly, Claire was unforgettable, I couldn't help feeling grateful for a day like today when maybe Maura had had a day without her.

"What's that?" She pointed to the strip of photos in Sam's hands.

"Those are pictures of the baby girl that's growing in my tummy," I said.

"There's a baby growing in your tummy?" Maura asked, wide-eyed.

"Yep," I said. "There is. Take a look at the pictures."

"Wow!" Maura said, her eyebrows almost disappearing into her hairline. Then suddenly serious and concerned, "Aunt Helen? Is she going to be my baby sister?"

I opened my mouth to explain the difference between sisters and cousins, but stopped myself, thinking about how it was Claire's egg that started it all. "Kind of," I said. "She's going to be your cousin, but you know what? She'll be just like a sister, just like Sam's like a sister to you. Cousins, sisters—it doesn't really matter, as long as you're all together, right?"

"Yeah!" Maura cheered. "We're having a baby!"

A few minutes later, we pulled into the parking lot of the Gymboree studio.

"Aunt Helen," Maura asked, "did you bring my blue leotard or my pink one?"

"Blue, I think. That's the one you like, right?"

"Uh-huh."

"Aunt Helen? Is Grandpa Larry going to watch me do gymnastics again?"

"I'm guessing he'll be here," I said. "He hasn't missed a class in months."

"Is he going to have dinner with us?" Maura wanted to know.

"Probably, unless he's tired of you choosing IHOP every time," I said, stifling a smile.

"Last week he drank six cups of coffee," Maura said. "I counted."

"That's a lot."

"But he never orders pancakes," Maura added.

"Grandpa Larry never liked pancakes, for some reason."

"Then why do we go to IHOP every time?" Maura asked.

"Gee, I wonder, knucklehead," I said, laughing. "Maybe because you love it?"

"Sam likes it, too," Maura said. "She likes the silver dollars."

We opened the door to the studio and Maura ran in, hollering, "Daddy! Grandpa!" She ran full speed onto Ross's lap, kissed him and then Larry, and then darted off for her warm-up.

I handed Sam to Larry and said to Ross, "You came!"

"I heard that we get pancakes for dinner afterward," he said.

"We do!" I said. "And eggs and bacon."

"I'd be crazy to miss it," he said, smiling. He stood up and walked to the window, watched Maura stretch her legs out and reach for her toes.

Larry looked at me, then at Ross. "Good news, huh?"

"He's coming around."

"Glad he's not a slow learner like me."

I sat down next to him, handed him the strip of sonogram photos, and said, "What do you think, Grandpa?"

# Chapter Twenty-Five

The following May, we gathered at Claire's gravesite to mark the one-year anniversary of her death. Maura danced around the grassy hill, the memory of her mother already blurred, the current events in her life now dominant. It was sad watching Maura forget her mother, to know that she wasn't capable of remembering that way. But it was also a blessing. No child should have to know that the person who loved her the most had been stolen from her, that she literally had been the victim of a thief. Let her forget, I thought. I would carry the heavy heart for my niece—a heart so full I could feel it in my belly.

I leaned flowers against Claire's headstone, placed my hand on the cool granite, closed my eyes. *I miss you, Claire. But I'll see you soon*, I thought, placing my hand on my swollen belly. *And Maura's doing well. Do you see how we're all loving her? We always will. I promise, Claire. I promise. I'll take care of her just like you took care of me. I promise to love all of these girls—none of whom is really mine, but all of whom are still my own. Whatever that means. What I'm trying to say is, I'll love them like you loved me, okay?*

I looked up at the marbled sky and then back at Maura. I would ask her occasionally about a memory, about Claire. She had already forgotten so much—the actual events. Sometimes she would recall a story, a day—"Remember when Mom and I picked apples?"—but then I would find a photo of the two of them at the orchard on her bulletin board, and I would know that much of Maura's memories were from pictures. But sometimes I would see her stop, as if she were trying to bring into focus a feeling that was buried a layer too deep. A hug, a touch, a smell—something that would make her pause and remember, a fleeting moment of "Oh, yeah." I knew because it had happened to me. Occasionally, in the last year, I had seen women on the street who bore a likeness to Claire and I had done a double take. Every time I ordered a vanilla latte, I would hear Claire instruct the barista to "go light on the syrup." In the days when the grief threatened to swallow me whole, I would hear Claire's singsong admonition: "Pull yourself together and put on a brighter shade of lipstick!"

I knew what Maura was going through, how she distrusted her memories, because I felt the same uncertainty about what was real and what was imagined.

The first week of July, I felt a twinge.

"Is it a contraction?" Tim asked.

"I don't think so," I said, tearing up at the thought of something going wrong, remembering the sadness that swallowed me after my miscarriage years ago.

"Let's get you to the hospital," Tim said.

Davis and Delia had come up from North Carolina the day before. The doctor had guessed that labor would start in the next few days. He'd given me the option of inducing, just in case.

Sam was on the deck with her grandparents when Tim and I came down the stairs.

"We need to get Helen checked out," Tim said to his parents. "She's feeling something. She's worried."

Davis and Delia nodded, assured us that Sam would be fine.

"Mommy and Daddy love you," I said to Sam, leaning over to kiss her mouth, just as another twinge grabbed at my abdomen. "Be a good girl."

Sam looked up briefly and then went back to blowing bubbles.

"Good luck, dear," Delia said, kissing my cheek.

"Delia," I said nervously. "Will you come with us?"

"Oh!" Delia danced, flustered. "I would be honored to," she said. "Thank you, dear!"

"I'd really like you there."

"Lucky you," Tim said to Sam. "You get Grandpa all to yourself. He'll probably feed you ice cream and Oreos for dinner."

"Yeah!" Sam cheered.

At the hospital, Tim checked me in, and once I was situated in a gown in a private room, the nurse came in to examine me. "Nothing's wrong," she assured me. "You're in labor."

"Oh, okay," I said. "Those twingy things didn't feel like what I thought a contraction would feel like."

"Those are just the baby ones," she said. "You'll see."

Five hours later, the contractions began in earnest. Seven hours later, I cried uncle and called for the epidural. An hour later, the anesthesiologist inserted the catheter into my spinal canal. The next few hours were calm. Delia and I played Scrabble; nervous Tim polished off a pile of candy bars. I even slept for a few hours. At ten o'clock at night, I felt a pressing. It was so low and deep that the burning pressure reached my thighs. The nurse checked. I was at ten centimeters. Ready to push.

Tim was on one side, holding a Styrofoam cup of ice chips ready for me to suck on; Delia was on the other, clearing the hair out of my face.

"Now, Dad, Grandma," the nurse said, "each of you is going to push her knee toward her face, and Helen, you're going to push for ten counts."

Tim put his weight into my one knee and Delia into the other.

"Now!"

I pushed and pushed, though my efforts felt impossibly weak compared to what was needed to see this through. I pushed more, harder, until it felt like I was turning inside out.

"You're doing really well," the nurse said. "Again!"

Again and again, I pushed. I lay back against my pillow, crying from exhaustion. Tim slipped me an ice chip; Delia folded a cool cloth on my forehead. I pushed again, and then again. Three hours later, the nurse said she was ready for the doctor. The baby's head was crowning.

"Oh, dear," Delia said. "She's almost here!"

*No, she's not*, I wanted to say, but was unable to speak through my exhaustion and tears. A sense of dread had filled me and an anxiety had wrapped around my neck and pulled tight. She should be here by now. If this was meant to be, it would be over by now. I'd have a baby in my arms. I never should have done this. I never should have tempted fate, messed with science, tried to find a loophole in my infertility life sentence. I wasn't meant for this. I was in the last mile of the marathon and all I wanted to do was to turn back.

When the nurse came back, she said, "Huh."

"What?" I asked.

The nurse stared at the strips of paper etching their way out of the machine that monitored the contractions. "Your contractions seem to have stopped. You haven't had one in over ten minutes."

My chest grew heavy. I fought for breath. Something was wrong. Of course something was wrong. My baby was dying inside of me.

Delia cupped her hands around my face. "Helen, the baby is fine. She wants to come out."

I shook my head because, all of a sudden, a fear filled me like cement, and I just knew that she wasn't going to make it. I wanted to see Mom and Claire. I wanted to tell them that it was no good on Earth without them, that I wasn't strong enough to carry on alone.

"She's afraid," Delia said to the nurse, her little voice ringing clear over the din of machines. "She's had a miscarriage. She's lost a lot of loved ones. She's scared."

Delia's words, making sentences out of my sad life, made me want to crawl into a ball and die.

The nurse nodded as if that explained it.

"The doctor will want to start Pitocin," the nurse said sympathetically. "But meanwhile, see if you can talk to her."

Delia bent down, her face just a few inches from mine. She pulled the cloth off my forehead, flipped it over so that it felt cool again. "Dear," she said. "It's time, Helen. It's time to meet your daughter. She wants to meet her mommy."

"Don't you want to see her?" Tim added. "I'll bet she looks just like you and Claire."

I turned my face away, squeezed my eyes shut. "I can't," I said.

"I know you're scared, Helen," Delia said, wiping my cheeks. "But you're not going to lose her. This baby is fine and she wants to meet her mommy."

Meanwhile, the nurse had turned the fetal heart monitor up loud so that I could hear the sound of the baby's heartbeat: whirl, whirl, whirl, whirl.

"Hear her?" Delia said. "Listen to her heartbeat. She's strong, dear. Just like you!"

I turned my face in the other direction and fought for breath.

"It's time, Helen."

"I'm scared," I said.

"You're not," she said. "Because there's no reason to be. This baby is blessed. She has angels bringing her in. Your mother, your sister—they're here, Helen. They're here to bring in the new baby."

"But what if—"

Delia cupped my face and forced me to look at her. "No what-ifs, Helen," she said. "This baby is strong. Now let's say a Hail Mary for the baby you lost, for your sister, for your mother. And then let's say one for our new girl who wants to come out."

My entire body heaved in a sob that was nothing short of a tidal wave. I burst into tears, squeezing my mother-in-law's hands, and then closed my eyes and said the prayers. The nurse nodded happily when she checked again and saw that the labor was progressing. Twelve minutes later, the doctor arrived, assumed his catcher's position, and received Grace as she was born into this world.

⌒

Forty-eight hours later, we were home with our new daughter. Grace—named for that elusive quality that I'd admired so much in Claire, the quality I now knew came straight from God. Sam clamored around her, kissing her hands and her feet, finding a spot to snuggle against my side. Maura, too, oohed and ahhed over her new cousin/sister. At one point, I had Sam on one side, Maura on the other, and baby Grace on my chest, and I was thrilled to see that my love unfolded like a blanket to cover all of them. I just looked up to the ceiling and let the tears slide silently down my face.

⌒

A month later, Dr. Elle Reese knocked on the door, ready to complete her final post-adoption visit. Today, she was wearing a shimmery, jade-colored tunic (maybe it was a dress?) over white bell-bottomed slacks. The blouse was open far enough to reveal considerable cleavage inside her silk camisole. Her silver heels were three-inch spikes. Her gemstone earrings hung down like dewy raindrops.

"Helen, Helen, Helen," she sang in her operatic singsong. "You certainly have been busy." Elle pointed to my new family: Maura and Sam sitting on the floor, sewing lacing boards, baby Grace in my arms. "When I first met you," she said. "I hypothesized that you had a hole in your heart left from your mother's death and that you were certain that having a baby would fill that hole."

"Good hypothesis."

"Has it?" she asked kindly.

"It has," I admitted. "Loving these girls in the way that I remember being loved by my mother—a love that was cut short—has definitely healed my heart."

"I'm so glad," Elle said. "That's the *goal*. The relationships in our life *should* be nurturing."

"In so many ways," I tried to explain. "I feel repaired. The old wounds feel repaired, anyway. As if what was taken has been returned. I don't get to be my mother's daughter ever again. But I get to be a mother and aunt to these girls. It helps. There's no doubt that it helps."

"And how are you doing with the loss of your sister?"

I looked to the ceiling, considered how to phrase my response. "That wound is still wide open, and that's exactly how I want it right now." I closed my eyes and steadied myself against the chill that tickled the back of my neck. "What I'm trying to say is that I want to feel the pain because that's when

I remember Claire the clearest. I'm not ready to try to heal yet. In time."

&#8994;

When we were finished with our visit, I scooped Grace into my arms and walked Elle to her car. I thanked her for being more to me than a social worker, for letting me revisit my history in the safe embrace of her counsel. As she drove away, I walked to the mailbox. Mixed in with the usual junk, advertisements, and bills was a yellow envelope from the adoption agency. I slid my finger along the top and pulled out the letter.

Dear Mr. and Mrs. Francis:

We are in receipt of your letter dated August 1 in which you expressed an interest in adopting a second daughter from China. We are heartened, in particular, to hear that you are interested in learning more about our Waiting Children program. The children in this group are oftentimes older and/or have special medical needs. But as they are "waiting children" already, *your* wait to adopt one would be much less than it was when you adopted your first child.

We recognize that it takes a special set of parents with an unusual amount of love and patience to open their hearts to these children.

We look forward to assisting you.

Sincerely yours.

As I walked back to the house, the memory of the day at Sam's orphanage played vividly in my mind: touring the baby room, the playroom, and standing in front of the room that the director said contained "hard-to-place" children. I thought of the beautiful toddler girl, the mentally challenged children, the boy with the cleft palate, the other with the missing arm. Most of them, clearly, were still there. Still waiting.

I opened the door and let the clatter fill my ears: Grace babbling in my arms, Sam and Maura clanking the tops of pots to the time of their marching band, Chip gnawing on his bone. I wiped the tears from my eyes, held the letter from the adoption agency to my chest, and took a deep breath. *One more.*

# Acknowledgments

My thanks go to Amazon.com for providing its Amazon Breakthrough Novel Award contest. I will forever cherish being honored as one of three first-place finalists.

Then, thanks to Amazon Publishing for offering me the chance to turn a contest manuscript into a polished and published book. Thank you to the expert eyes of the various editors, copyeditors, marketing and merchandising pros who worked on this book.

Thank you to my at-home editorial team, affectionately known as Mom and Mom: my mother and my mother-in-law who graciously read this manuscript in its many forms. Also thanks to Jen Pooley who generously offered industry advice and cheered me along every step of the way.

Thanks to my husband for allowing me to "play author," and in doing so, take time away from our business. He has given me support and praise and has been an all-around great husband.

Thanks to my three daughters who have provided me with enough material and dialogue to last ten books. Nothing imagined is as brilliant (or hilarious) as what comes out of their mouths. When my oldest was just a baby and she wanted more I would ask her "more what?" and she would respond "more some." That's what writing is like for me: each day I hope that I'll have something to say, that the thoughts and words will arrange themselves into nifty sentences; that there will always be *more some.*

# Reader's Guide
## A Q&A with Jennifer Handford

Q: In the beginning of the book, Helen is struggling with infertility. Was that drawn from personal experience?
A: Yes, definitely. I struggled with infertility for three years. There was nothing I wanted more than to be a mother. The desire to carry and birth a child was hardwired in me. Being met with infertility was not just disappointing, it was devastating, as if I had been robbed of something primal. The letdown that followed each "failed" month nearly consumed me.

Q: That begs the question: Did the infertility lead to adoption? Do you have a daughter from China?
A: I do. She's ten years old now, and we adopted her when she was one year old. But my story is different from Helen's. My husband and I were in the thick of the adoption process, only months away from being matched with a baby when we discovered that I was pregnant—something that had never happened in three years of trying. So we put our adoption on hold, had our firstborn, and then quickly hopped back into line to resume the adoption. My husband and I each had the strong sense that we were meant to do both: birth and adopt, as if our good fortune came in a bundle of two. Our "twin" daughters— one adopted, one biological—were a package deal for us.

Q: What was that like, adopting from China?

A: The waiting was the hardest part, but the process was smooth and the reward was great. It's a sad state of affairs in China with the one child per family law still alive and well in many parts of the country, but I have to give China credit for the efforts they've made to get as many of their abandoned babies adopted and into the arms of loving families. It's the silver lining to an unfortunate policy.

Q: We find out that Helen's fears about adoption aren't simple. She fears that an adoptive daughter may not love her and ultimately might leave her.

A: Helen's greatest fear is that she'll be left. A mother who died and a father who walked away have scarred her heart. She's uncertain about the staying power of even a child she has yet to meet. Helen's insecurity about her lot in life, as well as her relationships, defines who she is when we first meet her. She's self-centered and insecure because of what has happened to her, not because of who she is organically. It gives her a lot of room to grow. Watching her mature to the point where she is able to step up and stand in for Claire shows that she finally gets it.

Q: Throughout the book, you stop short Helen's happiness by imposing an obstacle. Why couldn't you just let Helen get what she wanted?

A: I was intrigued by the notion—a universal truth, really—that joy and grief fight for space in our lives. I liked the idea that Helen would have to find happiness—or at least, peace—with the notion that she did get what she wanted, a baby, the start of a family, but she also lost Claire. That's a tough one to juggle, and it's an extreme example of the cards we're sometimes dealt in life. I liked exploring the notion that life throws us curveballs, the idea that finally, *finally*, Helen got what she needed—a daughter. And now she was ready to play house, hang out with her sister, and even reconcile with her estranged father. She had a plan. The idea that we must deal with the good and the bad, simultaneously, all of the time, is ubiquitous. Helen—the younger sister who always relied on her older sister—now had the chance to be strong, and she was, proving it by not only caring for her new daughter, but also her sister's daughter, then ultimately, more children.

Q: You seem to have intimate knowledge of the "sister" relationship. Do you have one?

A: I don't have a sister, but writing about the relationship came easy to me; it was a bond that was natural to imagine: the tug of war for Helen between loving and needing Claire, while at the same time trying to break free to become her own person. Helen would have never wanted Claire to die, but it took Claire dying for Helen to see clearly. She would have never tested the limits of her strength and courage if Claire had continued to be her safety net. In writing this, the day I realized that Claire had to die was a sad one for me. The decision resonated well with me in terms of it being the right thing to do, but I mourned her loss from Helen's point of view.

Q: Why is Helen so determined to reconnect with Larry?

A: Larry represents the family she so desperately misses. Her mother is gone, and even while Claire's alive, she doesn't allow Helen to wallow in the past. Helen knows that Larry is her guy; he's the one to share in her residual grief. Neither of them have any interest in packing away the past; they want to hold it, polish it, treasure it. Helen sees herself in Larry, a guy who didn't always do the right thing, who was sometimes short on courage, but always meant well and loved deeply.

Q: Helen thinks in terms of food: "*My daughter*, the words that used to get caught in my throat as I thought about adoption, were now smooth and welcoming, like a caramel melting in my mouth" (p. 66). Is food a big part of your life?

A: I'm a huge fan of food—good food—and luckily, my husband is a wonderful chef who whips us up delicious creations more nights than not. Though I don't have the same skills, I definitely respect the curative value of food, the comfort that can be bestowed from a delicious meal. I'm the type of person who wakes up each day thinking about what I'm going to eat.

Q: After Claire dies, Helen admits that there are certain things that she likes about her new situation: Ross and Maura living across the street, Larry back in the picture. Is it okay for Helen to be happy even after losing her sister?

A: Definitely. Claire would have wanted Helen to be happy, just as much as their mother would have rooted for her daughters' happiness. Helen comes to see that there are no promises of the future, that we don't always get to play the roles we want for an entire lifetime. She says, "Sickness and accidents steal lives all the time, but that doesn't mean that we shouldn't live." Her acceptance that life is often brief is the greatest demonstration of her growth and maturity.

Q: You named your book *Daughters for a Time*. Is that related to this notion?

A: It occurred to me that all of my characters—Helen, Claire, Sam, and Maura—were all daughters. But each—in her own way—had been robbed of that position. That notion struck me as terribly sad, because who wouldn't want to be a daughter *forever*? Being a daughter implies that one's not alone, that there is parental comfort, security, and loving arms nearby.

Q: Helen admires the faith she saw in her mother, Claire, and her friend Amy DePalma. Can faith be taught or do some people "just have it?"

A: I quite admire the Catholic faith and the tradition and ritual that goes into each Mass, but I didn't grow up as a Catholic so still, so much of the time, I feel like I'm missing some elements that others—the truly faithful—have. Often, I admire true faith when I see it and I wish that mine were deeper. I do see it as a gift.

# Discussion Questions

1.  We meet Helen in the midst of her crisis with infertility. She has Claire for support, but she longs for her mother. Claire is efficient, demands Helen to "buck up" and to "think of a new plan" when Helen wants to wallow in her despair. Helen explains that Claire was the same way when their mother died—so quick to pack up and move on. Does everyone make their way through grief differently?

2.  Helen fears being left, so much that she worries that the daughter she's given through adoption will someday leave her. She thinks having a biological child would be easier, in that she would know where the child was coming from, no mysteries. Would an adoptive child "leave" any more readily than a biological child? Are Helen's fears misguided?

3.  It's not until Helen is older that she realizes that Claire has always been her greatest advocate. When Helen is in China—writing a letter to Claire—she recalls how her sister used to stop by to check in on her, slip her groceries, and check her cell phone to make sure it was working. Is a "sibling" relationship ever equal, or does one sibling always parent the other?

4. The concept of having one foot in joy and one foot in suffering is a theme that threads its way throughout the book. Helen admits to the social worker that it's a shame that she couldn't have it all, that she couldn't have Sam *and* Claire, just like she couldn't have her mother *and* father. Or her mother *and* Claire. Is something good always balanced by something bad?

5. Helen is particularly easy on Larry. She doesn't hold a grudge like her sister does. She remembers good times and is willing to give Larry a pass for the hurt he had caused his family. Why do you think that is? Why is her longing to reconnect with him so great?

6. Helen walks in on Claire while her sister is praying the Rosary. Helen admits her admiration, saying that it was so clear that Claire's is the penetrating type of faith, not the memorized version that Helen had learned through years of religious training. Where will Helen's curiosity and admiration for her mother's, her sister's, and her friend Amy's faith lead her?

7. Toward the end, social worker Elle Reese asks Helen if these children—Sam, Maura, Grace—have had the restorative power she was looking for, whether they filled the hole in her heart. Do some women have children to re-create, fix, or restore their own childhoods?

# About the Author

Photograph © Karen Dunn, 2009

Jennifer Handford was born in Phoenix, Arizona, where she lived until she moved to Oregon for college and graduate school. After graduation, she moved to Washington, DC, and has lived in the Virginia/Washington, DC, area for fifteen years. Jennifer is married and has three daughters. *Daughters for a Time* was awarded one of three first place prizes in the Amazon Breakthrough Novel Award contest. It is her first novel.

Please visit Jennifer at www.jenniferhandford.com.